THERE'S OLIVIA AND ODETTE.
AND THEN THERE'S CLEMENTINE.

*Sometimes, we were a team of three, but sometimes, there was them
and there was me. They shared a placenta and amniotic fluid, they
saw together with four eyes when they emerged, and used eight
limbs like a spider. They shared language and secrets without speaking, and when they finally spoke, it was in words only they understood. I was part of it, but not equal. I had never felt I could stand
beside one sister, Odette or Olivia, without the other shadowing us
both. Until now.*

*Maybe that's why I went to them each alone, maybe that's why
I had been digging into the crack of the arch, digging, cleaning like
a restoration, only instead of repairing, I pried at the keystone.*

**A poignant, compulsively readable story capturing the magic,
the mystery, and the dilemmas of sisterhood by critically
acclaimed author Gwendolen Gross**

ADVANCE PRAISE FOR *THE ORPHAN SISTER*

"A breathtakingly original novel. A haunting exploration of love,
loyalty, sisters, hope, and the ties that bind us together—and make
the ground tremble beneath us when they break. I loved, loved,
loved this novel."

—Caroline Leavitt, *New York Times*
bestselling author of *Pictures of You*

This title is also available as an eBook

"With exquisite language and an empathetic ear, Gwendolen Gross paints a gorgeous portrait of life, love, loss and sisterhood, and forces you to ask yourself: how far will you go for your family and what secrets can shatter even that bond? *The Orphan Sister* will linger long after you've turned the final page."

—Allison Winn Scotch, *New York Times* bestselling
author of *The One That I Want*

"This charming portrait of an impossibly gorgeous and gifted family is something rare: a delightful confection, filled with humor and warmth, that also probes the complex nature of identity, the vagaries of romantic and filial love, and the materialism inherent in contemporary American culture."

—Joanna Smith Rakoff, author of *A Fortunate Age*

"*The Orphan Sister* is engaging and sentence-perfect, wonderful in so many ways, but I love it best for its vibrant, emotionally complex main character Clementine. I felt so entirely with her, as she loves those around her with both devotion and complexity and as she struggles to achieve a delicate balance between belonging to others and being herself."

—Marisa de los Santos, *New York Times* bestselling
author of *Love Walked In*

"Even committed couch potatoes should enjoy the graceful blending of outdoor adventuring and wry immersion in family dynamics that distinguishes this engaging second novel by Gross."

—Kirkus Reviews

"Witty, smart, and inspiring."

—Jenny McPhee, author of The Center of Things

"Gross captures the erotic freshness of woods and avid outdoorsmen with perfect clarity."

—Christian Science Monitor

FIELD GUIDE

"The certitudes of scientific research yield to the unsolvable mysteries of emotional connection in this accomplished debut. Gross's deceptively spare style glistens with pungent language and precise aperçus."

—Publishers Weekly

"Stunning. A remarkable debut."

—Kirkus Reviews (starred)

"This beautifully written debut novel offers appealing characters and provides a unique view into the sensuous scientific world of field study with all of its attendant hardships and marvels."

—Library Journal

"Credible and inspiring."

—Booklist

THE
ORPHAN
SISTER

A Novel

GWENDOLEN GROSS

G

GALLERY BOOKS

NEW YORK   LONDON   TORONTO   SYDNEY

G

Gallery Books
A Division of Simon & Schuster, Inc.
1230 Avenue of the Americas
New York, NY 10020

First Gallery Books trade paperback edition July 2011

GALLERY BOOKS and colophon are trademarks of Simon & Schuster, Inc.

For information about special discounts for bulk purchases,
please contact Simon & Schuster Special Sales at 1-866-506-1949
or business@simonandschuster.com.

The Simon & Schuster Speakers Bureau can bring authors to your
live event. For more information or to book an event contact the
Simon & Schuster Speakers Bureau at 1-866-248-3049 or
visit our website at www.simonspeakers.com.

Designed by Julie Schroeder

Manufactured in the United States of America

10 9 8 7 6 5 4 3 2 1

LIBRARY OF CONGRESS CATALOGING-IN-PUBLICATION DATA

Gross, Gwendolen
The orphan sister : a novel / Gwendolen Gross.—1st Gallery Books
trade paperback ed.
p. cm.
1. Sisters—Fiction. 2. Triplets—Fiction. 3. Individual differences—Fiction.
4. Physicians—Family relationships—Fiction. 5. New Jersey—Fiction.
6. Psychological fiction. 7. Domestic fiction. I. Title.
PS3557.R568O77 2011
813'.54—dc22   2011004839

ISBN 978-1-4516-2368-0
ISBN 978-1-4516-2369-7 (ebook)

For

CLAUDIA ROSE,

REBECCA S. COLAO,

AND SAMANTHA R. GROSS,

my sisters,

and for

CYNTHIA H. STARR,

sister in words.

ONE

When my sister Odette called to tell me Dad hadn't shown up for rounds, my first guilty thought was that he'd had a heart attack on the Garden State Parkway, that his Benz had swerved, swiveled, and scraped against the railing near exit 142 until it flipped into the opposite lane like a beetle on its back, ready for the picking of crows. He'd fumbled for the aspirin he always kept in the cup holder, in a wood and silver pillbox he couldn't unclasp when it mattered at last. Blood would mat the silvery-red mix of his still-thick hair, his eyes would be open, he'd be dead, and I'd never have a chance to prove him wrong.

Of course, my second thought was to feel horrible for my first.

"No, he didn't say anything to me," I said. I almost suggested she call Olivia, but I knew she didn't need to, because Odette and Olivia, my twin sisters, know each other's opinions, their desires and mistakes, without speaking in words. Though sometimes I am party to this peculiar frequency, sometimes I stand feeling like the last chosen for a team because they are identical twins, and I am their triplet, number three. I don't match physically (they are four inches taller than I and my eyes are hazel green to their clear, cold blue) or hear as clearly in the ether of their silent communication.

"I think I'll try Mom again," said Odette. She was using her distinctive stage whisper that meant she wanted everyone standing in that hospital room at Robert Wood Johnson to know she was conducting important business on her cell phone. She was allowed to have a cell phone. She was a *doctor*.

"I can," I sighed, thinking I didn't want to.

"Just wait," asserted Odette, but we both already knew I'd procrastinate awhile and then go seek out Mom.

"Dinner he would miss—rounds, no. I'll start and give him another hour," Odette finished.

If I were talking to anyone else, I'd have been unable to relinquish my frustration. Even Olivia didn't root me to myself like magnet to steel.

I did feel calmer when I heard both my sisters' voices. And I could tell them apart—Odette's had an almost imperceptible deepness, a quiet, sad quality, a clarinet, while Olivia was all flute, in all circumstances. No one else could hear this, however.

We were polyzygots—they were identical, monozygotic, one egg and one sperm met and then split into two zygotes. I was fraternal—another egg, another sperm, but the same timing, which means I was like an ordinary sibling in terms of genetic material, and they were halves of a whole.

We had this special triplet quirk called Party Trick we developed in elementary school, time of Ouija boards and Monopoly (you would never want to play a strategy game with us; we knew how to team up and committed our own form of natural selection): we could speak word by word, each of us in turn, with the fluidity and natural cadence of a single person speaking. We were sleepover favorites when we were little; this was captivating, no matter how dull the subject. "We" "don't" "like" "ham" "because" "it's" "too" "salty." It wasn't practiced. We had a pact to do it whenever one of us asked—something we used rarely as adults, but still, it was always there, ability, connections, quirk, Party Trick.

In the middle of this crisis, I was struggling with my computer, trying to gain access to an online exam I needed to take in the next twenty-four hours. The server rejected my password. I was all ready, notes, coffee softened with Ghirardelli chocolate powder and half-and-half, a final exam indulgence. I had a bag of carrots and a bag of cheddar bagel chips and a giant sports bottle of water, even though I knew, from my undergraduate research, that bottled water is less stringently regulated than tap. I had my blanket and my most devoted mutt, Alphabet, who was lying on my feet as if he knew I wouldn't walk him until I'd at least half finished the timed exam. You could only log out and back on once. I had to get an A. I hadn't done as well on the lab portion as I meant to, but that was because I'd broken up with Feet (officially Ferdinand, an engineering graduate student from Spain who had fabulous dimples and little regard for my privacy), my brief boyfriend whose nickname should have kept me from giving him my phone number in the first place.

Sitting ready at my desk, I tried to log on. I used my password, dogdocClem, but the system said it was invalid. Dad always did this: he made us worry. He blustered in at family gatherings and brushed away queries about his lateness like lint from a suit. But somehow we all worried he was Not Okay—and I was the especial queen of worrying this—as if his Okayness held together the very universe.

I tried again, pounding the keys as I typed in my account number and the password. I was still invalid. I felt invalid. My head throbbed and I was still wondering whether Dad was all right. So instead of starting my exam, I apologized to Alphabet, restarted my computer, and got up to go see my mother.

Maybe he ran away, I thought, as I walked up to the conservatory. My father had built two additions for my mother: an art studio, because she had once casually mentioned she might like to take art classes again, and the conservatory of flowers, a long, inventive, difficult-to-maintain greenhouse that extended from the back kitchen into the lawn. She was usually there, my mother, though we had full-time gardeners for the roses and the vegetables that would be transplanted, after the last frost, into a raised plot by the three maidens' fountain. Mom made exquisite botanical drawings, having taken a class at the New York Botanical Garden before we were born. Sometimes I thought she was simply a woman of too many talents and opportunities—each was diluted in the soup of all her possibilities.

Maybe he went up to the house in Vermont because he is getting senile and thought it was summer vacation. Maybe he's had enough of keeping everything gripped in his fist and he let go; he went mad, like King George III.

I'd been mulling, for about six months, the possibility that my father might have early dementia, or even Alzheimer's. I'd researched the topic when I should have been studying chemistry.

Symptom one: memory loss that disrupts daily life. This was a disruption, for sure, though generally his focus on—and memory of—family commitments and plans had always been rigorously limited. Symptom two: challenges in planning or solving problems. No. Yes. Maybe. He had twice had Mom reschedule her plans for an anniversary party because he had forgotten about other commitments. But this wasn't new.

"I'm going to have to go to the golf outing," he said, the second time. "You don't have to come." My mother had sighed, dialing her party planner.

Symptom three: trouble with tasks at home, work, or leisure. No. He seemed to have no problems with work. Until now—not showing up for rounds. I was probably getting ahead of myself. I never used to get ahead of myself; I used to let the world unroll like a scroll, the beginning happening before the middle and the end, but ever since Cameron, I'd wanted more dimensions, I'd worried more about the unrevealed paper.

So when Odette called I should have just waited, I should have circumnavigated the mess of other people's early and late, but I was a triplet, and triplets have extra arms, extra eyes, extra marginally obsessive worries. I thought of my father standing by his car, staring at his keys as if they were foreign objects. Last week, I'd been witness behind the carriage-house curtain as he stood like that for a moment; was he thinking, or was he lost inside his own head? Was this the beginning of a crumbled father? The beginning of interventions and wheelchairs? No. No. Maybe.

TWO

All the way from the carriage house, where I was living, to the main, where my mother lived mostly alone, but for the occasional large presence of my father, A Very Busy Man, I tried to stop visualizing an accident. He'd been hit by a truck as he tucked his car door shut, giving it the love pat I'd observed with nausea—and, if I'm being honest, a simultaneous pleasing familiarity—since he bought the car. It was now almost ten years old, a top-of-the-line Mercedes sedan. Dad bought his car when the twins neared the end of Harvard undergrad; Odette had teased him and called it a Nazi car when he drove his prize into the drive. It was April, spring break, and my mother's three hundred daffodils from White Flower Farm smeared the lawn with cream and gold, trumpets of triumph.

Dad had turned the deep plum color of his quiet anger, and Odette giggled, Olivia giggling to match her anxiety. I felt the bubble of it, but refused to succumb.

"Nazis are not funny," said my mother, holding her hands like stop signs in front of the twins, two twenty-year-old women who were home from Harvard, finishing their medical school applications. Harvard and Oberlin were the first step in our lifetime of long division. I had to listen harder to hear them whenever we reunited.

"Yeah," said Odette, who was at the peak of her rebellion, which was a mild phase, and tolerated well, like many of the newer antibiotics. Olivia, because she was the same as Odette, rebelled quietly. She got a tiny, tiny tattoo of a rose just above her shoulder blade, much like the rose that had been named after our mother. She also had it removed in an operation she described as "excruciating, but elegantly successful," the next year.

"But Mercedes did use the Jews in factories—I read," I had said, wanting more, wanting my dad's face to blossom into rage. We were just post-teen years; we were pushing out the margins of family. My father, who controlled everything, the money, the order of the house, the comings and goings. As long as I could remember, we asked him to be excused, we asked him if it was okay to go out, we asked him if we could speak at dinner, in subtle ways, waiting for one of his lectures to subside, like requesting to speak freely in front of a superior officer. Part of me thought of it as civility and respect, but that part was dormant.

"This subject is closed," my father said. "The Holocaust is history, and this car is something I have desired for a long time and you girls won't ruin it with your delayed adolescent lashings."

"Hey," quipped Odette. "I didn't lash."

Olivia furrowed her brow with insignificant rage, but said nothing.

"It's okay," he said, cupping Odette under his shoulder. He took my mother under the other arm, and Olivia leaned on Odette. They were like a family of birds in a single nest. Olivia reached for me, and Odette silently told me to come in closer, but I could only hold their hands.

"Mom?" I asked, walking into the conservatory, as if she could be anyone else. My mother's hair was a perfect artificial light, blond-streaked brown that matched my sisters'. I didn't know why she didn't dye it red like mine—her original color was in-between. If it weren't for the crow's-feet, you might mistake her for one of her daughters. She used Botox, though we weren't supposed to know about it. The sad part was that she probably only did it because her friends did, not because she wanted to be smooth in that strange, paralyzed way brought on by toxic injections.

"Over here," she said. She was by the Octavia rose, the one named after her. There were specimens in the New York Botanical Garden, in the Conservatory of Flowers in San Francisco; the Octavia rose had won best in show twice in the mideighties. It was peach-colored, with tight, small blossoms and pale pink veins that made the petals appear almost like a light-skinned woman's translucent skin.

"It's got something," she said. "Maybe a must. Or bug—" She sighed and waved her hand over the plant as if imparting a magic spell.

Blight, gall, I thought. We knew these ailments from an early age. We helped her with grafting projects.

"Do you know where Dad is?" I asked her, casually testing the thorns.

"Don't break those," said my mother. "It's not good for her.

"He's at rounds I believe. You can check the Diary." She smiled, benevolent, but ignored my question and continued tending her rose.

"He isn't—that's why Odette called."

"Your father leads his own life."

Wake up! I sniped, but only internally. Olivia was the only third who could actually say things like that to Mom—some small piece of Dad was lodged in Olivia by nurture, or maybe nature; maybe a dad gene expressed itself somehow with louder song in Olivia than Odette. She had the tiniest pinch more confidence, the tiniest bit of directable anger in the chiaroscuro of her eyes.

I wanted to ask again, but I didn't want to hurt her. When my mother answered questions with obscurities, she was shutting down. I had to be gentle with her—this was the way we were closest—unlike my sisters, I avoided maternal conflict. I wouldn't scratch at her surface for the welling of sap.

Still, I tried once more. "Do you think he forgot to write it in? Has his memory seemed different lately, Mom? Do you think he forgot?"

She fingered a thorn. "No. He is getting older, but he's not senile.

"Sometimes I don't know why I bother with this prima donna flower," she deflected.

"Because she has a lovely name?"

"Maybe." My mother smiled again, but this time it was enigmatic. I could almost imagine her dumping the rose on the ground and dancing up the aisle of the greenhouse, freed at last from a single domestic obligation. My mother was talented, and kind, and thwarted, but I think she took the yoke of beauty and detail willingly. She could do more—Dad wasn't stopping her, he just wasn't paying much attention to her choices, I thought. Maybe her *maybe* marked letting Dad and his flower go just a little in return for his benign neglect.

In the front hall stood a tall sideboard that had belonged to my father's family. The drawers were lined with shoddy velvet, and silver teapots, six of them, huddled in the glass cabinets on the bottom. Paul Revere supposedly cast one. In the drawers Mom kept the two important books of our family lives, books I had resented for years and now looked upon as a ridiculous compulsion, my parents' control manifest. My sisters were both married, both pregnant, and in private practice—together—an ob-gyn and a pediatrician, nothing as fancy as Dad's career, but manageable, matching, and compatible, more or less, with motherhood; while at the same age, twenty-nine, I was living the single-student lifestyle in my parents' carriage house, so I might have to look at the books once in a while. I couldn't ignore them: the Diary, which listed where everyone important (being my mother or my sisters, mostly; Dad only put in his work appointments, but my sisters were tracked religiously. I had a spotty record ever since I left for college) was at any given time. Even now that Odette and Olivia had their own suburban minimansions in Princeton Junction, on the same street, three houses apart, Mom kept their work schedules, their own ob appointments (she attended the hearings of the heartbeats), their vacation schedules, in the Diary. They were so full, my sisters—I felt it when I was with them, the slowing of all systems after a meal. Packed patient schedules, occasional dates with their husbands; it would only be busier soon. I felt how wanted and whole and overwhelmed they were, each centered in the middle of a seesaw, unable to move for fear of losing balance. I knew it was easier for me; I was unencumbered, except for the tipping of my own concerns.

I checked the book for today and it just said *Rounds, Odette; Office hours, Olivia; Inspect conservatory, Octavia;* and *Rounds, Charles.* I sort of wanted *Final Exam for Organic Chemistry (prerequisite for Vet School) Online After She Gets the Fucking Computer to Log Her In, Clementine* at the end, but after I finished packing for Oberlin almost a decade ago, I'd ripped out a page of the Diary, swearing I didn't want to be part of such anal, weird, Waspy, Big Brother recording. Dad had agreed, calmly writing me a note that said Mother would no longer list my whereabouts in the Diary, but he'd like to know in general when tuition would be due and whether I'd please my mother with my presence at Thanksgivings and Christmas.

I was living in the carriage house behind my parents' mansion with my dogs, Ella and Alphabet, a ferret named Cheese I'd kept since someone abandoned him at Oberlin, and a boa constrictor, Skinny, whom I'd rescued from a sewer when I first moved home. Feet, my ex, was with me when I dropped my cell phone into the leaves, then kicked it into the storm drain like some physical-comedy act. I reached in, lying on the sidewalk while Feet stood above to make sure no one stepped on me, and felt Skinny before I felt the phone. Skinny, ever friendly, twined himself up my forearm, and I was not repulsed, which I took to be a sign. Also, no one claimed him, though I contacted the university, the shelter, and the police, who thought at first I was putting them on about a five-foot boa.

Skinny was puzzling; he often escaped his tank, though the cover latched on the outside. Sometimes I found him under the bed; sometimes bathing in light on my dining room table. Feet had convinced me to keep him. Feet liked snakes. He also read my journal—the main reason we broke up. He read what I'd written about our sex, that I preferred talking with my friend Eli to sleeping with Feet, that he drooled excessively when, well, attending to my needs. I have always felt that anyone who read my journal (and my sisters had done so, especially when they were afraid I was possibly suicidal) would have to be responsible for what he or she read. Odette and Olivia could handle it. Feet couldn't. He ranted at me, complaining that I didn't like sex (not true), that I spent too much time with my animals and Eli. That I didn't know just how good I had it. We fought vociferously, outside his dumpy graduate student housing, a cinder-block wonder two blocks from campus. When we finally broke up, it felt dirtier than anything else about our relationship, and I was still washing my hands of it all.

Anyway, now I had Skinny as part of the entourage. I'm fine with snakes, but I don't think they're meant to live in tanks, and Skinny required a massive tank, since he was a massive snake. I also minded buying frozen rats and baby chicks, but Skinny needed to eat. I helped him shed by letting him rub against the knobby oak table legs in the dining area of the cottage; my father once watched with a combination of admiration and what appeared to be feigned disgust.

It was a hidden side of my father; he loved being with the

animals, becoming as soft and fresh as Skinny with his new skin. He played tree for Skinny, eyebrows animated with the sensory delight of a huge snake wrapping and climbing. He was willing to look unsure of himself with animals—lying on the floor with the dogs, discussing things in barks and growls. Dad with my menagerie was younger, mischievous, unembarrassed by dog hair on his good sweaters. I remembered him as our childhood tree when he came to the carriage house—our rock to climb, my sisters and I playing in the water in the lake. He refused to communicate with Cheese, the only animal he didn't trust. But Ella was his secret love.

Once when he thought I wasn't in the carriage house—which had been his alternative lair when it wasn't the guesthouse—he came by to talk to Ella and told her all kinds of things, including how *lovely* she was, what a *good* dog, what a good *listener,* what a *beauty.* I'd listened from the bathroom trying not to laugh at my stodgy, serious father's sweet tone, and then emerged with a towel on my head, pretending I hadn't heard anything.

Still standing at the sideboard, I checked the other book, the Accounts. To my disgust, my mother—who had lived part of the sixties as a young woman, who had had her own career and an apartment in the Village and beatnik friends and who had smoked pot and designed her own Marimekko dresses and danced at Hepburn-like happenings—my mother submitted to having an allowance. My father recorded, on the front page of every month, what she was allowed to spend. She kept the books, paid the taxes, paid the gardener and the milkman, back before the money when we had two bottles of cream-top delivered in a silver, insulated box by the front door at our tiny, proud two-bedroom Tudor in Oakville, New Jersey. We girls shared the second bedroom and rotated outfits, fighting over who would get the one new dress of the season, bickering over socks. Wrestling for a tiny taste of independence. Later came the money. And Princeton, where Dad grew up, which was close enough to his new position as Chief of Pediatric surgery at Robert Wood Johnson Hospital. Now the monthly allowance was absurd, what some people made in a year, but still, everything was accounted for. The bank accounts were in Dad's name, and he wrote out a check each month for Mother, like some fifties throwback, as if he didn't trust her.

I don't know why she allowed it. I don't know why she didn't leave him when he jealously asked about her daily activities and then left for golf weekends without providing a number or bringing his cell phone. I once read that the jealous could anticipate their own guilt; surely Dad didn't really mind what Mom did with her hours when he wasn't there, unless he was asking in an obscured sort of language of love.

Sure, he had a beeper, but we knew better than to call pretending we were related to work. She had a busy life—and now that I'd seen it up close, I knew it rivaled a professional life, but it wasn't one—and she deserved one. Or maybe I just wanted her to want one. Odette and Olivia thought she was fine, that she had *enough*; neither of them had the same flood of fear when Dad was late. I imagined she still smelled the collars of his shirts when he came home for dinner, breathing him in like a woman in love.

The Accounts showed a lot of expenditures this month. Two parties, one a joint baby shower for my sisters—just over, virgin

mint juleps and all—and one an anniversary party for my parents, to be held in three weeks. It would be catered, of course, with
tents in the backyard and a dance floor. A jazz band that also
played standards. My mother had given me a CD and asked me
whether they were good. The New Black Eagles. They were fabulous, I told her, wondering whether I could bring myself to wear
something formal. Whether I was willing to wear heels to humor
her. Whether I could bring my friend Eli, now that Feet was history and I was tired of dating unsuitable men. Odette said she'd
set me up with a sweet, young intern, but I said no without needing any words.

"Nothing here," I called to my mother from the kitchen door.

"I'm sure he'll turn up," she said, as the phone rang. She made
an entrance with an armload of roses, clippers, and thick leather
garden gloves. She smelled green. I answered the phone, as
requested: "Lord residence, Clementine speaking."

It was Olivia. Her voice was strangely nasal, as if she'd been
crying. Since she was pregnant, she'd been more visibly different
from Odette, in a way even those who were not part of our trinity
might observe. Olivia's belly grew up against her ribs in a firm
half-sphere like an embedded balloon. Odette had a pillow, the
bottom curved like a teardrop. Odette's azure blue eyes looked
tired; Olivia's were vivid and wary. Odette was working with a
midwife-doctor team, but Olivia was having none of that non-
sense. She told me she wouldn't mind a C-section. Odette was
shocked.

"Clem," said Olivia. She sighed.

"Is it about Dad?" Knowing it was.

"Is Mom okay?" she hedged.

"She doesn't seem to care that Dad's AWOL."

Olivia was quiet. I tried to read the quiet.

"What? What?" I asked. "Do you know what happened? Is he okay? Why are you suddenly unreadable?" She knew what I meant—I couldn't know what she knew.

"No. I mean he's okay. I mean, I don't know exactly what happened."

I was the only one skilled at holding a secret for long. I knew her need to tell was almost physical, almost autonomic. She was suppressing a tell-sneeze.

"Still," I said. "You can't fool your sister."

I'd felt this need myself, but I was good at resisting. I imagined it was squared with my sisters; an exponential urge.

"Clem, I know why Dad's gone."

My heart started anticipating fight or flight.

"Okay—so where is he?" I asked, thinking, again, that he could accidentally have stepped in front of a bus; that he went to his parents' former house, wherever that was. That he was at their graves right now, communing with the dead.

He could have fallen in a manhole in Manhattan. He could be having an affair with a prostitute in Red Hook. It happened all the time, respectable men, afraid of growing old. I thought it, but I didn't believe it. Heart attack, I thought again. If he had a heart attack, if he died, I'd never have a chance to be his favorite, even for a moment.

"I don't know where he is," she said. "Just why he's gone."

I was speechless.

"He did something," she said, and now I could tell this wasn't pregnancy congestion; she'd been full-on sobbing. "A long time ago, actually. And I'm not going to be the one to tell Mom."

"Olivia?" I pushed away all my odd fantasies. This sounded real.

She didn't answer.

"What did he do? Embezzle? Have an affair? Fake his medical license? Murder someone?"

"It isn't funny, Clem. He left me a message," she sighed dramatically. I couldn't read her sigh. I hated that.

"Okay, okay, so what did he say? Where the hell is he?" *Why you?* I wondered. But Olivia had always been the tiniest hair ahead. Loved more by a fraction of a nose. I'd suspected it, and now I knew it. She got the first heavy-as-a-fist hug hello. She'd been born first by a minute. I was last, though the family joke was that I was still a middle child. Olivia's birthday phone call was first. Dad trusted her just the smallest bit more—no one else would ever notice, but I read it as well as the secret language of my sisters' faces.

I remembered, swimming in my own little lake of self-sympathy, that one year when we were kids, he brought us gifts from a conference—I'd gotten a pen that contained a floating, plastic, small intestine with a sandwich that moved through if you tilted the barrel. I thought it was the best thing ever, making throw-up jokes with abandon. Odette received her very own reflex hammer (with a drug-company name etched into the handle), and tested it on us each. I hated that funny-bone sensation. Olivia's souvenir, however, was a real stethoscope. A real one. For listening to real hearts. He gave her something functional and grown-up and different. He trusted her more, and because I'd been eight or nine and prone to bathroom jokes, I hadn't realized until later how unfair it had been.

Then my sister Olivia said something akin to blasphemy, something so horrible coming from her I half expected a thunderclap.

"I can't tell you," said Olivia. "But I listened to his message and then I did a little digging. And he's an asshole. We'd be better off if he were dead."

THREE

Here are some words I would use to describe my father: stubborn, loyal, handsome, secretive, important, distinguished, powerful, charismatic, bossy, charming, brilliant, unfair, prejudiced, magnanimous, uneven (with long legs and a short, bullish torso), and occasionally, in small and dangerous ways, spiteful. I'd kept a journal, my version of a confidant, since I was ten and had probably used each of those words in my rantings. Also, in the past two years, perhaps just because we'd fought so long in our quiet ways and then I came home—and saw him up close more than I had in about a decade—he was beginning to shrink, both physically and in terms of his power over me. He was getting old.

For all my resentments, I loved the man. I loved the way his hair was slightly too long and too wild. I loved the way he clasped my hands when he greeted me, as though I were an honored guest. I loved that he actually cared what I did with my life, enough to be nearly constantly peeved with me.

On the day I came home to live in the carriage house, Dad helped me lug my bags and pets inside. He lowered a suitcase and held open his arms inside as if to call the air in as welcome. He carried the sedated Ella into the house and set her atop the throw pillows on the couch, tucking a cashmere blanket around her. I relinquished a tiny gasp—dog on furniture.

"She's special," he said, patting Ella, who panted and drooled and twitched with a desire to leave the realm of chemical sleep.

"Like you," he finished, turning quickly back to the door as if encumbered by the emotion.

In the doorway he looked out and said, "Remember those neighbors who kept sheep?"

"The Bells. They had goats, Dad. They were having a go at cheese, remember?"

"No, it was sheep." He stomped his foot, a recalcitrant child. "Well, that's it then," he finished, and trudged off, leaving me to rebalance my internal scales. It was goats, I knew it was goats; we'd had to shoo them off the driveway more than once. Maybe that was the first time I thought Dad might be more than just a little forgetful. I had neither of his parents as reference of aging, so I just thought about it, patting my sleepy dogs in turn.

We never met our parental grandparents; Dad kept the details of his family contained like internal organs, vulnerable to light and air, safe only in the confines of translucent muscle, fat, skin, and skeleton. Dad's parents died long before we were born, late babies that we were; my mother was forty and Dad was forty-four, and Dad obscured all the rest of the family history, genetics and stories alike, as if they were valuable, volatile secrets. In third grade all three of us had to make family trees, and Dad wouldn't even tell me whether we had any aunts or uncles on his side of the family. In our room, Odette said, "He was an immaculate conception," and Olivia and I laughed and tried not to think about our parents having sex.

✦ ✦
✦

Though my mother liked to say we were New Yorkers like her—
she was Upper East Side raised with a driver and a doorman—we
were actually born in Red Bank, New Jersey, in the Riverview
Medical Center, because we were four weeks early and Mom and
Dad were down the shore at a cousin's engagement party. Mom's
ob-gyn had said it was safe to travel. To this day Mom says it was
eating excessive quantities of shrimp cocktail that started her
labor; she couldn't stop dipping them in the spicy sauce, it was as
if we craved the iodine. Even thinking about that, I imagine it was
O&O, my sisters, who demanded that luxurious overindulgence
in a single prenatal voice. I was probably content with cranberry-
orange juice mixed with seltzer, and little toasts with red-pepper
toppings. I wouldn't have complained, even though I don't like
red peppers.

My mother is fond of calling us her three wishes—she always
said we were the first multiples in the family since before the *May-
flower*. Supposedly there were several sets of practically prehis-
toric twins, but we were the only ones in recent history. If you
asked my dad whether multiples run in his family, he'd answer,
"Only multiple intelligences," and launch into a subject-garroting
lecture on frontal-lobe electrical impulses or his colleagues who
ignored the hand-washing mandate in favor of less effective
squirts of sanitizer.

Our first house was in Oakville, New Jersey. Before the
money. The radiator covers looked like flowers if you stared at
them, or like birds in flight, or the thousand disgusting geometric
seeds of a green pepper. We spent hours listening to our five

records on a kiddie record player we received collectively for our birthday. *The Jungle Book, Free to Be You and Me, Hair,* which was completely inappropriate, but no one noticed, James Taylor's *Sweet Baby James,* and *Abbey Road.* When I was eight, I wanted to be a rock star, or to sing on Broadway. I wasn't sure how these were dissimilar, but I stood in the center of our room being a powerful entity, collecting all the heat and light from the world by giving it song. Of course, in chorus at school I sang quietly, afraid to make loud mistakes.

"Cut it out!" said eight-year-old Olivia, marching in, holding Odette's hand as easily as one might hold a pen when writing.

"Too loud," said Odette.

"I thought you two were playing four-square in the driveway," I said, hoping they'd go away, and wanting them to stay. It was a crowded Sunday, and time alone in the room was precious. When they were with me, I felt squeezed and possessed—like a swaddling: comfort colliding with desire for freedom.

"We're done. We're playing Sorry now."

"I don't want to."

"We do. You're yellow," said Odette.

"Ha ha, you can't make me play," I said.

"But you want to," said Olivia, and sadly she was right. Odette soothed me more; Olivia saw my darknesses and light. I lifted the record player arm from "William Wants a Doll" and sat on the circle of green nylon rug Mom had bought to match our pale green bedspreads at the store in town where you could get stick candy in the front if you were a good customer. We loved the lemon stripes.

We played Sorry. There was an unspoken balance; if you

bumped a sister back to start, you turned for the other sister next, even if you had to reverse your progress to do so, even if you had to give up a good play in the name of silent fairness.

That time, though, Olivia bumped me twice. The second time I glared at her, feeling both an inexplicable peace and expected fury.

"No," I said. "I don't want to go back to start, and I don't want to be yellow and I don't want to play anymore."

"Spoil," said Olivia.

"Sport," said Odette, but she smiled. "I don't blame you. Yellow always loses."

"No," said Olivia. "Clem just doesn't want to play fair. And she didn't want to play in the beginning."

"So you're punishing me?" I laughed and rattled the board, just enough to disturb the little Hershey's Kisses shaped pieces into chaos.

"We don't punish." Odette looked at Olivia. She was saying something silently, and I couldn't hear it. I hated that. I squeezed my eyes shut to listen, but all I saw, all I heard, were the fireworks of squinched eyes and the percussion of Mom emptying the dishwasher. I suddenly longed for my mother, who braided our hair, who made mine French braids because my hair was easier to manage, because I wanted them. My mother who sent me kisses from across the room, who didn't read my mind.

"What?" I said, but I wasn't asking. Olivia had moved in close to make me play, but now she shifted away. Odette packed up the game. Odette could never bear to let a fight erupt into full volume.

"Clem doesn't have to play if she doesn't want to," said Odette.

"But she did, she wanted to." Olivia gripped the box top.

"I don't want to do things just because you say I do," I said.

"But I only say so if you want to in the first place," said Olivia.

Odette pulled at the box top and the corner tore.

"I'm tired of being so known," I said. *Not really,* said my sisters, and I heard them, and they were right. I kicked the box when I left the room, in search of a privacy I would never have and never wholly wanted, either.

The money came after Dad finished his residency; this was stipulated in some kind of trust, and even more came when our grandparents—my mother's parents—died. I had a limited repertoire of memories about my Me and Da, as Mom taught us to call them. I remember Me had musky mink coats and wore dark red lipstick and diamond-chip earrings. I remember Da smelled of limy cologne and pipe tobacco, and that he coughed like a sick seal. They always brought us dresses with crinolines and gave us savings bonds in crinkly, flag-embossed envelopes, which Mom put in the Accounts ledger and we never saw again. We were meant to make a big show of thanking them, though it meant nothing to me at the time, savings bonds. Once when we learned to play Monopoly (Odette and Olivia arbitraged and traded the best properties so they each could purchase hotels), I asked my mother if I could use my savings bonds as get-out-of-jail-free cards in Monopoly. She laughed and held her hand to her thin, white throat, Mom's nervous gesture. She didn't answer, which meant I wasn't supposed to ask.

Even then, my mother and father went away without us sometimes. Our father often had business trips, conferences, doctors' retreats that I now know were sponsored by drug companies. We never went along, though we were invited. There were a few family vacations, but they were mostly at some mysterious relative's house in the Hamptons, or, after the money, the house on the lake in Vermont.

When they left us when we were young, Me or Da or my mother's sister, Aunt Lydia, would come to care for us. Lydia still lived in Manhattan and was six years younger than Mom, which meant it was almost okay that she wasn't married and had a job in an advertising agency as an artist. Lydia wore silver rings on every finger and braided our hair. She brought a hatbox full of makeup and tweezed the twins' eyebrows. I was tempted to submit to all that attention but was repulsed by the idea of tearing out hairs. We always stayed up late with Lydia, but she would suddenly become an authoritarian when we became too silly, rolling on the floor and saying potty words to delight each other.

"Up to bed," she'd say, slapping her thigh. At that moment, we didn't know whether she was being funny anymore.

"I mean it," she'd say, making no eye contact. So we went. That slap on the thigh made it seem as if she might actually strike us, though she never did.

The weekends with Lydia were fabulous, though. We made homemade wheat-crust pizza and ate sauce and cheese from the bowls while it baked. The sauce came from a jar but tasted like metal and mouthfuls of basil.

Lydia always brought art supplies—sketchbooks and Cray-Pas and charcoal sticks that sat light as a bird in the hand. I wasn't very talented, but I loved watching her hands move. My drawings were lumpen, rigorously wrong, but she never wiped away my work or said anything other than "It's all about the process."

She sat with me, sketching, even after Odette and Olivia lapsed into boredom and traipsed off into their collective world of stick forts beneath the hemlock trees. Lydia would set up a still life of pears, grasses from the backyard, a cracked rubber Pinky ball we never played with anymore.

"We're alone together!" I said to Lydia.

"Like sisters." She grinned, her mouth barely asymmetrical, like Mom. She liked the idea of being one of us.

"No," I said. "Sisters are together but not alone."

I didn't feel as if I had to be one of three when O&O would talk without words, looking at each other across the lawn to communicate—*we're going biking, we're playing hide-and-seek*—and there was someone else who didn't always know what was going on without asking. It was a pleasant feeling, but naked, off-kilter, like having one eye covered while dancing.

Once, we were left in my grandparents' care at their apartment in the city. I remember this because it was unusual; because Me wasn't the kind of person you climbed onto or engaged in play. She was a person who sat in white chairs. She had clothes that crinkled if children looked at them. And yet I thought she was beautiful in an old sort of way; I aspired to her calm and elegance. I couldn't get mad quietly, but Me couldn't get mad any other way, as far as I could tell.

That time we went to the apartment—which was larger than our entire house—for a weekend so my parents could have some kind of anniversary celebration. Even then I knew there was something of a currency to it, sex between them. We knew about sex; our parents had explained it matter-of-factly when we were young enough not to be disgusted, and it just seemed like an ordinary piece of information until our friends began to learn, and then we squealed along with them and made gasping noises when they brought out books with pictures. Still, even at eight, I knew how much my mother worked at being attractive; I knew my father was in charge of almost everything, but when it came to romance—or later, I realized, the act itself—my mother held the purse.

That stay at my grandparents' was a long weekend of enforced quiet and enforced fun. We were nine years old. We each slept in our own twin bed (mine was a cot squeezed between my sisters' matching lilac duvets, but I didn't mind, because the cot seemed adventurous, like camping), in the room my mother and her sister had shared as children. It was hard to imagine Lydia and my mother talking with each other at night—did they discuss boys, or play dolls together? How could Lydia pierce my mother's formidable silences?

The apartment wore the aroma of the blood-orange linen water my grandmother kept in a crystal spritzer on the tiny glass table by the door. Our pillows were goose down; you could feel the thin spines of the feathers if you pinched them. There was central air-conditioning—something we didn't have in the Oakville house—so the rooms hissed quietly and the air felt dry and clean. Odette had an asthma attack and Olivia didn't, an imbalance that rarely occurred.

My grandmother took us places in the back of a town car that visit, gliding through the streets in interior quiet. It was August, and women were wrapped in short dresses that showed the glitter of sweat on their legs and arms. A deliveryman on a bicycle tapped the side of the car, leaning against it for balance, and Me gasped. Odette tried to scroll open the automatic window, but Me pressed her hand over my sister's and pressed her lips together. "We do not," she said simply.

We went to the Museum of Modern Art. I wanted to stand by the water lilies because the longer I looked at them, the more I felt as though I could enter the watery cool of the painting, leave the sad lump of missing my mother and the strangeness of my grandmother's house and the rules behind and dive into the swirl of blues.

"Let's," said my grandmother, her hand over my hand. She looked into my eyes, and I noticed hers were the same green as mine, only softened by age. Her hand wasn't a reprimand the way it had been on Odette's in the car.

"There's so much to see," she said almost kindly.

We went to Serendipity and Me let us order whatever we wanted. Odette and Olivia had butterscotch sundaes with maple walnuts, but I got an explosion of decadence called Forbidden Broadway.

Odette nibbled daintily at the nuts, complaining, disappointed that they weren't what she expected.

"Yes, they are," said Olivia, her mouth stuffed with warm butterscotch.

"What do you know?" Odette began spooning her walnuts onto Olivia's dish, and Olivia flicked them onto the plate with her spoon. They were tired. *Punchy,* Me would later say, which meant Olivia grew bossy and Odette mercurial. They kept fighting, sniping silently, and I gave up trying to listen in.

My grandmother overlooked their scuffle and shared with me. For once, unlike when we offered a taste of dessert to my father and he took enormous bites that made me regret allowing his spoon, she shared in slow, pleasurable nibbles that made me slow down, chew the chocolate cake, the thick, buttery hot fudge, and notice more notes than simply sweet and cold. I held an iota of inherited elegance in my pinkie finger. Occasionally I could hear my sisters internally, but choose not to listen.

One morning, Me outfitted us at a boutique near her house, where nothing had a price tag. My sisters were well behaved, but I suddenly felt silly. It was the penultimate day of our stay, and I missed running around, missed the smell of my own house, butter cookies and lemony furniture polish.

"I want to try this!" I said, snatching a sailor blouse with matching skirt and cap from a display.

"Settle down," hissed Odette, who had been reprimanded enough for all three of us during the stay. Me's quiet, gentle, terrifying reprimands.

"And this!" I pulled a pair of high-heeled silver shoes from a top shelf, and ten pairs of shoes toppled on my head.

"Ow!" I yelled, and my grandmother's forehead and cheeks pinked.

"Girls," she said. "You must behave like ladies in here."

"Well, well," said Odette, looking at me, unable to resist. She pretended to sip tea, lifting her pinkie—what was elegant before was now ridiculous.

"My, my," said Olivia, flapping one hand, pretending to be fey.

"La-di-da!" I said, feeling a part of a swell of pleasure in being rude. Olivia was thinking of torn cloth; Odette imagined stains. I thought at them—chocolate-covered faces, a pile of rumpled fancy pantaloons, satin and velvet. I could hear them thinking back—spilled honey on a cashmere sweater, initials dug deep in the heirloom dining table.

"Girls," said my grandmother, holding out three gingham dresses decorated with ribbons of happy Scottie dogs. We let her buy them for us, each of us guilty of the collective wild thoughts. We didn't want these baby-girl clothes, but somehow knew it would help Me feel important, would somehow assuage our shame at feeling spoiled and ungrateful. We were nine years old already, and we'd accidentally scuff all three pairs of patent leather shoes on the back steps, coming home.

The town car took us all the way home to Oakville. I laughed privately but out loud with my sisters—we'd stayed up late, talking about how odd Me and Da were, how Da disappeared for hours, and he must be constipated. We were kids, after all, and this was hilarious. Me had "made" us breakfast by ordering things from the chef. But she let us have hot chocolate with homemade marshmallows in the lilac bedroom and didn't complain when I spilled a small comma of chocolate on the pale purple rug. I gasped, a little bit of our imagery manifest. We decided it was more fun to make our collaboration visible and had developed a silly sign language— holding our heads—to imitate how Me's hair stayed all in one piece on her head, a stiff brown helmet. We flapped our hands at each other and said *la-di-da*. Little did we know we'd be actual rich girls soon.

When we came home, our parents kissed in front of us more

than they used to. Mom positioned her hand on Dad's thigh; Dad dipped her as though the two of them were dancing. It felt like a show, but at the same time I knew they belonged together, congruence. Odette groaned and Olivia said, "Ugh," but I didn't mind all that much.

Despite the way he pulled all energy to himself—his lectures about his work successes, his theories of politics, and subtle embedded preferences for colleagues who had Ivy League educations—Mom had a particular way of listening to Dad, a pursed lip, almost kissing, a leaning in across tables, a glossy expression that I thought, when I was younger, was the epitome of romantic love. I wanted that. But then, a few semesters into courses at Oberlin, I began to think theirs wasn't abiding love, but an unsubtle gender bias. What Dad did was better, more important, more meaningful, more profound, not just because he was a doctor, but because he was a man. I seethed against it, but I also wanted to forgive her, because she had obviously been brainwashed by a generation, by her parents, by the lack of financial diversity in her upbringing.

As much as she taught us we should put ourselves first, before we had families, that we should build careers and then proceed to childbearing, as she had—she had been a marketing manager for a high-end women's clothing store, a job she once said she loved, though her love seemed to fade with distance, and she began to say, "It was easy to give up for you girls," with an artificial ease— as much as she taught us this, she was a horrible example of how to be in love. If my father was excited about something, she buzzed around him waiting to help him, waiting for a role to be cast her way, though it rarely had to do with her. He got excited about medical research he read, about participating in studies for his patients—he was a pediatric neurologist and semifamous neurosurgeon. Sure, he would defend her forever; he insisted we apologize when we'd mistreated her. It was a subtle puppetry, and I resented it.

FOUR

I jabbed at my fingernails with the top of a doggie-treat pack while Olivia's cell phone rang. I'd put it on speakerphone so I could repeat dial. After three rings, it went to voice mail, which meant she'd pressed the little button on the side to send the call away. Again. This was my fifth call since our stunning conversation.

"O," I said. "Me again. You need to talk with us. I'm calling Jason if you don't call back."

I wanted to read her. I wanted that feeling I'd had all my life when I felt my sisters' feelings; when I'd picked up their frequency, an electric current of pleasure just under the alternating current of my own heart. With Odette, I knew she was as anguished and confused as I. We were shut out. We heard the same outgoing "This is Dr. Lord . . ." blah blah blah.

"O," I said, amending my previous message. "Just talk to me. I won't make you do anything you don't want to do."

This was something we told each other as adults. "We're dolts," Olivia joked at our latest dinner when Olivia didn't want to eat the broccoli rabe with pounds of garlic. "And dolts don't make each other do things they don't want to." Because we could—because we knew how to make each other feel too directly to resist. "It's a pact," Olivia had said, pushing aside the greens, and Odette and I didn't need to nod or say anything in order to agree. We meant everything, not just dishes that might generate dyspepsia.

But now I wanted to make Olivia tell me everything—as if she'd held secrets about Dad all along. Maybe I shouldn't have threatened to call Jason; that would only infuriate Olivia, who liked, much more than Odette, to maintain a margin between her husband and the rest of us. Jason had an awkward side; he would answer for Olivia—yes, we'll make pie for Thanksgiving, and, yes, we'll bring in your mail, and, no, we don't want the desk Mom remodeled out of the study—and Olivia would feel grudgingly obliged, but she hated his definitive, undiscussed decisions in the realm of the Lords. I wondered, sometimes, who initiated their sex, and whether there was ever a tiff over location, timing, position, or pleasure.

I stared at my desk and at Ella, who stared back and thumped her tail. The first thing I do in the morning and the last thing I do before bed and sometimes in between is to walk the dogs. Sometimes Cheese wants to come, too. I put him on a goofy little ferret leash and he winds his furry self around my neck and I feel dressed like a pimp.

Alphabet always has to be in front. He pulls the leash and I can feel the possibilities of my shoulder joint and I yell at him, or I use my firm, terribly important voice, when I'm feeling patient. Poor Ella. Alphabet was the squeaky wheel while Ella was the patient, unrelenting love.

"Oh, El," I said. "At least you'll always talk to me." I scratched her back and she rolled over, still giving me her sweetest look. *Love me.*

I had to look up Jason's cell number because I didn't call my brother-in-law all that often.

"Clementine!" he barked. "Planning a surprise second shower for my wife?"

"Oh, you've been prepped, haven't you?" I said. "I just don't think Olivia realizes we need to be in this together."

"She passed her nonstress test beautifully," he said, stalwart man. "Since I know you're calling out of concern for her health."

"Okay, Stonewall Jackson—can't she just tell us where to reach Dad, or whose number she has?"

"His lawyer." He coughed. He wasn't supposed to tell. He changed the subject, as if I'd forget. "Her heartburn is awful, though. Do you feel that, too? You know, that triplet thing? Do you feel her heartburn?" I had to admire this unrelenting focus on his wife.

"His lawyer? We *have* his lawyer's number, I'm sure," I said, leaning down and scratching Ella's soft, warm belly, as much for my own comfort as hers. She groaned.

"A different lawyer. Now I'm done talking about that. I'll tell her you called to see how she's doing. It'll mean a lot to her, bye!" he barked again, hanging up.

"What the hell?" I asked my dog. Alphabet stood by the French doors and growled at a leaf. Part of me admired Jason's doggedness. And oddly enough, I did experience mild heartburn when I was with them.

"Odette," I said, happy to easily reach my other sister on the phone.

"Yes," she began, knowing without my saying why I called.

"Though I don't drink coffee, not even decaf anymore. Shall we meet at that place in town you like so much? I could use a pastry or two."

I could tell from her voice that she felt like me, as though we were both ripped loose and vaguely lost, wires stripped akimbo.

"You know what this is—some secret lawyer?"

"Lawyer? Let's deal with it over something gooey," she said, and I pictured her manicured hands digging into a brownie with a pile of frosting.

Despite our closeness, my sisters were sometimes a unit without me. All my life I'd mournfully watched the walls of their castle, wishing they would crumble and let me march in. But now that they were looking vulnerable, I was terrified.

A new man was working behind the counter—dreadlocks and a tan, barely scruffy, warm face. He asked the question we'd heard all our lives, only this time it was just one rounded sister and me. He leaned into the counter grinning goofily and said, "You two must be twins!" to Odette.

Odette stared at me as if I'd just been invented.

"We are," she said, putting her hand over mine.

"But we have another," I said. "So really, we're triplets." When did I ever bother with all this? I missed Olivia's deadpan habitual answer, *no*.

Over coffee—I had coffee, and one of those gooey brownies, and Odette nibbled demurely at a scone and sipped her ginger-chamomile tea sans sweetener—I told her what Jason said and she sighed and said it was time to hire someone to help us with all this.

"Like another lawyer? Don't we have enough lawyers?"

"A private investigator," she said, offering to ask around. Odette was taking crumbs off her scone as if she could parse it into individual calories.

"Why did she?" I asked. "Why did he?" It was all I needed to say, and Odette started, quietly, to weep.

"Now don't do that," I said, not really meaning it. She was allowed to cry. Along with Party Trick, we played other games—mind-reading games such as pick a number. When Odette picked a number, she could sometimes tell us one at a time—usually Olivia first, then me, but once in a while, she thought "eight," obscuring it from her twin like a covered hand of cards. Olivia would get irritable when that happened, and even though Odette found her easier to read than I did, she'd reveal her number to me before Odette. I didn't have the same control either did—if I thought a number, either they could both read it or neither could. Winning, for them, was just a matter of the fastest call-out. I felt as though I would never learn their perfect language, their control. But now Olivia was hiding from us both.

"It's hormones," Odette said, pretending. "The crying. I think Olivia did it because somehow he made her. She's closed right now, Clem, it's the oddest thing—I've only once or twice felt I couldn't read her. It's like not having a telephone, or worse—it's not having a reflection in the mirror." She paused to shake with sobs, almost as though she were laughing.

But then she cleared her throat and said, "But you know, it's kind of a relief that it's her and not me. I don't know if I could bear it right now, whatever *it* is."

"I know," I said, only I'd felt closed out more than once or twice. I didn't need to tell Odette that, she'd remember the numbers game. She'd remember hide-and-seek, when I was always left wandering the third floor while they snuggled like den rabbits under Mom and Dad's bed. "She'll come back."

"He might not," said Odette. "He might have gone off to become a yoga instructor at a school for orphans in the Congo."

"He became a fashion consultant at a couture house in Milano."

"He joined Doctors Without Borders and is leading an expedition to the south pole. To see if there are any borders there."

"He left Mom."

"That one's not funny."

"It's not supposed to be," I said.

My sister's beeper began its alarm, and her BlackBerry buzzed, and her cell phone rang, all within seconds. She groped the devices and sighed. "Just a patient," she said. Odette abandoned her dissected scone and we left the bakery together.

My sisters are not beautiful by the ordinary standards; they have light brown hair and clear blue eyes and slim, plain bodies. Their hands are long-fingered and agile, their voices matching pale sopranos that peak to girlishness when astonished or afraid. But there is beauty in their motions, in the assuredness about their destinies and capabilities. I used to think of them as a pair of queens—they don't embody the soft romance of princesses. And, of course, everyone is captivated by their doubleness. Including me—but they belonged to me.

My sisters aren't the same—I know them each the way you know parts of your own body—left hand and right—without examination you intuit the differences. And now the left had an injury, or a weapon, or a coin.

As I came home from the café, Princeton looked aggressively pretty—clean, upkept Victorians, excessively green grass. I let my eyes cool from my own small bout of tears and breathed deeply. I had to focus on my own goals, see past the green and my family.

I opened the door to the carriage house, dropped my keys, and sat on the floor in front of my computer, petting the dogs, who circled me as if I'd been missing for days. My exam—I needed to get to it, to get past it, to move on. This time it let me log in, and I wondered why some things were easy some of the time, and some things lead nowhere. Odette would find us a private investigator, and I had a chocolate smudge on my arm, and suddenly I could do whatever I wanted on the server.

I needed to get at least an A-, though my applications were already in. I'd finished Genetics and Statistics (which my friend Eli called Sadistics) and Organic Chem was the final prerequisite before I was ready, actually ready, fully prepared, fully committed to vet school. Of course I had to wait to hear whether I was admitted. I could wind up in Wisconsin or California. I could have a mandatory Food Animals section, I could be moving somewhere I knew no one at all—for the first time in my life. Even when I went to Oberlin I knew two guys from the grade ahead of me, who had joined the Can Consortium and played garbage-can instruments in joyous concert with fifty other enthusiasts on the quad. We all danced.

I wanted to stop thinking about the importance of the results. If I didn't get in, I'd be unplugged, purely aimless. The GRE had been bad enough; I had to retake it since my scores were eight years old. I'd sat at the thick oak table in the carriage house leafing through the practice books, feeling as if I were sixteen again and practicing for the SATs, sitting out on the lawn by the pool, hoping to get a tan even though I wore sunscreen so I wouldn't burn, hoping Odette would bring her boyfriend, Larry, by so I could flirt with him—he obviously liked me, not that I'd ever betray her. I'd loved the power of flirting back then, before I knew what could be lost.

I needed to get into vet school because after many false starts, I had finally decided what I was going to do, and I needed them to see me succeed—my parents, and my sisters, too. Of course, they'd be wrapped in the milky gauze of new motherhood—which they would juggle perfectly with their work and sex lives—but still, I knew a little piece of them wanted me settled in some way.

I typed in the last answers on my exam, hit save, then send. I was finished. All the eggs were in the basket, and I had to wait to see whether they'd hatch.

My father was missing, and still time ticked on, the grass grew, and the team of silent gardeners amassed on the estate—my mother hired a service that used no power tools, so our entire two-acre lawn was mowed by hand, with a second worker following behind to rake up the cuttings and put them on the compost pile by the back of the property, where my mother brought eggshells and ceremoniously flung them over the six-foot white pickets the neighbors had been sorry to see, even though they kept the eyesore out of eyesight.

"O." I left another message for Olivia. "Call me and tell me you're okay."

When my phone beeped, I jumped.

"Olivia!"

"I'm okay, Clem." Then, before I could read anything from her tone, as if she suspected me of putting an emotional trace on her phone call, she hung up.

I threw my cell phone across the room, where it bounced on the plush couch upholstery and landed in a tasteful big-bellied crystal bowl full of river stones. It didn't crack.

My mom would talk about anything except my father.

"Would you like lunch?" she singsonged, rapping on my front door.

"I haven't heard anything—except that Olivia's okay," I called out to her. "And Dad has some other lawyer? Do you know about this?"

"I know Olivia's okay. I asked about *lunch*."

"Just finishing up here. I can't eat much because Eli's coming for dinner."

"Oh, Eli," she said, raising her eyebrows.

"No, Mom, Eli's my friend. Only my friend." It didn't matter what either of us felt—he'd been off-limits since he was my boy-friend's roommate in college.

"Either he's gay or he has a crush on you," she said, picking up the blood-orange spritzer she kept on the table by the door. It was hard for me to remember this was her guest home sometimes; it felt entirely mine until she waltzed in and reminded me her air needed freshening in case some real guests came.

"Okay. Chicken and watercress sandwiches," she said. My mother *looked* like tempting company. She had lip gloss and updated makeup—light foundation that made her face sunny, and shimmery, subtle eyeliner. She was reading a biography of Napoléon and would tell me all about his jealousies and motivations. She wouldn't talk about Dad, but she'd charm me the way she charmed everyone. It was possible that, with her makeup and clothes in place, my mother looked younger than I. I wore sweat-pants and a coffee-stained white, short-sleeved sweater. Sighing, I followed her over to the big house.

It was ridiculous, infuriating, and wrong that Olivia wouldn't tell any of us any more about what she knew. I called her relentlessly—or at least five or six times—and all my calls went to voice mail. I knew she was pressing the button. My sister was holding out against me, against Odette. Olivia had never done this before, and Dad was puppeting her, and I was confused, furious, and jealous. He must have known we would be jealous. Or maybe he didn't even consider us. Maybe I had too often imagined he thought of us; he was a narcissist. He was selfish. And yet I cared what he thought of me.

When I let myself think about it, I wanted to shake my bulbous sister, but I was doing my best not to think about it. It had been two days, and my mother had said as long as she knew he was safe, she didn't mind.

"If he were my husband," I told Mom, chewing on the delicious, thinly sliced sourdough, "I'd hire a detective." *I'd command Olivia to tell,* I thought. *I'd threaten divorce.*

"Do you like the bread? Mary Beth gave me the culture. She brought it back from her trip to San Francisco. Well-traveled bacteria!" My mother smiled.

I tried to smile honestly, but felt as though I were acting. My jaw ached. I took another bite.

I had eaten four meals at the house in the two days since he vanished, partly to keep an eye on her, at Odette's insistence. It was pleasant and uncomfortable, like an elaborate wool dress: itch and splendor. I leaned back on the kitchen chair, waiting for Mom to tell me to put the front legs down. We'd had almost an entire bottle of cabernet, probably worth more than my car, a ten-year-old Toyota with a dent in each fender, as if it had been hugged too hard. Mom tugged the watercress out of her sandwich and nibbled.

"Delicious," I admitted.

We used to have a full-time cook, but never a maid, only a cleaning service once a week. The Accounts. It amazed me that my mother, with her doctorate in comparative literature and executive experience, could spend more than three hours a day vacuuming an empty mansion without going mad.

"Don't you want to know?" I asked her as I washed and she dried. Never mind that we had a dishwasher, with just a few dishes my mother insisted on hand washing.

"No," she said. The room smelled of mayonnaise and the custom organic, lavender dish soap. I had eaten too much, my whole sandwich and Mom's scraps, two helpings of new potatoes in butter with parsley. I was supposed to be saving my appetite for Eli's genius work, but being around my mother made me nervous, so I ate to fill the hole.

"Mom, you have rights, too."

She dried my dish, once, twice, drying it over and over as if it had absorbed water and needed the constant attention of a dish towel to return to its ordinary state.

"I have that meeting at the Morristown Museum tonight," she said.

"He just *left*, Mom. And you go on as if everything's okay." I knew she didn't like how I patted the cutlery with the dish towel.

"I think you underestimate your father sometimes. I've had my more difficult moments." She sighed, and I could almost hear her editing her words before she spoke them. "And your dad was unfailing in his attentions. He's always encouraged me, supported me . . ."

"But, Mom, he's just gone off—"

"I used to dislike being left alone. But now I actually crave it."

"Left alone is one thing. Abandonment is another."

"When you have a husband, my dear, then you can make your own decisions about how you treat him. I trust your father." She put the dish in the cabinet and started rubbing at a spoon.

"Dad?" I asked his cell-number voice mail. "What the hell? We're worried about you, and Mom's calm, which means she's panicking, and how dare you? You're killing her! Call her, okay, Dad?"

I look like him. My father is seventy-three now; his hair has yielded to a faded silvery-red. He has a freckled forehead, a freckled chin, a freckled neck, and freckled chest, as I do. My sisters are smooth as cream. I don't mind the hair, though; it's dark enough to almost not be red. I think it's my best feature, suggestive of another color, suggestive of wildness when really I've been subdued since I decided to return to school.

After Mom left for her Morristown Museum meeting, I lingered in the big house, telling myself I'd just check the Diary, one more time, for clues. The Diary was the same, but I started fingering the table's little drawer pulls, tarnished brass, heavy curves like binder-clip handles, holding things together within. When we were little, we'd extract a rubber-band ball, risking the wrath of our organized mother. We'd bounce it in the hallway of the little house, peeling off the bands, counting, chaining, entertaining ourselves with the limited properties of afternoon and rubber.

Here was a packet of bills from the landscapers, all stamped PAID. Here was a tiny bundle of potpourri, bound in one of my mother's old stockings, dried rose petals that smelled uniquely of the Octavia rose. Here were old report cards wrapped in a ribbon. Odette's A A A A and a handwritten note from her seventh-grade teacher: "Olivia is an outstanding pupil!" *Olivia.* On *Odette's* report card. I didn't remember this story, but it must have felt wretched to Odette. It was one thing to be one of three wishes, and another entirely to be called by your sister's name—not just by a confused person, in person, but on a report card. I tucked the report cards back in the drawer. The house was ticking. Clocks in the living room, the grandfather in the hall, moon phases and exquisite serif numbers, and I realized I needed to climb up to Dad's attic office; I needed to hunt for more.

My steps required stealth; I'd outgrown my privileges to romp up the stairs. Of course, Dad was the one who encouraged romping. Dad, despite his seriousnesses, was playful in the privacy of houses. He played hide-and-seek with us in the couches, let us get wild, never reminded us not to bang our heads on the corners of furniture—so sometimes we did. Dad could tickle all three of us just by wiggling his fingers in our general direction, at least until high school. Possibly he could get me to laugh if he did it right now.

His office smelled like Dad. There was a paper smell, old books, and maybe something like cloves—probably aftershave, or something Mom used to press his shirts. I bit the inside of my cheek. I loved her care and I hated that she pressed his shirts, and that he was gone.

The desk itself was neat; the top drawer held fountain pens accompanied by their cartridges or ink bottles, mechanical pencils, felt tips, Sharpies, a regatta of writing instruments. The next drawer was just the office supplies—rubber bands again, paper clips segregated by color, a slide rule—a slide rule!—a metal protractor, a compass (the kind we used to stab holes in our paper when we were supposed to pencil perfect curves). Nothing suspicious. But then, beneath the drawer dividers holding this supply bonanza, something crinkled. I extracted a packet of papers, messy, very un-Dad-like, tied with string. Here was my sixth-grade report card. Math was only satisfactory. Here was a program from Olivia's production of Ionesco's *Rhinoceros,* first year at Harvard. Here was another report card—Olivia's? No. Not Olivia's. The first page was missing, but I didn't recognize the form. There was no year, only onionskin paper grown thin enough to hold to the light and trace. Someone had earned three A's and two B's. I couldn't remember a year anyone other than me had such a dismal record. Maybe it was Dad's—maybe Dad himself got two B's!

Here was a picture of Ella. I was beside her, but you could only see my leg. Here was a picture of my apartment in San Francisco. I felt a welling of love for this man who collected evidence of my life in a messy string-collated bundle. A school photo from third grade, my lower lip red and chapped, my shirt pastel blue, pansy-patterned, my eyes like his. Odette and Olivia were here, too, eyes so blue, clean, and distinct to me—the smallest fold around Olivia's mouth, I knew it was a secret sarcasm, even in third grade. And then there was an extra photo—sometimes whole sheets of the wallet-size ones never made it out of the school-photo envelopes because we had so few relatives with wallets to fill with our faces. It was someone I didn't know at all.

A quick poison ran through my veins—why did my dad have a photo of another kid? A mistake. Someone's stuck to ours in the envelope. I had to think it—Dad was not a pedophile. Olivia had said we'd be better off if he were dead. No. My dad—no. Maybe this girl was Dad's sister—we never knew if he had a sister, maybe he'd kept her photo bundled with ours by accident. I looked on the back but there was nothing. The background was like ours, mottled indigo of a fake sky. Would a photo of Dad's sister be in color? The girl herself looked a little pissed off, but her mouth was sweet in a smile—it was only her eyes that held irony. Straight, mouse-brown hair. A barrette and a middle part. A pink button-down shirt on a narrow chest. She looked maybe nine.

My dogs were barking—I'd left them far too long. I reassembled the bundle, tucking in the mystery photo. Maybe the photography studio sent home one of our classmates to keep the three of us company—I didn't know this girl, didn't remember her. Just one more look—Dad's yearbook from high school. I flipped through to his picture. Charles Lord, so young, so vulnerable and simultaneously stubborn. The dogs. I closed the book and put it on the shelf next to Chaucer. I wanted to read the Chaucer. It called me names—*science geek, procrastinator*—I should have taken the photo or the yearbook, but instead, still feeling guilty for intruding at all, I grabbed the volume of Chaucer and went back to my carriage house to let the dogs out.

I acquired my love of science from my father. I used to think we all inherited it, but I think Odette just loves being in charge and Olivia loves the drama of deliveries more than anything. She's the kind of doctor to whom patients ascribe undying love—during deliveries she tracks down the anesthesiologist and persuades him to bump up her patients in the schedule when they've changed their minds and don't want natural birth, but an epidural, and pronto. She finds private rooms when the whole hospital is full. The patients think she's a goddess and send her gift baskets of cheese, homegrown honeycomb, even jewelry. If I ever have a child, I want my sister to deliver it. I want my other sister to examine it. I want to be safely bracketed in their parentheses—whether I have a child or not.

Both my sisters glided through medical school because they inherited Dad's ease with learning, his quick mnemonics and methods and whole-page memory. One Thanksgiving my father laughed with glee as Odette recited, "Skip lifted Brian's law book heartily," then grinned and finished, "the five heaviest human organs: skin, liver, brain, lungs, and heart!"

Not to be outdone, Olivia chanted, "Old people from Texas eat spiders—the bones of the skull are occipital, parietal, frontal, temporal, ethmoid, sphenoid."

"Ethmoid schmethanoid" was all I had to add. I didn't have that kind of memory. School was hard work. If I saw the insides of something—an equation, an eyeball, a work of art—I understood it better, but I wished I could swallow whole ideas the way the three of them did, whole ideas that they could regurgitate whenever needed.

Odette knocked on my door, smiling seriously. She was on her BlackBerry, and she gave me the eyeball. As my dogs rallied around her, giving her the physical greeting I wished I could, too—smelling and wagging: you're you! I'm me!—I picked up my own phone and dialed her number, knowing she was going to patch me into a conference call.

"It's one of *those* birth plans," said Olivia, her voice the even, bright sound of her doctor-self.

"Well, her best friend is a militant midwife," said Odette, smiling at me as the phone clicked. "Not like mine—she's doc-friendly."

"Hello?" said Olivia. "Who are you talking to—O? You there?"

"Yep," said Odette, nodding as I listened in.

"*But under no circumstances shall the mother be anesthetized* makes it complicated . . . hello? That's Clementine?"

"Party Trick," I said, feeling a little mean, and a little nervous that she wouldn't do it. We always did it.

"Argh," said Olivia.

"We," Odette said.

"Need," I said.

"A," moaned Olivia.

"Family."

"Meeting."

"All right, already," said Olivia. "I'm not trying to protect the bastard; I just didn't want to waste all of our time."

"Tomorrow," said Odette.

"Fine," said Olivia. "Now about Mrs. Hindenberg."

Odette laughed. "Hillsmith."

"Good-bye, Clem," said Olivia. "You know, patient privacy and all that."

Where was Dad? What was he doing to the three of us?

We needed to, Odette wrote on a Post-it before she waved and left.

But as I watched her go, I was afraid that even though *we needed to,* Olivia still might shut us out, that our triple-hold would weaken for twin grappling, and if anything was worse than a constant harmonic, it was two notes, empty without their third.

FIVE

On the third day of Dad's absence, we held an afternoon family meeting in my diminutive living room. Mom refused to come at first, so we started without her, but as Odette predicted, she couldn't stay away and appeared bearing a tray of limeade garnished with mint leaves she'd grown in her conservatory. She had dipped the glass rims in sugar before she filled them.

"So," said Odette, continuing what we'd started without Mom. "There's this other lawyer, whoever she—or he—is. If you won't give, O, I say we make a list of possibilities. And split up the contact list on his cell phone. If we can unlock it. Mom, surely you know the code?"

Our mother hummed and distributed limeade, acting mysteriously deaf, as if, if she pretended she couldn't hear, other people would forget she was listening. If I cover my eyes, you can't see me.

"Mom?" said Odette.

"O, this is ridiculous." Olivia had been sitting in the big chair, an enormous plum with sticks for legs in her graceful mauve maternity dress. She'd told us already, six or seven alternative ways, that Dad was safe and he'd contact us soon. That she didn't want to talk about it. She looked like Mom, lips thin, containing confidences. All I could read from her was a fat, fuzzy thought caterpillar, with occasional shock-shots of food. A fudge-filled shortbread cookie, a single slice of pink ham. That must be how pregnancy felt—at least one where you were keeping your father's secrets.

"No, you're ridiculous," said Odette, sweating a little. She had been pacing my living room. I felt Odette, her anxiety in my own stomach, an acid lining. She was guessing numbers for Dad's code—7/7, our birthday; 11/20, Mom's . . . I was awash in her worry. But Olivia only emanated the blur and the food, no thoughts, no distinct feeling. It was as if she wore a lead apron against the two of us, using her triplet superpower to reveal or veil.

Odette kicked off her clogs because her ankles were swollen. Her maternity dress was much like Olivia's, only black. Every now and then I thought I saw an elbow or a knee make its way across the surface of her belly.

"You know better than to keep this from us." Odette addressed Olivia with a teary look.

"Girls," said my mother, her voice high and childish. "It's so nice to have you here all together."

"Jesus," said Odette. "Don't be ridiculous."

"Ridiculous, *ridicularum, ridiculas* . . . ," Olivia started, as if we were holding Latin class.

"O," said Odette, her eyes mildly desperate.

"You all right?" I asked her, because my sister never panicked. She succumbed to anger, sure, but she had a lawyer's steadfast intent. She never looked like this. As if she might cry. I might cry. I still imagined him dead. I walked over to Olivia and put my hand on her shoulder, trying to divine the source of her hermetically sealed information vault.

"Why does he have some extra lawyer?" I whispered. "Is he divorcing Mom?"

"It's not that," Olivia said. "It's not about Mom, not really." Olivia closed her eyes. "I don't like this," she continued, pausing to catch her breath, though she sat still, almost motionless except for her worried mouth. "Any more than you do. If he hadn't asked me to keep this to myself—anyway—he's being a jerk, but that doesn't mean I can't respect his wishes."

"Planning a funeral, Olivia?" I asked, because I saw a crack and wanted to pull it apart with my fingers. *"Respect his wishes?"*

"He's fine." Olivia's eyes opened: sudden blue. "Really." She took my hand in hers briefly, then dropped it. "I don't think he called me on purpose. That is, I just answered. I thought it was about this case he was helping me review—"

"Since when—," Odette interjected. "I didn't—"

"Shh!" I said.

"Fine. I'm not talking to you," asserted Odette childishly.

"Dad gave me his lawyer's number in case I go into labor," Olivia said. "Or—"

"Why would a lawyer care?" Mom looked sharp, but softened, a wave reaching knife edge, then receding, liquid.

"What about me?" Odette pouted.

"You aren't talking to me," said Olivia. "But I was about to say in case you go into labor, too."

"It's inevitable," I said, unable to help myself in the face of their fecundity.

"He had some old family business—but I know about it because I read his papers, not because he confided in me," said Olivia.

I thought of the child's photograph I'd found among our report cards. Obviously I wasn't the only snoop—and maybe I'd been too late to get any real evidence—of what I still didn't know.

"You know, it's the first time he ever did anything that was just *me*, not me and O—O and O and O and O and O . . . ," Olivia continued. "Clem, you may not have grown out of wanting negative attention, but I still—"

"Hey!" I interjected, but stopped myself. I wanted to hear everything she was willing to say. Or at least I hoped I wanted to hear it.

"Still," her voice was mellowing; a decrescendo. "It was something *just me*. And now I realize this was only because I was convenient that he told me, not because I was special." She pouted—a recalcitrant, stylishly plump mama-to-be. I thought she got more than her fair share of attention.

"What old family business? What old family? Mom, what the hell?"

"Don't swear, Clementine," said Mom. "I don't know," she whispered. "I don't know."

"There were just some people from his, um, childhood," said Olivia. "I think he realized he's mortal. And he has some old friend who's dying or something."

My mother looked wounded. "Some old friend I don't know?" she pondered. "Your father and his opacity."

"He's mortal?" Odette said.

"I hope so," grumbled Olivia.

"What old friends?" I asked. My mother put her hand over my hand like a punctuation mark. A musical *fin*. End.

"He's fine," said my mother, picking up my glass and placing a coaster under it, though the table was glass.

"If that's all, girls . . . ," said my mother. "Anyone hungry?"

My mother, brilliant with a conservatory of flowers, a multi-tasking Library Friends volunteer and country-club member, was sometimes like a toddler. Sometimes, when I saw her stamping her foot as she argued with my father about something—his last-minute weekends away, his insistence that I could only move in if I didn't bring my ferret (Mom won, and I kept my entire menagerie)—she looked like a three-year-old having a tantrum. Her face contorted, she was threatening to cry. But as I watched her now, since I'd been living at home, as I'd watched her with my sisters, with the gardeners, with the woman who delivered organic produce twice weekly in reusable baskets, I realized this was just her way, that it had little to do with marriage.

"We're hiring a private investigator," said Odette, walking over to the window and looking out at the lawn.

"You don't need to," said Olivia, almost conciliatory.

"Yes, I do," said Odette. "*We* do," she said, looking at me, and my sister. "And if you're not going to tell us what you know, it's going to cost more."

"This isn't necessary," said my mother softly.

"I have work," said Olivia, heaving herself out of the chair.

"Fine," I said. Ella began to bark; she wanted out. Alphabet joined in with his houndlike howl. I picked up the leashes and nodded to the women of my family. "Thank you, Odette. Gotta go." If no one would tell me anything else, I wanted them all to leave. I wanted to strategize with Odette over the phone. I wanted Olivia to crack. But it wasn't going to happen like this. I looked up at the house as I came out of mine, hoping the Mercedes might suddenly appear. He may have been opinionated, sometimes even small-minded, but I didn't want my father dead. And it was hard to imagine why he would need another lawyer. What kind of fight was he waging? Was it for money, or love, or his family we never knew? It was hard to imagine Dad needing to fight for something, perpetual king of the castle. We played that—he was the castle and we climbed atop his shoulders at the lake in Greensboro, wrestling to be the girl he'd dunk into the water. He was rarely there, rarely with us, but when he was there, he was there in body, playful, when we were young enough for that sort of play. What would make Olivia both tight-lipped for him and furious at him?

By the time I came back from letting Ella and Alphabet sniff all around the pool, dig around the mossy base of dogwood at the back of the property, and finally pee in the hostas (a little uric acid wouldn't kill them—hopefully), I saw Eli's little frying-grease-rigged Corolla parked on my little gravel driveway. He was sitting on the stoop, and my sisters and mother were gone.

My friend Eli came over to the carriage house twice a week for dinner. I bought ingredients and he cooked; that had been our arrangement since college, when I was in a dining cooperative and he was scraping by to afford his fifth year—he was getting double degrees in piano performance and biology and was one of the smartest men I'd ever met—and I'd pilfer the stores at the co-op, bringing home a block of cheese, two avocados, six slices of bread, whatever seemed extra enough to take.

Eli is a brilliant cook. His mother was a chef, and she became a TV personality, a celebrity chef, just as the concept took off. Food TV. She was half-Indian and wore wrap dresses and exotic hairstyles that made her every bit as gorgeous as her food. Eli grew up in Manhattan, sometimes attending school, sometimes substituting with a tutor on the set. She was glamorous and he was a geek. She died in a small-plane crash in the Alps two years before college; Eli went to live with a father he'd hardly known in Cleveland, and then on to Oberlin, which is where we met.

"I couldn't get portabella mushrooms," I said. "They only had these little thingies." I pulled out a bag of the tiny soldiers they'd had at Whole Foods. Gorgeous objects with fat, smooth heads and a gorgeous, woody scent. And at $18.99 a pound, I could only afford a thimble-size bouquet, but I didn't point this out to Eli. Eli's mother had had a lot of money, but it was tied up in probate court; he had to live on very little as he finished his Ph.D. in biology at Princeton, teaching his way through grad school, living in a nasty apartment in East Brunswick I refused to visit because I was afraid to walk the six blocks from the bus to his door. He was studying food science—he specialized in the health benefits of food diversity, but it came down to hours and hours of lab work.

"Oh, goodie, criminis!" said Eli, carefully extracting them from the bag. "They're baby portabellas, Clem, even better—these are delectable. I'm not going to make the frittata then. These deserve more of a showcase. Spring rolls, I think. Do you have the carrots?"

I handed him a bag of baby carrots. "Organic."

"Oh, I would've preferred real, live long carrots with the tops on." He looked up at me. I was scowling. "But of course. Just what I wanted, these." He kissed my nose.

"So," said Eli, chopping scallions, his elegant hands dangerously close to the blade of his knife—which he brought with him everywhere the way someone else might bring a cell phone. Eli rarely remembered his cell phone, and it usually needed a battery charge. "What's the word on your dad?"

Of course I'd told him everything. Well, almost everything. I hadn't told him that in my secret heart it gave me pleasure that Dad was gone, gave me a tiny sense of peace I hadn't known I was missing. There was a lot in my life I was missing, but until now, I hadn't known I was furious enough with the man to wish him gone.

"Maybe he's dying, or maybe he has Alzheimer's," I said, thinking aloud. "God, I hope he's not dying." I was unable to avoid it—what had happened to Cameron made me go there, to unexpected endings.

I looked over at the framed family portrait from my sisters' wedding on the desk and noticed how my father's head was bigger than everyone else's, how there was something almost vulnerable in the way he curved around my mother, trying to conform to the shorter stature of everyone else in the picture. My brothers-in-law stood square and proud; my father slouched. I couldn't bear his face because it made me think about his mortality, all the possibilities, so I put the photo facedown on the desk, but gently.

"Clem?" Eli put down his scallion work and touched my cheek. Just friends, but he still made me blush. Eli dried his hands and sat on the floor with Ella, tugging gently at her ears in play, the way Dad did. "Who's a beautiful girl?" he whispered to her.

"I really resent this drama. You know I love the man, no matter how difficult he might be. He may have been frequently late and emotionally absent, but, Eli, he knows me, and he eventually arrives, and I think he wants me to be whatever it is I am—only better, of course. He wants," I stopped to pat Ella, who was nudging my hand and woofing gently, having lost Eli to another hand washing and his kitchen prep.

"He *wants* to be proud of me. I do love him."

"I know you love him," said Eli. "But sometimes I'm not sure you *like* him all that much."

"Neither am I." I tasted a scallion, the slippery sliver between my teeth like the taste of a pond, like the taste of something slightly disgusting, and slightly wonderful.

SIX

We moved to Princeton when we were eleven. We had been ordinary girls, except for being triplets, in Oakville. There the questions at school were about why I didn't look like them, whether I had been held back a grade, how we could all be the same age, and, in shrieking, giggling, private sessions in friends' houses, how our parents had conceived us all at the same time. In Princeton, there were questions of objects and services; basically, we were measured by our wealth.

Suddenly we had our own rooms. Mine was on the third floor; in a moment of extravagant fairness, my mother had us draw straws to choose our rooms, and I won first pick—the longest piece of a cut, red-and-white-striped bendy straw from a box of one hundred. I wasn't sure, despite trying to listen, whether my sisters wanted the top room, but it had the most privacy, and its own bathroom, and secret eaves with short doors and tiny, silver-chained latches.

"I want the third-floor suite," I said, feeling grandiose. "Can the bathroom be mine, too?"

"Yes," said my mother. "But the other two rooms are for your father—he wants an office up there."

The idea of sharing a floor with my father made me nervous.

— 63 —

What if I was taking a bath and he needed to use the bathroom? Still, he was home so rarely, it was worth it. What if my father was different around just me—would I recognize him? Would I want or eschew the possibility of unplanned attention? Without testing this in my sisters' heads, I wasn't sure.

I wondered why he traveled so much, but knew I wasn't supposed to ask. He had recently attended an alternative-anesthesia seminar in Las Vegas; he'd let me keep the wax ear marked with acupuncture points and Mandarin characters telling what they were for. He'd pointed to a red dot with his long-fingered hands, saying, "I think this one's for the spleen, and this one's for the tickle spot." Then he'd tickled my armpits, making me squeal and twist away.

Dad was absent during our relocation, so my mother was left to instruct the movers, six short, powerful Irishmen wearing green T-shirts and flirting with all of us, where to deposit our things. They hauled crates of books atop their heads, stepping heavily up three flights of stairs, grinning and winking. I loved their accents.

There were nine bedrooms in the house, and eleven bathrooms, so there was no dearth of choices, but mine was clearly the most secluded, like a penthouse in a posh hotel. My windows were original glass from 1910, and they blushed mottled and uneven sunlight. We chose wallpaper from catalogs; we picked rugs and curtains (I chose a mint-green, lacy fabric labeled Spring Fever, and my mother laughed a short sound of surprise when she saw the price, but bought them anyway).

We had been ordinary girls, and now we were rich girls. Of course, the other girls at our school were richer; their mothers didn't keep Accounts books, didn't bring them to Nordstrom but limit their expenditures, looking nervously in a tiny notebook, mumbling about sales tax. They shopped at the Lilly Pulitzer flagship store in Manhattan; they bought chunky, white-framed sunglasses at a counter at Saks Fifth Avenue. Still, our house was huge, and there was a gardening crew, and a cook and a cleaning service, and we had ponies.

My sisters took to it all with natural ease—not that they were greedy, they were just adaptable. While before we had gossiped wistfully about birthday parties at the roller rink in Montvale, now we were invited into air-conditioned limos that conveyed us to Broadway and hip plays at the Little Red School House. I wore my Gap jeans and polo shirt from Nordstrom, my sneakers from a former life instead of pumps—who could walk in pumps? And besides, our mother didn't want to cast away our old clothes just because we were living in a state of endowment.

"Those jeans still clothe you," she said to us when we told her in concert how our classmates all wore Jordache instead of Gap. "You aren't going naked, but we aren't spending more unless we need to. We *have,* but that makes us all the more responsible," she said, squinting at the parsley she was chopping in the new kitchen, which had a walk-in fridge and so many cabinets and drawers that half were empty.

We played hide-and-seek, climbing up above the water glasses where our new friends would never look for us.

At first, we three went to the same parties, all had the same friends, before we branched out, before we were differentiated— me, and them. Until I met my friends Sophie and Mary, I was part of The Clump of girls, the vaguely popular group—neither most nor least. I felt that I was acting. My sisters felt secure—it was a distinct imbalance. They couldn't comfort me, though, or didn't want to. Sophie and Mary changed things for me—a pair of girls who wore dark lipstick and cast spells from a book of Wiccan magic and had their palms read in Greenwich Village—and who also read books all the time and liked not just riding horses, but caring for them.

After we rode the trails together, we sat on our ponies—mine was a fat, black, walleyed sweetie named Giselle who seemed asleep except when there were sugar cubes. We groomed them and French-braided their tails and read aloud to each other and our animals from a collection of Elisabeth Bishop poems, not entirely understanding.

I wasn't part of The Clump anymore, but in sixth grade I tried out for the school musical, even though that was a highly Clump-like activity. Mary and Sophie scoffed, but they respected me for doing something I wanted. I wanted to sing. I wanted to act. I wanted to be on Broadway, though I was shy and my classmates were stunned, sitting like flies waiting to be shooed from a windowsill in the auditorium, when I belted out the audition song, "I've Never Been in Love Before," from *Guys and Dolls,* with passion, volume, and surprising talent. I'd been singing to the Beatles, warbling along with Ella Fitzgerald records our father kept in a wooden crate beside the record player he'd built himself, balancing the arm in a pool of glorious liquid mercury.

My sisters tried out, too, and won parts as Hot Box girls. To everyone's surprise, I was cast in the starring role of Sarah, the missionary who falls in love with a gangster. And to my pleasure and mortification, Sky Masterson, my romantic partner, was played by Grey Munro, who had moved from South Africa in fifth grade, when we were new to the school together. Grey was tall and was redheaded, like me, and he saw snow for the first time at age eleven. We'd been talking about electricity and were taking turns at a board assembled by the window, trying to complete circuits in pairs to light a bulb. Odette was my partner, and she was working so quickly I just stared out the window. Silently she told me, *I've got it; don't bother.*

"It's snowing," I said quietly, wondering at the way the world was suddenly muted.

"Snow?" asked Grey, knocking over his chair as he ran to the window. Any other teacher would've told him to sit down, to wait his turn, but Mrs. Carrigan, whom we all adored, told Grey he could go outside. By himself. Smack in the middle of the electricity lesson. We all watched him out the window as he held his hands up toward the sky, coatless, wearing brown corduroys and a striped T-shirt that made him look like a kid from *ZOOM.* His face was glorious with recognition, with joy and a tiny bit of fear as the snow kissed his face.

"He's weird," said Odette.

"That's okay," I said. She looked at me, recognizing something, but being honorable, not teasing.

Grey's eyes were very, very blue. I loved him from that moment.

Unfortunately, there were two Sarahs and two Skys in our production of *Guys and Dolls,* and we'd each get two nights, one with each partner. And unfortunately, the other Sky was Gary Waters, who was shorter than me and always tried at lunch recess to snap my bra strap or steal my lunch or trip and catch me. I didn't realize until later that he had a crush on me as potent as my crush on Grey. Meanwhile, Grey had kissed one of the Clumps, a girl named Nicole, at a boy-girl party I hadn't attended—though my sisters were there and offered thorough reports that made me wince and ask for more. Nicole was claiming she and Grey were boyfriend and girlfriend, though Grey didn't seem particularly involved in this endeavor.

My mother came to rehearsals and sat with her knitting, embarrassing me just by being there, by knitting, by wearing a dress she'd made herself with the Marimekko fabric left over from our couch slipcovers. Often, she missed mortifying me as she drove Odette and Olivia to matching Suzuki violin lessons, to figure skating and twirling, all of which I'd forgone after a lesson or two. After the show, I'd ask for voice lessons and study for three years with a divorced Princeton grande dame who'd been on Broadway for sixteen years before retiring to the suburbs. She wore scarves on her head and had scars from melanomas that had been removed—she'd been a serious tanner—and she smoked between lessons on her screened-in porch. I had already taken two years of school clarinet lessons—I knew outside lessons were expensive, and despite the house, despite the money, Mom still checked the Accounts every day; she still made slipcovers and her own dresses, so I couldn't help worrying about money in concert with her silent obsession.

I would be a fine singer, but I wasn't good at clarinet. If I practiced, I got a perpetually chapped lower lip and a little improvement. If I didn't practice, the sessions in the basement of the lunch hall were somewhat more bearable, as my teacher, the spindly and sweaty Mr. Peterson, would demonstrate for more of the half hour rather than sitting through my squeaks and cracked notes, wincing and encouraging, which consisted of patting my shoulder with his gigantic, blunt hand.

Sixth grade was a year of longing: for my mother to give me more attention than my sisters, but also not to embarrass me, the way all sixth-grade mothers embarrass their girls; for Grey to kiss me—which he would, onstage—for real; for my father to come to the play, even though he was away all the time now on business trips. Oftentimes he brought Lee, the nurse-practitioner who worked in his practice. She'd been working with him since we moved to Princeton—an oddly chic woman, wearing the fringe and flowers of the seventies, and no makeup except for thick kohl eyeliner, which made her exotic. She was always in his office when I came to visit. She was young and she brought us gifts—when I said I was interested in learning French, she came to dinner with six storybooks in French. When Olivia said she loved horse figurines, Lee brought a little white shelf to hang in Olivia's room, and three tiny Hagen-Renaker ceramic horses—one prancing, one with ears erect and tail asway, and one speckled pony. She brought flowers for my mother and kissed my father on the lips. To be fair, she kissed my mother on both cheeks, like a Frenchwoman.

We adored Lee; she was exotic and amazed us with what she could accomplish without the benefit of a husband. I never knew what my mother really thought of her; she flushed when Lee kissed her hello. Mom always included Lee at Thanksgiving and Christmas parties. She chose Lee's holiday gifts and consulted with us; I helped her the year Lee received a music box that had tiny brass animals spinning while "Für Elise" rang out of the speakers like a discussion.

Later, Lee left the practice and had a baby out of wedlock. We still said that, then, *out of wedlock*. She adopted another child from Guatemala and moved to Boston and, like that, left our lives. It was the special disempowerment of childhood that kindled a small fury in me. If Lee could leave, anyone could leave, and I had no choice but to administer my affections elsewhere.

All through dress rehearsals for the play I was worried my father wouldn't see me, hear me sing and fake hiccup, playing drunk after drinking *Dulce de Leche* in Havana, sets painted by my friends Sophie and Mary, who had stopped wearing black lipstick in favor of clumpy mascara and peachy lip gloss pocketed from Sophie's mother's vast collection of cosmetics. I was afraid my father would watch me when I kissed Grey, or Gary, and that he would mind. Or that he'd miss it, so he wouldn't.

Closing night was my night with Grey. On our second night, which was my first performance, I'd kissed Gary, and he'd tried to push his tongue past my teeth, a fat slug of tongue, tasting of Bazooka gum and pizza. I pulled away and delivered my line, about feeling dizzy, and stepped back on the stage. Then I'd sung "If I Were a Bell I'd Be Ringing," and thought about Grey, about how just last week he'd crouched down on all fours, offering me his back as a step stool in gym class, so I could reach the first knot on the climbing rope. How I'd been embarrassed that I could do more push-ups than all the other girls and some of the boys. How Grey's back had felt warm under my sock-clad feet. How his eyes were dark blue in the stage lights, how I couldn't even remember what it felt like to kiss him in dress rehearsal; I'd been so nervous, it was as if it had never happened.

My father wasn't in the audience, or at least he hadn't come in with my mother, who was wearing the same embarrassing Marimekko dress and holding little gifts for my sisters and me in her lap, little wrapped things from the town's gift shop that were probably beaded bracelets my sisters had coveted for weeks.

Then I was singing, and kissing Grey—this time I remembered, because I pulled away as quickly as I had with Gary, feeling the eyes of the audience on us, feeling how dry his lips were, and my own, how hot it was under the lights. He smelled of wool and limes, delicious. He grinned at me, but he was acting. I wore a blue wrap skirt that had been my mother's, and a high, white blouse. My hair was back in a bun, and I had chosen Chinese slippers so I wouldn't be taller than Grey, who wore loafers with a little heel. Mrs. Carrigan had wanted me to wear character shoes, but I didn't have any. I cast my focus into the audience, wishing I'd let the kiss last, wishing he had, wishing it had felt like more than the lightest moth-brush of mouths, like the momentous opportunity it really was, instead of brief, too brief to make an impression on this boy I adored, just a stage kiss, nothing real. Despite the lights, I could see my father in the back, having come in too late to get a decent seat, and he held an enormous bouquet of flowers in his lap.

I drew out the audience with my fake hiccups; I sang, holding the notes the way Mrs. Carrigan had instructed me. I ran backstage in my Chinese slippers at the end, and Mrs. Carrigan squeezed my arm and told me to pull my socks up. Then we went out for bows. My father came to the front of the auditorium and handed me the bouquet. Never mind my Hot Box sisters, who wore supershort skirts and sparkles on their lips. My father brought me a fat bouquet with roses, African daisies, freesia, and orchids. It must've cost a fortune. He was wearing a suit and smelled like the airplane he'd been on less than an hour before, but he brought me the flowers and kissed my cheek and I adored my father, in that moment, more than Grey, more than the whole stageful of classmates who had been stunned that shy Clementine was their star. Then Grey's mother brought him a bouquet of garden flowers—heavy-headed peonies and poisonous, handsome lily of the valley, and Grey turned and handed them to me. He may even have said something, but I couldn't hear it for the applause. And then I made a mistake I would rue forever—in that moment of pleasure and confusion, I walked over to Mrs. Carrigan as she took her own drama coach's bow and handed her all my flowers, as if they'd been intended for her all along.

For the last week of school, I walked by her classroom and visited my flowers from afar. They had been meant just for me, from my father, from Grey's mother, who must actually have looked at me, who must have said something about me to Grey—such a titillating possibility, that my name had come into their house like a visitor—and I hadn't been able to bear all that attention, but I wanted it now, when it was too late to take the gesture back.

Even back then, Odette and Olivia never faltered—they'd planned on medical school forever. "Pass the butter. Cornell is pretty good" was the sort of thing my father said at dinner. We sat around a huge table in Princeton, oval and teak, which smelled of the Murphy oil soap my mother used to clean it herself.

"Our daughters can do whatever they want," my mother said in a rare moment of assertiveness. We were eating meat loaf, which the cook had made at the triplets' request. My mother made the mashed potatoes herself, and my father grunted that there was no point in having a cook if she was going to waste her talents making plebeian food.

"I know," said Odette. "But we *want* to go to medical school."

"Speak for yourself," I said.

"She can speak for me," said Olivia, wadding a buttered roll into her mouth.

"This isn't an eating competition," said my mother.

It's okay, said Odette silently. I didn't want to listen.

"And Columbia," said Dad. "Of course you'll be legacies at Harvard."

"I want to be a vet," I said. I'd been waiting for the dog they'd promised me when I turned ten, but Dad lied and said Mom was allergic. I had rabbits in a hutch in the backyard, the ponies, two chickens that I tended until the neighbors complained about the noise and odor—from over an acre away I couldn't imagine they'd have any idea, but mother agreed and the chickens went off to be fricasseed, or whatever. I ate meat; I wasn't rabid with rights or anything, I just loved them, the differentness of animal bodies, their quiet attention to the world. When I told my father I was planning this, I hoped he'd give me a little smile, a little redemption, since I was the odd one out, the runt, the unmatched spoon. Instead, he'd made an odd growling sound.

"Ha," he coughed.

"Or an artist," I continued. "Or chanteuse."

"She makes wonderful pots in that class," said my mother, and I silently thanked her for defending me. She took a bit of oily salad, and a speck fell on the front of her shirt—it was enough to make me want to leave the table.

I could hear Olivia thinking, *Mom is mortifying.*

And Odette: *Poor Mom.*

"You think you'll get into vet school?" my father asked.

"Yes."

"We'll see," he said. "Anyway, why would you want to work with heartworm and ticks? You'd spend most of your life excising the reproductive organs of cats and dogs."

"Charles," said my mother. "That's not necessary."

"I'm not trying to be cruel, Octavia; vets mainly neuter and vaccinate."

"And doctors cut out the reproductive organs of people, too," I said. "And make their noses look like other people's noses instead of their own. And make old ladies look like they're in a state of perpetual surprise. If it's just about money, almost any profession has its limitations."

"Enough," said my father.

"Your father helps children," said my mother. "You know that."

"And I can help animals." I meant it, that helping animals seemed every bit as important as helping humans.

"May we be excused?" Olivia asked for both of them. Always for both of them.

If my sisters ever wanted to do anything else, they never let on. Sure, their anticipated specialties changed, from emergency medicine ("It's sexy," said Olivia, when we were in seventh grade, trying to shock someone. "No," said my father. "It's underpaid and dangerous") to pediatrics ("the least-respected specialty," said my father, though later he recanted, when Odette finished her rotation and found she held a lingering love for babies and toddlers and even teens) to psychiatry, for a while, for Olivia, when she was fifteen and thought our parents were repressed. Which they were.

In our eleventh year, shortly after we moved to Princeton, Odette once ran away—she left the house and went to the Big Rock, an island at the end of the block where you could watch boys ride by on bikes and ants navigate the preposterous cavern of a crack in the glacial erratic that stood about four feet high and was a perfect cool spot for thinking. Odette took a whole packet of graham crackers and the peanut butter jar, though she forgot the knife. Olivia, of course, went after her. We were all in fifth grade, and Odette had gotten a B on a paper about mummies. It was fall and the wind washed my face of the long red hair that usually covered my eyes, caught in my mouth like a question.

"Mom," I said, calling out to the hallway. It was always too quiet in the house when my sisters were out; I could hear the floorboards agonizing under my weight as I walked to the stairwell.

"Mom!" This time I yelled it. This was the way it worked: Odette did, Olivia followed or judged; I told. That was our natural order. Sometimes we were protecting each other; sometimes we were simply illustrating the autonomic responses of triplethood.

"You can come up here," said my mother, who was arranging leaves in a vase on the landing. Dad was away again; this time some drug company had flown him to San Francisco for a conference on postoperative-pain management. Lee was with him. I wasn't sure whether I was more jealous that she was with him or that he was with her, but mostly it didn't matter, except that Mom seemed more distracted when he was gone. We had pancakes for dinner, the cook was off, and when Olivia had asked for bacon, Mom had just sighed, never answering.

"Mom," I called up the stairs. "Odette ran away. She took the peanut butter."

"She'll be back," said Mom, humming the Schubert quintet.

"She got a B."

"Okay," said Mom.

"A B. Does that mean she won't get into medical school?"

"Honey," said my mother, looking at me in a way she never did at dinner, "not every minute of every day is about medical school."

"I know. Odette doesn't run away, though."

"She won't go far," said my mother, suddenly wise. I wished I could turn them off the way she could. Sometimes I didn't want to listen; I didn't want to know them before myself.

"Why does it bother her so much? It hurts," I said, showing Mom the vulnerable spot in my throat where I felt Odette's tenderness.

"Sometimes I'm not so sure you girls have a balanced attitude." Mom picked a tiny ant off her leaves and squashed it between thumb and forefinger, then casually wiped it in a tissue. *You could've put it outside,* I wanted to say.

And at that moment I felt more alone than I had, probably, since being born. My mother was trying to reach out, but her arms were short. I wanted that comfort—I wanted her all to myself, and here we were, alone together, but we were still each alone.

"One of us does," I said.

SEVEN

I did belong at home in some ways; just a few days after I moved into the carriage house to take classes and apply to vet school, I volunteered to help at the Princeton Junction animal shelter, three days a week. It was close to my sisters' McMansions, but not too close—there's no way the property values would allow for the inevitable barking and urine odor of a shelter. Each time I newly loathed the stink, though after a dozen or so minutes each time it blended into a sort of acrid background. The manager kept the shelter very, very clean because the most dramatic drain on a shelter's finances is veterinary care, and with so many animals—often sick with worms or viruses or infections—in close quarters, sickness spread. I spent most of my volunteer time sterilizing cages, with bleach and hot water and scrubbing brushes wearing a pair of enormous rubber boots. "Are you using the boats?" I would call out to the other volunteers. We took turns wading. My hands were raw, inflamed, and parched, but I felt as though the world was a slightly better place for my work.

After I was done scrubbing, I would give the dogs a little playtime, walks, and the kind of examination someone who has not yet been to vet school can give them, in hopes of solving the mysteries of their appetite loss, hoarse barking, limps, or dry noses. It wasn't that I neglected the cats (though since watching *Lady and the Tramp* at age five, I have never had the same love for elusive, claw-bearing felines as dogs, who were all habit and trust), it's that the majority of the shelter was filled with dogs, and because of the neighborhood, those dogs were often purebreds—golden retrievers, Lhasa apsos, Pekinese, pugs, a veritable breeder-ville of expensive animals who had jumped their invisible fences, whose owners were too busy at work to notice that Jessica the Labradoodle was gone, off in search of entertainment, skunks, and garbage cans unfettered by the rubber straps that challenged toppling.

Walking around the neighborhoods of Princeton Junction three days after Dad went AWOL, I scanned all the empty houses, their open-eyed windows looking out on geometrically mani-cured lawns.

One particular dog had been my favorite for the past three weeks—I was calling her Pony because she was a Harlequin Great Dane, and tall enough for a small child to ride. My own animals were quite huffy when I came home smelling of Pony, but she needed attention, needed to play ball in the tiny patch of grass by the parking lot, needed to tell me, in her silent, drooly way, that she was sorry she was taking up too much time and space. Poor thing—she hadn't been underfed, and she showed no signs of ill-ness, but she was the most apologetic dog I'd ever met, and though she wasn't hand shy and showed no signs of abuse, I kept thinking she'd had a family expert in psychological torture of some kind, to make her seem so embarrassed by her own presence. It was a glorious presence, too. When I walked her down the street and back, she was so light on the shelter leash you hardly felt her, and people stared openly from their car windows, oogling the dog as they might a movie star.

I've always been a softie for the orphaned. Dead birds on the road made me weep for their children. My God, these poor dogs had no families! It seemed so lonely, so cast-off. I couldn't imagine not knowing my sisters existed—for whatever fights we had, we'd gouge out the eyes of anyone who betrayed another of us. Alone, so alone, poor Pony!

"Pony," I said as I brushed her in the little grooming room behind the reception desk. "You know I'm waiting, right?"

Pony looked at me quizzically, her tail straight down, her eyes averting when mine met them.

"He's not perfect, but I only have one Dad. It's like there's a shoe about to drop somewhere."

Pony tilted her head. I wanted to take this one home.

I wrested my cell phone out of my pocket for the fifth time in about ten minutes and checked. I felt his missing, a glowing pain, almost pleasure.

Pony's tail waved, a low, quiet gesture. She gave my hand a swipe with her giant tongue. I would not cry, and I would not take her home unless she didn't find another one. I bit my lip, drawing a little blood. Then I changed the subject.

"And I'm waiting for my Chem grade, which may help and hopefully won't hurt."

Pony's soft, beautiful flank quivered.

"Is that too hard?" I put the brush down, a rubber groomer we stored in a jar of disinfectant like a barbershop comb.

"Hello?" queried someone walking into the shelter, calling through the open office door.

"Oh!" A woman wearing a Versace suit and carrying a patent leather briefcase. "You're getting her ready for me?"

"Excuse me?" *We are not your groomers,* I wanted to say, *you selfish, irresponsible lady. Maybe* lady *was too generous.*

"I was going to send the nanny, but she doesn't like driving with Alexandria in the car."

"Alexandria?" Of course, people sometimes came to claim their pets at shelters—I'd volunteered on and off for years and had seen happy reunitings and the angry relief of dog owners who had left the fence open, who had meant to keep the collar on, who had moved and forgotten to relicense, who let their dogs run off leash in the park and stopped too long to gossip. But somehow I hadn't expected Pony to go home. I knew better than to grow attached—I had enough in the way of furry and scaly attachment waiting for me in the carriage house.

"There will be paperwork," I grumbled, watching closely to see if Pony—Alexandria—was afraid of this woman.

"I called ahead, I simply can't do it now—I have to be in court at ten—" The woman waved her hand at me and opened the half door that separated the office from the lobby with deft, beautifully manicured fingers.

"No," I said. "The manager will be back in twenty minutes—or so." She had left to pick up her daughter at preschool because someone had thrown up in the water table.

"No," said the woman. She held out her credit card, like a threat. *Take this and nothing else matters.*

"No," I said. "You didn't look for her for three weeks."

Pony barked.

"You'll have to come back later."

"I cannot accept this," she spat. "You are not entitled to judge me."

I started to feel not just annoyance, not just a mild flush of anger, but an explosive rage. The kind of rage I hadn't felt since my father and I had fought about my switching out of premed, since I'd watched my mother pack my father's suitcase for yet another trip, folding his shirts with a mechanical expertise, never questioning how much time he dedicated to his research, his work, his extracurriculars. This woman thought she could cavalierly lose and find her dog, leave the responsibility to the nanny and the volunteers at the shelter. She probably bought the dog just to show off—giant-breed owners either really loved dogs or were especially vain and thought of them as unusual accessories. I couldn't see this woman, whose heels were thin enough to sew with, walking Pony. I couldn't see her remembering to feed her dog since she clearly rarely ate herself. How dare she, how dare people expect other people to simply fuel their lives, to flock around them in adoration or be off with the will of a waved hand. I knew that feeling, of trying to live up to impossible expectations. If I wasn't going to be a doctor, couldn't I still be *enough*? How dare people not respect the other people—or animals—they'd brought into their lives?

"*Out,*" I said, and Pony yelped.

The woman's face contorted, and she reached for her cell phone like a weapon.

"We're back!" called the shelter manager.

I loosed Pony's shelter lead. There were things I couldn't control. Many, many things I couldn't control.

✦ ✦ ✦

At home, I threw down Pony's lead, which I'd been gripping since I slammed my way out of the shelter. I wasn't a rageful person, usually. Sometimes impulsive, and certainly I had moments of temper. Ella circled around me, wagging and sniffing, wanting reassurance that I wouldn't forsake her for the dogs whose scents I'd conveyed home on my clothes. Ella stuck her nose on me, wet spots of claim.

Ferdinand had adored helping me walk my dogs. Maybe we shouldn't have split up. I was thinking about people peeling off from me like faster runners. When we broke up, I thought I'd out-run Ferdinand, but now I wasn't so sure. I remembered the last of Us, standing outside the college library. I was wishing I didn't have to smell the cigarettes of the smokers, and that maybe it would be okay to be alone for a while.

Feet had yelled at me, "You are selfish, girl." His Spanish accent made him half-appealing, half-menacing.

"Ferdinand," I'd said, thinking *the bull*. "It's not just me—you don't trust me—I can't trust you, you read my journal—"

"These are small things," he said, kicking a wall as if he could punish cinder blocks. "It is you who is unwilling to ever wholly—" He paused, searching for the English. "Hold a hand."

Maybe that was true, at least with Ferdinand.

My sisters held my hands just by being in the same room, and I only had two hands, so maybe what Ferdinand meant was just that I was full. But in fact I was empty—empty from losing Cameron, empty now at one side, Olivia swept off in the wave of my father's departure. If I worried only about losing someone, I might never notice who was standing with me.

I wasn't just going to wait for information to fall upon me like a burning bush. I checked my e-mail. Two spams.

I looked at the Princeton website where my grade would be posted. Nothing.

I checked my e-mail. Nothing.

I picked up my phone and put it back down. Checked my cell phone. Nothing.

I checked my e-mail. Nothing.

Why was it my father could make everything too quiet and too loud all at once? I couldn't stand the buzzing in my head, waiting to learn something, waiting for something to unspool.

"Want to hold my hand, Ella?" I asked, petting the dog, and she lifted her paw, always obliging. The dogs didn't withhold love; none of them had a hand, but they'd offer what they had. I checked on Skinny, who was basking in a single sun spot in the corner of his cage.

On my way to the kitchen, anticipating the cocktail nuts beside the bar for some mindless worry-eating, I stopped and picked up the Chaucer I'd pilfered from Dad's office. I remembered attending a student recital with my friend Lily sophomore year—there were free concerts almost every afternoon and evening at Oberlin, some spectacular, the future of classical music resounding in Kulas Recital Hall at the conservatory, voices that rang again and again with all the passion of history. A soprano portrayed the

Wife of Bath in *The Canterbury Tales*; she seemed wise and condescending, and, if I remembered correctly, fairly bawdy, singing about marriage and being the whip.

Looking for that part I'd heard sung, I flipped through the book. Wife of Bath.

Experience, though noon auctoritee
Were in this world, is right ynogh for me
To speke of wo that is in marriage . . .

I looked at his notes, Dad's notes in the margins. *Experience tells us marriage is a woeful thing—this wife of Bath married five times! (Love stinks) What an appetite! She wants to know what's wrong with that.* Dad in college—it seemed incongruous with the grown man. His handwriting was legible before he became a doctor—fancy that, it was a cultivated specific sort of inarticulateness. *I'm more important than you are, so you have to work to read even my notes.*

I flipped forward through the tale, and a photo fell out of the book. It had those scalloped edges you never see anymore—a woman's bridal portrait, painted the way larger portraits were retouched. Was this in the fifties or sixties? Who was this woman? Her eyes were dark, but painted in with a little green. Coiffed brown curls. Her dress was vast, but cinched at a tiny waist. She had real eyebrows—little fermata marks without the dots (I'd looked at a lot of music with Cameron), and she seemed joyful, full of promise, full of expectation. Her flowers were painted blue and white, the brushstrokes so oddly primitive and obvious. She had a distinctive nose. Probably hated it, I thought, but it made her look strong. Bow-shaped lips. Cheeks brushed roundly pink. Nothing, once again, on the back of the photo. Was she someone Dad knew in college? Right after the Wife of Bath, a bride, how ironic. She looked a little ironic. She looked smart. I wanted to introduce myself.

My phone rang and I jumped up, knocking over my desk chair.

"Bakery?" said Eli.

"Excuse me?" I asked, though I knew he meant *Let's meet at the Bent Spoon in town.* We were both done with classes, and he was getting ready to start his summer job. He had two days in between to swim at the university pool, cook for me, watch me fall apart over Dad—or not—no, I couldn't—and probably find a new girlfriend, something he tended to do in moments of gap. We'd talked about a day trip to the shore, but now I felt I had to stay close to home.

"Any word from your wayward father?"

"No, I haven't heard anything about my stupid father. I need to crack Olivia. I need my Chem grade."

"Say what you want about him disappearing like this, but he's not stupid." Eli respected my father. The two of them talked about wine together, and Dad pretended to know about cooking to impress my friend. I didn't like the two of them together, vaguely chummy—it made my skin itch. At least he'd resented Cameron outright.

"Bakery," I said, slathering lotion on my dry, bleach-perfumed hands. Maybe I had just been waiting for Eli to call all along.

EIGHT

Gripping an amazing pecan-and-glaze-encrusted bear claw, I grappled in my purse to check my phone again. Eli was late, and I was peeved, because if he hadn't suggested the Bent Spoon, I'd still be checking my e-mail every few seconds and moping at home, which would've been satisfying, and much less embarrassing than gobbling a bear claw on my own, wondering whether I should add some artisanal ice cream à la mode. I smiled at the dreadlocks guy behind the counter—he was always there now, and I loved him for his vulnerability, his baby skin, even the small chapped patch under his lip. I wanted to offer him lip balm.

"Dad." I was talking to his voice mail again. "It's not fair. You're not fair. This doesn't make you mysterious and cool. It makes you a jerk. Call, Mom." Maybe he forgot, though. Maybe he wasn't a jerk, but ill.

Finally Eli arrived, flirting with a woman who might've been with him or might coincidentally have been walking into the Spoon.

"You're totally hilarious!" the woman shrieked, patting Eli's shoulder in a proprietary sort of way.

"And you're lovely," said Eli, giving her a long towel-dry of a look. *Disgusting,* I thought. The woman was lovely—she was lean and taller than Eli, her eyes were shaped by perfect liner, and her skin was bronze, her hair down to her waist, supershiny, deep brown. She had gold eyeshadow, and it actually looked stunning. Her lips were lush and just lightly glossed. I almost couldn't stand to look at her.

"This is my Clementine," said Eli, sweeping his generous arm toward me. I swallowed a wad of bear claw and nodded.

"Oh, my darlink, oh, my darlink," the woman sang, her accent vaguely Russian. I almost spat out my next sweet mouthful because I hadn't had to endure such childishness since grade school.

"I'm Elainamartella," said the supermodel.

"Pleased to meet you," Eli said, bowing and kissing her hand. Elainamartella looked longingly at the food cases, then kissed Eli's cheeks, waved at me as if erasing something, and left the premises without ingesting a single calorie.

"Did you get her number?" I spat at Eli.

"Of course," said Eli, blushing.

"Elainamartella. She was probably born Roberta Blackhead or something."

"Now, now," said Eli.

"You're the one who called, and then you brought *that* with you."

"Meow. I just met her while I was waiting for you."

"*You* were not waiting for me." I gestured toward my bear claw. I felt, inexplicably, like crying. Eli always had someone new. He had a mysterious universal sex appeal, and he responded to most overtures. But he was still my best friend.

Eli had been there after Cameron—he led me around Oberlin

like a skittish whippet. I didn't want to eat, but he took me to the café in the basement of the student union so I wouldn't have to face the overwhelming mashed potatoes and bulk cereal of the dining hall.

There was a woman named Maya who worked at the café and made Adjective Sandwiches. You gave her an adjective—for your mood, for an idea, for the pure pleasure or pain of it—and she expounded in a sandwich. I remembered one time in particular— I wore sweatpants that hadn't been washed for a week, and a T-shirt Cameron had lent me before break. It was just a plain blue T-shirt, washing-machine stress-holes worn at the neckline, and it fit me badly, gapping at the shoulders and clinging at the belly, but I couldn't take it off.

"We're getting you an Adjective Sandwich," said Eli. "And you're going to eat it."

"Whatever," I said. "I'm not hungry. You get one."

"Fries, please," Eli said to Maya, who was famous for "blustery" sandwiches, and "amnesiac."

I hated food almost as much as I hated breathing.

"I'm going to get, um, let's see—'contemplative.'"

"Sure, that's easy," said Maya. She asked him a few questions about taste and texture, then started with wheat flatbread, then layered sautéed portabella mushrooms, roast beef, baby Swiss, and papaya chutney. She slid it into the oven to toast, then topped it with radish sprouts and olive oil, salt, and pepper—it was a beautiful choreography. "What are you getting, Clem?"

"I can't," I said.

"She's going to eat. How about 'fortitude'?"

"That's a noun."

"Okay." Eli looked at me, as though he might read me the way my sisters did. He patted my head, which felt bruised. *Ow,* I thought, but no one could hear me.

"Okay," Eli repeated. "How about 'recuperative'?"

"You got it," said Maya. She sliced Eli's sandwich into wedges. I was almost hungry. Somehow I felt able to absorb the colors—the delicate green of the sprouts, the melancholy red-specked gold of the chutney.

She made me "recuperative": ciabatta bread with red-pepper mayonnaise on the bottom and honey mustard on top. She filled it with roast turkey and white cheddar and put a hurtfully red, succulent tomato slice on top after she toasted the sandwich. I managed to eat the whole thing, the best food I'd had in my life, the only food I'd had in my life. Eli fed me half his "contemplative," and though I wanted to feel guilty for eating, instead I was incrementally restored.

Eli helped me pack up at Oberlin, though he said he'd be miserable when I left. He was relentless in caring for me—I couldn't lose him, though I was rude to him sometimes, and when I went to California, I took his friendship for granted and sometimes ignored him. I wasn't mad at him—I was mad at Cameron for leaving me.

"What, are you jealous, my Clementine?" Elainamartella was long gone from the Spoon. Eli put his hand over my sticky one.

"No, I'm worried. I'm a wreck."

"You are not," said Eli. Then, quietly, he said, "I'm sorry you have to experience this." Suddenly, it felt real, and I did cry. My mouth opened and I gasped and made silent, awful sobs. Everything hurt. I cried because I was furious, because I wanted to know where Dad was and why he was gone and I didn't want to cry and I didn't want to care so much. *What about me?* I thought. *When will something be about me?* I looked up at Eli and stopped crying. I was pathetic, a narcissist. Maybe I was about to get my period. I was glad I hadn't said my thoughts out loud.

"How's the bear claw?" my friend asked, tearing off a piece.

I looked at Eli's calm face, the face that would never abandon me—a trait I found both essential and infuriating. He wouldn't leave, but did I ever really *have* him? I loved the mess of him, the lost, sturdy, assuredness. Drop him in the middle of the woods and he'd look up at the sky and just start walking. Cameron had needed me, had made me exquisite with the pressure of watching me, the pressure of his wide mouth. Eli just sat beside me. I brushed a crumb from his mouth with my sleeve.

At Eli's suggestion—and after seeing him off at the library, trying not to notice how his T-shirt clung in the right spots: around his shoulders, his lean back, trying not to always be a little bit in love with someone I couldn't have and shouldn't want—I went to see Olivia at her office. Eli had been Cameron's roommate, Cameron's nemesis. I could never expunge it from me, losing Cam, but I was beginning to wonder whether we still had to pretend the dead man was in the room, kissing me.

Maybe she'll feel more forthcoming away from that castle of yours, Eli had suggested, sending me off to Olivia's medical offices. I didn't admit that it was killing me that she knew more than the rest of us, but of course it ate at me. And puzzled me. Never before had our father shown any preference for the right bookend (Olivia) or the left (Odette). At least, not in front of me.

My sisters worked in Siamese-twin offices within a new brick building in a new brick office park landscaped with the art of a local sculptor: giant bronze reclining women and horses, the bronze still brownish, the green years yet to come.

"Do you have an appointment?" asked the receptionist, who sat in a low chair behind a tall, cherrywood and glassed-in wall.

Do I look like I need an obstetrician? I almost asked. Of course, it could be the gynecological portion of the program, but I hated her efficiency. Instead, I said, "She's my sister."

"Really? I'll see."

You'll see? I thought. Sure, I hadn't been to my sister's office since the grand opening party, and sure, there was Odette, identical and also swelled like a fruit, and here I was, wearing jeans and a shirt I'd had since high school, tie-dyed in art class, a bit too tight, but not unfashionably so. A bit of bear claw frosting stuck just above my chest. I rubbed at it, licked the spot, and then looked around to see whether anyone had seen me sucking on my clothes. Maybe I really needed to go next door, for a pediatrician.

The receptionist came to the door, the opening to the chambers—while I was ogling the tall play structure designed to look like a tree. Two computers were set up with slide shows of gestational stages. The few developmental toys still looked clean, despite the daily grubby hands exploring them. I wondered if the receptionist boiled herself along with them, sanitizing her sour face and the happy talking telephone in one evening's endeavor.

"Ms. Lord?" she called as if I were a patient. "The doctor will see you."

I half expected the nurse to prick my finger or ask me to pee into a cup, but instead, when the receptionist handed me off, she ushered me into a little exam room, squeezed her lips whitely together, and said, "Hm, you look nothing like her."

"Thank you?" I muttered.

My sister left me waiting for thirty-eight minutes in her little exam room. I sat on a chair, then the crinkly-papered table. I took apart the little model of an ear. I studied the pamphlets on STDs, preeclampsia, gestational diabetes, and herpes. I counted sixteen wrapped swabs in the culture drawer. I checked my cell phone three times, but I was waiting. It was time to have it out, even if it was on her terms, even if she was infantalizing me by putting me in her exam room. When she finally flurried in wearing her lab coat and her stethoscope with a panda bear gripping the cord, she sighed deeply when she saw me.

"Clem." She put her arm around me as if we were not just sisters, but friends. "I'm so tired. All my patients brought their other children." She waved the panda at me. Then she sat down on the chair and propped her feet up on the counter, which was surely a health code violation. *Depleted,* she thought. *Exhausted. Candy bar. Babies.* I was listening to her thoughts as deeply as I could, but that was all I could divine.

"Did you wash you hands?" I asked, reciting the question from above the sink.

She heaved herself up and started foaming up her hands under the water at the sink.

"I was kidding," I said softly.

"So, want to feel the kicking?" She took my hand in her still-damp, now scrubbed one and put it on her belly.

I felt nothing but taut skin.

"Did you feel that?" she asked, a bright tone in her voice.

"Wow," I lied. "I'm here about Dad."

Olivia pushed my hand off her belly. "Right. Forgive me for thinking you actually cared about me."

"Of course I care about you. I just think it's weird for you to know where he is—"

"I have no idea where he is. I only have a number—"

"A number we should call," I said.

"No one's in labor. Yet." I felt a sliver of her fear—a sharp splinter invisible under the surface. My sister was afraid of labor.

"This is exactly what I'm talking about," I said. "All this mystery. Who's going to die if you tell? Dad? It's just not fair to any-one—to Mom, or O, or me—"

"It's not about fair," Olivia started.

The nurse knocked at the door and poked her head in. "Sorry. You're getting backed up, and I know how much you hate backup—"

"Just a minute," said Olivia, her voice commanding and pro-fessional. "I'm almost done here." I couldn't read her at all now; her doors were up, ramparts.

"Olivia," I said. "Don't you think you should share what you know? It's been almost a week. Mom's pretending she doesn't care, but I swear, she can't take this. She'll go nuts, or she'll get a lawyer and start divorce proceedings—"

"She wouldn't. She loves him."

"So do I, but I think he's being an asshole. Where is he, Olivia? Where is he? Is he going senile?"

"He is not going senile." She grimaced and took a breath. "*I don't know.*" Olivia held on to her belly as if I were attacking the child therein.

"Everything okay?" the nurse asked, opening and knocking at the same time.

"On my way," said Dr. Lord. She stood up and looked at me, teary-eyed. Her face was puffy. My sister looked awful. I actually felt guilty. I wasn't sure whether it was her guilt or mine.

"Fine," said Olivia, relenting perhaps because of her pregnancy, or because she hated backup, or because she couldn't stand my pressure, though I doubted that—she'd always withstood it with hauteur and extraordinary strength.

"Dad gave me the number of his lawyer, that's all. He said to call if there was an emergency. But I know something else because I did a little research on my own."

She was half out the door, and I stood up, reached out my hand, but didn't touch her.

"He's gone to see his wife."

"Um? Mom? No, he's not *at ho*me—" I felt as though I were talking to a recalcitrant child.

"He's married," she said.

"Duh. Hence us."

"No, I mean, to someone other than Mom."

"Excuse me?" My mouth suddenly postdentist fuzzy, half-hot, half-numb. Nausea, evil nausea.

"Our father was married before Mom—before we were born.

He's been supporting her for years. Don't feel sick now; you'll make me barf."

I said nothing, staring at the bear on her stethoscope. *This can't be true,* I wanted to say. How was this possible? How could he get married to Mom without telling her first? Our father, the bigamist. It sounded like a joke. The bridal portrait hiding in the Wife of Bath. Was that woman—?

I cleared my throat, hoping the funny feeling in my mouth would pass. "Does Odette know?" I should have asked a thousand other questions first.

"No. Neither does Mom, unless she's an incredible actress," said Olivia. "And I won't be a beheaded messenger. It's his job, the asshole. Not mine."

"O? Why didn't you tell us?" I sucked in air—there wasn't enough oxygen in the room.

"I didn't want to be the one to ruin everything. I guess I thought if I didn't tell, it might not be true."

For a second, I didn't recognize my triplet, her face smooth as stone, her eyes desolate, pupils tiny. Then she turned to the door.

"I have to go," she finished. "I hate backup."

NINE

The third place I lived was Oberlin, Ohio, where I went to college. There I met Cameron Kite, whom I loved, and who died in an accident in his backyard pool in San Jose, California, where he grew up and was home for break. There was blood in the water from a scrape on his leg, his mother told me, her voice a closed calm, confessional, lost in her own perpetual panic, describing everything, the weedy look of his white-blond hair in the blue.

First, though, there was the rebellion. Beginning in junior year of high school, my father hired a college counselor for us—paying some ridiculous sum, not subtracted, as most of our activity fees were, from the Accounts and mother's allowance. By my teen years, I was disgusted by our father's tight grip on every activity of the women of his house.

He chose when we took vacations to the Vermont house—a glass-and-wood beauty perched above Caspian Lake in Greensboro, Vermont, the Northeast Kingdom. Even if our father was staying in Princeton, he mandated our trips there with Mom; he told her what to pack, what to buy at the supermarket before we left, and what to get at the Willey's general store once we arrived. He had her schedule lessons at the odd tennis club up above dairy farms, and private sailing lessons on the lake. It wasn't a Princeton sort of town, but for some reason people from Princeton flocked there. In junior high, I discovered that Grey, whom I'd loved in elementary school, and who had left for a private boarding school in Boston because his grades were lacking (probably he was distracted by snow, by the three girlfriends he supposedly juggled in sixth grade—but still—I harbored a secret desire to kiss him again, for real, to tell him I wished I'd kept those flowers his mother brought to our musical), had a house on the lake as well. His parents had been coming to Greensboro for three generations. They owned farmland worked by a dairy farmer and woodland logged periodically by teams of Clydesdale skidding horses and the last of the big Vermont men whose hands were cracked and muscled by work.

I spent my high school summers enduring tennis lessons, and savoring riding lessons at the Greensboro riding stable, where girls my age from town looked at me sidelong, left my girth strap loose so I might easily slip (luckily I'd learned about bloat and walked and cinched Melody, the horse I rode, whenever I could tell she was holding her breath), and clearly resented the Summer People. My sisters and I played at the private beach on the lake below our house. We wrestled on the raft and sailed across the lake together in one of our two matching Sunfish, Odette trailing her hands in the water, leaving an instantly erased seam in our wake. We got along sometimes, and sometimes we fought. We went to square dances at the town hall and Olivia flirted with the sons of dairy farmers and kissed one behind the barn—no one ever knew except for the three of us. We were so bored; we had to read each other for lack of enough books to consume us.

Then, the August before senior year, after a month of college prep courses (Odette and Olivia went down to Johns Hopkins for a summer program for supersmart premed geeks, and they sent me postcards making fun of their classmates. I didn't get in. I worked at the Baskin-Robbins and sat in the verdant backyard pretending to study SAT review books), we were followed to Vermont by a college counselor, a young woman who'd grown up in Paterson, New Jersey, and had crawled up the cliff to Harvard by grabbing at every tiny crack in the wall between her bottom-level life and the top. She had tenacity. Now she had her own business coaching the children of the rich on how to fatten their applications, make them juicy, appealing, and make the essays relevant, brag without bragging. Her name was Juliet, and she was a mocha girl, she said, half-black, half-Hispanic. She stayed in the only bedroom that didn't have a lake view and wore khaki pants and polo shirts every day. She didn't bring a bathing suit, so while we dived from the dock, she sat on a towel with her pants rolled up, reciting vocabulary words to us as if we weren't obnoxious and privileged. It embarrassed me to remember just how snotty we could be.

Odette and Olivia took her seriously in the evenings, though. They convened at the big oak table, bought at auction along with our brass beds and the cuckoo clock in the front hallway. They reviewed what they had yet to learn because they both planned to apply to Harvard early admission, with Princeton, Yale, Brown, and Cornell as the second-tier choices if they didn't get in.

I had a hard time taking it all seriously. All I wanted to do was sail past Grey's place across the lake and wonder whether he still remembered me. I'd had a boyfriend by then—I dated a senior my sophomore year: Drew McFarlane, who was six foot five and played no sports, much to his parents' chagrin. He wrote dark poems and painted his toenails black and kept his hair short and precise and threatened his father, a partner in a management consultancy firm, by saying he planned to apply to West Point. He'd had the requisite summer volunteer job with a senator, living with his sister in D.C. and not getting carded at bars. Then we dated, and he told me he really wanted to be a poet. He'd been shaving since he was ten; I pretended to braid his chest hair, and he was the best kisser I'd ever met. Of course, he was the only boy I'd ever really kissed.

We slept together twice, and I decided I loved sex, that I always wanted to have sex, that sex was all it was cracked up to be. Drew smelled like sweet timothy—a green, good scent. He seemed sweet and pale at the core—innocent, his heart radiant with the light sap of summer-starved fields.

My sisters were horrified when I told about the sex, even though we'd used condoms, even though he spent at least an hour on my relatively undefined needs before and after his were satisfied. Then he applied to West Point—and got in. And my longing for sex was still there, but I hoped for love now, too. Drew wrote long letters, with poems in them, for a few months at West Point, before he disappeared into the maw of the military and we broke up—I always felt as though we were mutual sounding boards, warm bodies, just friends.

Juliet had several bibles of college information. The best one was a comprehensive listing, the one book I was willing to study that summer. I had narrowed down my preferences to Oberlin, Brown (though I didn't really want to go Ivy, and I didn't think I could get in, either), Hamilton College, Rutgers (which would mortify my father), Ramapo College, Swarthmore, Wesleyan, and UC Berkeley. Juliet didn't approve of my list, but she did agree that I shouldn't try for Harvard, Yale, MIT, or Haverford, which was just fine with me. I took picnic lunches of Cabot sharp cheddar and Granny Smith apples out to the raft via canoe. I lay out on the smooth, wet wood watching the sky change, thinking of the smell of the lake, overripe and ancient, and wondering whether there could be a beast at the bottom, a Loch Caspian Monster, as we'd half-joked, half-believed when we were little. My sisters, however obnoxious they were when Juliet asked them to define *voracious* or *vainglorious,* took the bible work in earnest. They were both applying early decision to Harvard. I dreaded their collective departure; I looked forward to being apart.

Our third week in Vermont, that last summer before we knew where we were going, the August heat came hard and heavy, unusual for Vermont. The window tapped with the sounds of flies hatching and battering themselves in an effort to enter the world. The lake was still, and Juliet had finished her work; one Friday Mom drove her to Burlington to the airport, where she exchanged our tutor for a new arrival: Dad. It felt as if he were a visitor, as if he didn't belong in the realm of women that was our house. My sisters had grown apart from me somehow—clearly closed with their common goals. I didn't want the same things they did, Harvard, excellence, but I wanted to be part of them, I was part of them, and I hated how they were hoarding their conversations and competitions, working in tandem on their applications, swimming together and taking a Sunfish without at least asking if I wanted to come along. It seemed that way to me—as though only separating from my sisters could provide the true rebellion I desired. My mother, I feared, would remain placid whatever I did, silently hurt; my father wouldn't notice. I consoled myself that three was too many for one little boat, anyway.

I wrote a bored letter to my friend Sophie. I listened to the cracking of the maples and white pines in the heat. There was no air-conditioning, so I descended to the dock, lowered myself into the water, floating on my back with my legs dangling down, sipping air like a sweet libation.

I heard the car rumble up the gravel drive. I didn't move; if they didn't see me, I might not have to talk to my father for another hour or two. Staying still, I was almost cold in the water, feeling the striations of chill from the deep lake to the shallow bathing water where my face lay. I moved my arms just barely, pretending I was a mermaid, a jellyfish. Even with my ears mostly under, I heard my mother—she was wailing as she slammed the car door behind her.

This is it, I thought. *He's leaving. Or she's leaving, or something else—some crack in the still mirror of their limited relationship.* I hated him for abandoning her so often, hated him for making her who she was, not letting her be who she was in the pictures on the mantelpiece: valedictorian at Bard, scholar in white pants and a burgundy silk blouse, holding her happy black mortarboard hat as if it might float off her head, lift off into the sky.

I had heard my parents having sex, in the acoustically exposed Vermont house. I had heard my mother gasping and moaning, my father grunting as if he were swinging an ax into wood, which the men from the farm did sometimes, the handymen, the men whose skin was prematurely aged around the eyes from squinting into the thin lemon of Vermont sun. Now that I'd had sex myself, I understood something: it wasn't just the bodies, longing for each other, it wasn't just a sort of cupcake consumption, half-visual, half oral; sex was a form of correspondence, and a form of currency, like electricity. I felt as though it would keep them alive, keep me alive, keep the world animated. I also knew I was waiting to be part of a pair, that I would surpass my parents when I was: the man I chose wouldn't ever want to leave me for the rest of the world.

I lifted my head slightly, enough to hear more, but not enough to be witnessed, hovering like a weed by the dock.

"You have no idea what it takes!" she was crying, her voice embarrassingly shrill. "You are always gone—going, going, gone. Is it someone else? I swear, I've trusted you so long I'm afraid not to—"

"Don't be hysterical, Octavia," said my father, his voice low, which made her seem even more pathetic. He heaved his unzipped garment bag out of the back of the car, leaning heavily on one side. I willed him to fall over, to stumble, to grind dust and Vermont gravel into his Armani. I hated his suits. Scrubs were one thing, the beeper, the uniform of a surgeon, the hat, the mask—I'd observed my dad in surgery once, sitting between my sisters, feeling like a witness to a crime. They leaned against the glass of the theater observation room, ogling the blood, the innovative laser work he did, the fineness of everything, the finesse, as he manipulated someone's brain, her core, the what made her herself. He was removing a tumor, burning away bad cells with a tiny wand. Our father, magician.

"I'm not hysterical!" my mother screamed. "You promised a week!"

So it wasn't anything new. He was just departing sooner than he said, as usual. He was just leaving and leaving and leaving, but he was never gone. He was in our planning for college, he was in our mother's purse on her trips to the store; his name was on her credit card: Mrs. Lord.

My sisters sailed up to the dock just as my mother stamped inside. Our father posed as if he hadn't just scolded our mother, as if there were nothing to fight about. He strode down to the dock and held out his arms for my sisters, possession. They jumped off the boat and into his arms, now just wearing a button-down, the suit jacket shed in the oak and flybound house.

"Girls!" he said. "I hear there's great progress to report." He kissed the tops of their heads. I watched, still floating, hoping no one would notice that I was being left out, hoping someone would.

I was almost hatched from high school—I felt independent and contemptuous in my separations, all of them: division from my mother, who seemed to fade as we set about cleaving from her (I scrutinized the dull gray roots of her hair; they grew out more in summer in Vermont and accused me of letting her get old, letting her fade as we acquired the shine of young adulthood). We were dividing, too, my sisters from myself, a pair in harmony and me, an entirely different melody. My father, most of all, began to irk me, began to appear didactic when before his firmness had simply been a fact, an order that kept the world moving forward. I hated the way my sisters basked in his approval.

"I wonder whether you'll get your letters the same day," he said, glowing at them over black raspberry pie my mother had made with berries we'd picked—Juliet performed the lion's share of the work without sampling a single berry.

"I wonder whether you'll both get in," I'd sneered because I wanted to change the subject.

"Clementine," scolded my mother. "Jealousy is not becoming."

"And subservience is?" I challenged her.

"Enough," said my father.

"Yes," I said. "Enough. She does more than enough for you, and you reward her by spending most of your time and energy elsewhere. What's with the allowance, anyway, Dad? Is this 1952? You think your little Ph.D. lady can't be responsible for money all on her own? Your little wifey?" It felt scandalous to say these things, but awful and true. He'd hurt her even as he arrived; I hated the way he drained her of power and joy.

"Enough!" yelled my father.

"Clem," said my mother, appeasing.

"She's just a child," she said to my father, looking almost fearful.

"And that's how he treats you," I said. "I'm seventeen years old. I'm as much a child as my sisters, only the difference is they'll be virgins until they marry—"

You suck, Olivia said silently. *I'm sorry,* I replied. *I know*—this was Odette. *And we might.* They were talking in my head and I wanted to be angry alone.

My father stood up, thin-lipped. "I won't tolerate this kind of behavior. You need to treat your mother with respect."

"The way you do?" I said, but I was already running out of steam. It was my age, I told myself, I wasn't a hateful person. What came out of my mouth was bitter.

On the other hand, the pie was delicious, buttery crust, a lattice cut with a fancy crust-crimper. My mother made things beautiful. I was just pretty sure she wasn't happy, and it didn't seem fair. He was.

"Enough," my parents said in unison. Mom looked at Dad, her lips in the tilted bow of her adoration. I wanted to wipe off the expression. I wanted her to stop loving him that way until he earned it.

My sisters were holding hands under the table. I hated the way they clung to each other, an English fence, impenetrable, grafted together. Sometimes, I was surprised they hadn't been born attached. I could easily join hands; they were there for mine, but I didn't. Even if I was the one who made it so, I was deeply, deeply jealous that there were two pairs: Mom and Dad, O&O. I was always the odd one out.

That night, we heard our parents making love, once again, only this time my sisters and I looked at each other, horrified by the brazenness of their shouts. My mother was yelling, "Like that! Like that!" as we sat at the table drinking tea we'd made ourselves from pineapple weed and chamomile.

"Ugh," said Odette, wrinkling her face.

"I do believe we need to go swimming," said Olivia, out loud for my benefit, as Odette had already taken in this information by merely looking at her twin.

We shed our clothes on the dock; the night was still hot, the sun finished, the lake glinting with the eye of the moon.

My sisters dived off the dock and wrestled, giggling in the water. Neither of them had had sex. It seemed odd, the two of them naked together, but then, we'd been a trio of naked babies in the womb. Our father had told us all he was proud of our plans, though he nodded at me, showing mild disapproval. Just wait, I thought. I'd decided to apply early decision to Oberlin. Even without visiting, I knew I'd love it there. I'd talked with alums on the phone, not formal interviews, but a chance to ask the kinds of questions I really had, such as what do people do at night? And what if you decide to change your major? Of course I'd enter pre-med. Otherwise my father might not allow the tuition. But Oberlin itself would bother him, would itch at him like contact dermatitis. And I wanted to make him itch, make him squirm.

So while I thought I was rebelling, that I was finding my own way, in fact, when I went to Oberlin, I was in search of a mate, and while college was about other things, underneath it all I wanted to be paired, plain as the pathetic girls looking for an MRS at other schools (this would never do at Oberlin), only I didn't know it then.

TEN

My first roommate at Oberlin, Lily, had a theory about college.

It was our first night, and we'd arranged our belongings—her guitar near the middle of the room, my books claiming more than half of the insufficient shelf—in a cautious sort of self-deprecating territory-taking. Lily grew up in Wisconsin, an only child, and she could juggle, write songs, and weave her own fabric—she was also pixie pretty and liked the room much colder than I did, so she left the windows open in winter. I closed them. She opened them. After having my own room since we moved to Princeton, I'd been cautiously optimistic that I'd meet a best friend instantly, that we'd share clothing and enthusiasms and chemistry notes. We shared the middle of the three and were best of friends once we no longer had to divide about seventy-five square feet into two realms.

"I think first we'll cast off old skins, you know, kiss random boys and take that experimental college class where you examine your own cervix." She giggled.

"Really?" I asked, but I didn't find it shocking, only a little odd as a collective activity.

"I might, but probably not; I'm a prude, deep down, are you?"

"I guess not." I was experimenting with identity—I'd told Lily

I had two sisters; I hadn't yet told anyone I had twins with whom I was tripletted. I was going incognito. It felt quiet and noble.

"Anyway, we'll shed that first skin and then we'll get weird calluses on the new skin, you know, from sleeping with the wrong random boys or learning we didn't really want to see our own cervixes—"

"I wouldn't mind." A stain was on the ceiling above my long, narrow bed, a stain shaped like a comma, or an apostrophe, depending on which way you laid your head.

"Really? I'd be way too nervous to look with other people there."

"I suppose I wouldn't—if everyone was doing it," I said, thinking the stain on the ceiling shouldn't be there already; the room was freshly painted.

"And then we'll actually start to learn how to live in the world."

"Isn't that a poem? 'Learning to Live in the World'?"

"William Stafford," she said. We belonged here. We belonged with each other as freshperson roommates, even if we'd bicker over who left a banana peel in the trash can and attracted clouds of fruit flies. But I wasn't sure about her theory; I thought I already knew most of the things I needed to know. I thought I already had my final skin.

We walked in packs to the dining hall. Lily and I held hands like sisters, only it never felt the same. I ate six bowls of Cap'n Crunch for dinner one night, sitting at a table of new-team camaraderie, feeling flush with all possibilities.

Probably Lily kissed more random boys than I did. She fell in love with music history, art history, and a philosophy major who worked as an RA in our dorm and offered free, nonsexual back massages for anyone feeling really tense.

"I'm not tense anymore," said Lily, returning late one night.

"Really?"

"Well, we didn't sleep together, even though he wanted to. Almost. But you know what, Clem? It's even better when you know you can actually say no, and maybe save it for later."

I didn't remind her that this RA's nonsexual massages migrated—with me, with at least three other women I'd talked with. It felt like an invasion of her personal fictional narrative. If she'd been able to read me, like Odette or Olivia, she'd just know. I had to get used to telling people everything, to revealing what I wanted when I wanted to let it free. I was swimming in a sea of unknown plants and animals, dazzled and afraid I'd lift my head to the dun-colored sky.

Then I met Cameron Kite. He had white-blond hair, and grand passion for the violin, which he practiced when he wasn't in the biology lab. Cameron was so pale he was almost transparent; his blue veins at the surface of his skin were like rivers; I wondered if I could see the white boats of the blood cells rushing toward a bruise. He sat behind me in Human Biology, and he was premed, but not because someone else wanted him to be, because he was planning to become a developmental pediatrician.

I'd seen him coming into class. He was stunning, a white-blond California boy whose walk belied an ease in his body, a sense of self I could never achieve but witnessed with pleasure and awe.

His was one of the hands raised with astute questions in class; his voice made us all turn to him. Lily, who was taking the class, too, told me she'd seen him watching me. I was trying too hard to keep up with the lectures to pay attention. I'd vowed to myself that I'd only play—date, dance in the 'sco—the campus dance club—with its flashing lights and retro music and deep coolness that made it possible to dance like an idiot and feel like a goddess—when I had finished my work. It wasn't easy, because homework required thinking; reading required thinking, ideas required the fourth dimension of time to become whole in my brain. Sometimes I struggled, and I didn't want to get lost before I'd started the marathon of learning.

One day after class I said good-bye to Lily, as she headed off for Music History 100 at the conservatory, and turned to see Cameron fidgeting with something in his backpack, clearly waiting for someone to come out of class. I looked behind me at the chorus of faces, but when I looked back, he was looking at me.

"Are you going to lunch?" he asked. I was, only Cameron belonged to Harkness, a dining co-op, so he offered to bring me as a guest. It felt like another freshperson experiment in possible friendships—because somehow, though of course I'd noticed he was beautiful, I'd never imagined he'd be half of a couple with me.

"You are missing someone," he said as we walked across campus to Harkness. "Maybe two people."

"Not my parents," I said, smiling, hoping I hadn't seemed ungrateful when I asked what kind of vegetarian food they had at the vegetarian co-op. Cameron wore a T-shirt, HARKNESS, WE

WEAR LEATHER, and I enjoyed the irony and also wondered whether I was going to have to wash dishes; I'd read that everyone helped out at the co-op.

"Are *you* missing someone?" Unnerved that he could smell my triplets, because I knew that's what he was reading, I almost asked, but then my cards would be splayed on the table and the game would be finished.

"Not really," he said. "Maybe my brother."

He knew. How did he know? Cameron was someone who paid attention. Later he told me he had synesthesia—sometimes he smelled color or saw sound. When he first waited for me, he said, my voice was the color of California, yellow-gold, and he missed home.

But right then, I wasn't sure I really wanted to have lunch with him. He was sort of prying—asking right up front about my feelings, and my sisters, and I was in the happy cloud of forgetting.

"Why your brother?"

"He understands me." Cameron's voice made my bones resonate. I still wouldn't tell him. We ate a delicious chickpea salad with feta cheese for lunch, and Cameron explained the co-op arrangement—he signed up for duties, everyone had dishwashing crew, but other jobs were assigned different points. He was a bread baker; he got up at four to start the bread. He loved the smell of yeast and heat. He served me some of his homemade bread with lunch, and I relished the wheatiness, the work to chew. I relished him, his beauty, his voice, and most of all his attention. I realized that while I'd had a thousand intense conversations since school started, they'd had such a frenzied flow about them; I had felt splashed, obscured by the movement of it all. Something about lunch with Cameron was quiet. Something about the way he watched me when I spoke made me feel heard, in a way no one had ever warmed me with absolute attention.

Of course, his parents had hoped he'd go to Berkeley or Stanford or Santa Barbara—somewhere closer to home. They hiked together as a family; they tasted wine; he made them whole, too.

Cameron had been a boy who loved books, who surfed and played violin with equal ease, who had grudgingly been popular, who had known all along he was unusual. His older brother was autistic and lived in a group home; Cam showed me photographs stuck with Fun-Tak above his bed: his tall, easy-limbed brother, also sunshine-headed, open-faced. Cameron told me they'd had a private language of gestures that still made them both laugh like mad. Reed could talk, read, work, but he hadn't been able to attend regular school, and he couldn't bear loud noises or the smell of broccoli. There wasn't anything simple about him, Cameron said; he was more sensitive, and more hurt by the world.

And I told Cameron, the first person at Oberlin, that I was a triplet, and he didn't ask to see photos of my sisters, he just said, "I knew there was something extraordinary about you," and kissed me for the first time, on the cheek, slightly too close to my mouth, so my lips burned with wishing.

The motto at Oberlin is Learning and Labor, and although it has been years since students put in hours in a cornfield, it was still a place where we learned to learn—and working at the dining co-op (it was much cheaper than the dining hall; we pooled our money and relative skills, which sometimes led to a tragedy of the commons brought on by undercooked beans), menu planning for 120, running dishes through the giant Hobart dishwashing machine, I learned a little bit more about labor than I'd known before. I learned education was a tool to avoid some of it. I learned that I wanted to be good at things—at art history, at writing essays about division of household labor—not because I wanted to be better than the other students doing the same, but because I wanted to be a better person myself.

I loved listening; I loved the idea of music, I loved to hear Cameron play, and to watch him, too, his square fingers and wide palms attending to his violin in a way that made me jealous and aroused at the same time. I wished I'd started something young and fallen into it, like learning to swim as a Pollywog at the Y and later becoming an Olympian.

Cam had come to Oberlin because he knew he needed distance to see more clearly. His parents were accomplished and energetic and always watching him. His father, still working full-time as a space engineer, also wanted Cam to join in his projects—learning to cook Szechuan, playing the piano, building tree forts, buying an orange orchard. Cameron told me they never yelled at Reed, and that was a gift. Cameron was more ordinary, at least in terms of what they needed to provide him, but when he took violin, so did his mother. They weren't hoverers, he explained, they were joiners. They'd practiced something called Floortime with Reed and focused on circles of joining in, circles of communication.

Sometimes, though it wasn't their intention, Cam said he felt dizzied. He didn't blame; he loved his parents and his brother—he just needed space.

Cameron and I studied together, but I couldn't concentrate because I swore he smelled like oranges. He was quiet in class, and so intense when we met in the library, I thought he'd never be interested in me; he was too interested in drinking in the whole world of school. We swam together at the pool, and the first time he kissed me for real, on the mouth, we'd paused in the hot, chloriney, blue light to chat while clinging to the wall. I asked him what he thought of current genetic research, whether the genome project would be the panacea we hoped it would be.

"Do you really want to be a doctor, Clem?" he asked, adjusting his swim cap, which was black Lycra. His eyes were a fierce blue, his eyebrows so light they were almost invisible.

"No," I said. "I have no idea what I want to do."

Cameron grinned at me, and I thought he was going to push off the wall, the way he sucked in a lungful of breath, but instead, he kissed me.

At Oberlin, dating was either sleeping together and acting casual as you strode across campus, maybe even looking at other students with the sort of possibility that belied a lack of seriousness, or it was like a trial marriage. I spent my nights in Cameron's room because my roommate, Lily, couldn't sleep unless the room was very, very quiet, and she swore Cameron snored, though I never noticed, and I was the one pressed up against him in the narrow, extralong twin bed. We ate our meals together, studied together, bought books together, slept breathing the same air, sharing oxygen, almost like sharing a body.

Cam had told me his roommate was a slob—mostly the roommate was absent when we were there, and I didn't see all that much evidence; some laundry left lonely in the corner, unemptied trash. But Cam said he'd borrowed Cam's jeans—without asking—and returned them with a heap of stains: mustard, grass, paint, maybe blood. He'd bumped into Cameron's violin and popped a string. The bridge was more important to Cameron than his own body; it made me wonder that an object could be so close to self, but I sympathized. "He should just not touch your stuff," I said, thinking it might not be that easy in a small room.

The mutual dislike had started young; the roommate—Eli— had brought a woman back to the room on their very first night at school, and Cameron had come home to find her lying on his bed. It was prudish, Cam knew, he said, but he'd put masking tape across the floor: your side, mine. So then when I met Eli for the first time, I didn't recognize him—the shadow across the room at night was a real person, and not so greedy for space and attention as I'd imagined.

Still, when we were in bed, sleeping together for the second time, someone came in the room, someone coughed and interrupted a particularly intimate session of licking, someone said, "Excuse me, but do you expect to be here all night?" as though we'd thought this out—which of course I had. I did.

Once, while Cameron was in the bathroom, I'd moved Eli's books and notes from the floor—just shy of the tape border—and put them on his desk. I didn't want to trip. And I felt a little guilty; we dominated the room, and he didn't seem *that bad*.

When Cam came back, he looked at the desk, then at me. "Why'd you do that? He's a slob—and you're not his mother."

"Jeez. I didn't want to trip."

"Oh, well, that's fair," he said, eyeing the neat pile I'd made. Then he tucked his leg behind mine—tripping me, folding me like a bedsheet, disarming and charming me, and laid me on the bed.

With the exception of Eli, Cameron looked and took in people before he judged them. He opened before discarding—willing to believe in possibilities whereas my East Coast sensibility taught me to assume limits and frauds. Cam assumed friendship and the magic of anyone's particular senses.

"He sounds like a French horn," he said of Professor Steinberg, who taught human biology. We were eating real fall apples we'd bought at a farm stand, riding our bikes out into the expanse of corn and soy fields, away from Oberlin, away from everyone but the two of us.

"And your roommate, Lily, is a Meyer lemon—more sweet and watery than bitter tang." The sky was more open here than Princeton, a wide palm of possible blues.

We tossed our apple cores and filled our backpacks with the rest of the apples. I felt fat and happy as a pony. I felt full of the greens and tangs of outside.

Cameron's luminosity came from where he grew up, his parents, his brother's special sensitivities, but most of all it came from his own inner light, an elegant synaptic originality. Some people, those who held sarcasm on the surface like a thicker skin, made

him politely temperamental. Maybe that was the issue with Eli—
Eli's sharpness, his harder humors. I was lucky to meet Cam when
I was flush with learning to crack open ideas for the various nut
meats of discussion. I'd turned off just enough Princeton to
believe.

It didn't hurt that Cam was stunning and played the violin as
though each note were sexual devotion. He took longer steps than
the rest of the group of us parading from place to place—Cameron
strode headlong into whatever came next.

He was a virgin until we met. In all my fantasies about finding a
mate, I never imagined a virgin. He was vaguely embarrassed by
his body the first time we slept together, watching himself and
watching my face as if there were clues to successful lovemaking
that could only be revealed by eyebrows, elbows, and of course the
angle of his penis. We took our time. We did it repeatedly, our first
night, we loved each other's body in a way they hadn't been loved
since we were infants, and even then, it was caretaking, not the
kind of honor we bestowed upon each other.

The sex made me wonder why I had been so thrilled about sex
with Drew. This new invention was long and slow; we spent hours
in the morning exploring each other's body as if they were new
countries. After that first night, Eli spent most of his nights at a
girlfriend's off-campus house. Cameron and I consumed each
other like chocolate. It wasn't just that we loved each other's body
and mind; we loved what we'd discovered, as if no one else had
lived in the land of new love. I missed my classes and barely passed

the Ethical Biology elective for which I'd waited in line over three hours to register. His skin tasted of oranges. His mouth felt like bee's wings against the smooth contours of my back.

After a brief relationship with the RA, who, to his credit, stopped giving indiscriminate backrubs while they were going out, Lily had a crush on Cameron's roommate, Eli. We talked about him ad nauseam, his job at Mudd, the main library, his laugh, which made people turn around all across campus. I didn't tell Cam; I didn't mind noticing the fellow, either, purely reconnaissance for Lily. She also had a crush on her piano teacher—she was taking lessons from a student at the conservatory. We went to concerts together and let music seep into us like oxygen. I'd never heard so much music before, and such variety, Schubert piano concertos, Bach cantatas, the visiting Swingle Singers, jazz ensembles, a microtonal opera.

In our room, when I wasn't with Cam, Lily played guitar and we sang harmonies together; she was the kind of person who'd make a superlative friend—if only we hadn't needed to live together. In fact, we became much closer after we lived apart, able to pick up harmonies in conversations as well as songs. We still talked on the phone two or three times a year and sent old-fashioned snail-mail letters from time to time.

But Eli and Cameron weren't charmed by each other. It was small bickering—Eli left mean notes about Cameron's smelly dirty laundry; Cameron accused Eli of loosening the strings on his violin. Cameron allegedly broke Eli's coffee mug but swore he hadn't done it. The resident junior who was supposed to advise the freshpeople had to step in—he told them he could mediate or find them each another roommate. Cameron said mediate; Eli said mediate; but they were both too agitated, and eventually they were each reassigned to transfer students. It was an ugly side of my Cameron, but I forgave him. I didn't understand how anyone could escalate such pettiness, but I didn't really know Eli, so the story just lived in the mythical history of first college year.

At the beginning of sophomore year, Eli and I were in the same Indian Religion class. I watched Eli listening intently to the professor, who was passionate about the devotional poems we studied and also knew Eli's history. She didn't favor him in a traditional sort of way; she was much too fair for that, but we could tell, just from the way she said his name when he answered a question, that she had a little bit of a crush on him, too.

Lily reported that Eli, however, was in love with a million women, and none of them were Lily or the religion prof (who was happily married anyway). He was in love with a swanlike modern-dance student who wounded him by sleeping with other men whenever she wanted and telling him the details. He was in love with an environmental-studies major who left him notes that said things like *I am your nubile love slave. You must cook me for dinner. Be gentle but firm* and posted them on his door for all his dormmates to read. She wrote in Sharpie on bright white paper. She realized she was gay and asked Eli to have sex with her one last time before she gave up on men forever. Though he was ultimately heterosexual, Eli fell in love with his piano professor, who was so charismatic you knew when he came into the concert hall even if it was packed with a murmuring audience getting ready to sit down. He could come into the back entrance and a wave of faces would turn toward his light like sunflowers.

One winter evening, Cameron and I sat side by side in the famous womb chairs at Mudd, studying, spinning, dreaming. At least I was dreaming. Then Cameron left his chair and climbed into mine. We were like puppies in a pile, all limbs and heat. Outside, winter had crusted everything with cold; our feet were always cold, our faces. In the womb chair, we were a bucket of warm. I couldn't stop giggling, though, because there wasn't enough room. A woman in another chair shushed us. The chair made an ominous cracking noise, and Cameron started to laugh outright, and just then, Eli wheeled by with a cart of books to reshelve.

"Can you ask them to relocate?" asked the shushing woman. To her credit, it was almost midterms, and we were in a library. Still, this made me laugh harder, and Cameron was weeping with folly.

Eli didn't look inside the chair. He paused his cart and said, "Madame and monsieur, might I recommend the Days Inn in Elyria?"

This made us both laugh harder, though Cameron looked up at his former roommate and saw who it was, or maybe he knew from his voice.

"Dude," he said, "I hear there's a vacant room where two guys who couldn't get along used to live."

"Yep," said Eli. "I use it all the time, don't you? I believe you are the famous Clementine?"

I couldn't stop. I was crying with the pleasure of it, and now I had to pee, and people all around us were huffing off to study elsewhere. Only Eli understood.

"I am!" I said, extricating myself from Cameron's limbs and running off to the bathroom.

When I came back, Cameron was sitting alone at a table.

"He's not so bad," I whispered.

"No," said Cam. "He never was."

"Maybe we should have him over for cocktails," I joked.

"Shh!" said two women in chorus.

Cameron grinned and put his fingers on my lips, a sexy *Quiet, please.*

On our way out of the library we saw Eli again, manning a desk. Cameron saluted. Eli stood up and bowed. It was a relief to know Eli wasn't a monster, to tell Cameron how Lily had a crush, how she asked me about Eli all the time, how Cam and Eli's fighting had made him more mysterious.

Cameron was quiet and took my hand. Then, as we wrapped ourselves in scarves and hats and mittens and arctic-worthy coats, he leaned in and whispered, "Just please don't like him. Don't like him more than me."

I wasn't sure I heard him. I was sure I heard him. It was the only unreasonable thing he ever asked of me. I asked him not to look too closely at the jet-haired twin geniuses who played cello and viola in his chamber ensemble. I asked him not to go out for 3.2 beer and fries at the pub with them after rehearsal unless I went, too; I saw the sexual current under the music, or maybe I was just threatened by anyone who might speak a different language with Cameron.

"Really?" he'd asked.

"Just invite me, too, and I won't mind."

"The beer is awful, anyway," he said, agreeing.

I asked him not to take the same ethnomusicology class I did because I would be too distracted, plus I knew he'd just be so much better, I wouldn't ever feel flush with new ideas, I'd feel as if I were catching up. Mostly, I was a trusting and reasonable girlfriend, but I had moments of insecurity, so I could give him this. He hadn't asked me not to talk to Eli, or be in study group with him, or laugh at his jokes. He hadn't asked me to hate the man. Maybe he saw something I didn't, because to me, Eli seemed jovial and sharp-witted and fun and even handsome, but certainly no threat to the brilliance of Cameron Kite.

Over the summer, I visited Cameron in California, and he visited me in Princeton. I wasn't sure what to expect when we met him at Newark Airport. My father had offered to drive us, and I'd been surprised, but too far out in the sea of my lust and longing to remember how odd this was, my father, taking time out to drive me to pick up my boyfriend.

"So," said Dad, parking in short-term parking. "What can we expect, besides a dramatic decrease in the phone bill for the next week?"

"What can *we* expect?" I unbuckled before the car was fully parked. I wanted to taste Cam's mouth; I needed to feel his square fingers and the smudge on his chin from playing violin. "The royal *we*?"

"Your mother and I," said Dad, glaring at my unclipped seat belt.

"You've talked about it?" I opened the door, and Dad tugged the parking brake with dramatic force.

"Of course, Clementine," he said following me as I rushed to get out. "We talk about you. It isn't just paying your tuition, you know." He patted his car as we shut our doors behind us. "We want to know if this young man is treating you with respect. If he's worthy of your attentions."

"Oh my goodness, Mr. Bennet, sir, I'm pleased to know you care about the sensibility of young Mr. Darcy," I said, teasing him with Jane Austen. But I was pleased. I was flush with attentions— Dad's, sudden and unexpected, and Mom's, by proxy.

"Don't be rude. Your mother cares a lot about the choices you make."

He paused; I was pacing, waiting for the crosswalk sign near the entrance, deeply impatient, thinking of talking to Cameron, how much I needed to be with someone who didn't know what I was thinking but really wanted to know.

I stopped pacing for long enough to consider my father. "Thank you," I said, meaning it, but also meaning *Leave me alone.*

I saw him first and felt as though I were riding my pony over a jump, those seconds airborne, flying, possibilities and inevitable landing. I kissed Cameron in front of my father. I held him long and hard and he laughed because he was trying to see my face and I couldn't let go.

"Well," said my father. "I can see someone's glad to see you. I'm Dr. Lord." He held out his hand to Cameron, who shook it, looking my father in the face even while his other hand reached inside the top of my jeans waistband to press against my lower back. I felt capable of stripping him right there, of having sex at the baggage carousel, I'd wanted him so much my body felt charged, electric, lightning seeking ground.

"Pleased to meet you, Dr. Lord," said Cameron. I realized just how far the body can go in betraying propriety. It hurt, and it was exquisite to want him like this.

In the car on the way home Cameron sat in back. I twined my arm behind the seat, not minding the sharp cut of the strap, and held his hand.

"Well," said my father, his voice an exaggerated baritone. "You two should remember there are other people present and not just the two of you in the world. I hope you're not planning anything expensive in the near future. I have a lot of college tuitions to pay, and I'm not in the market for a wedding."

Cameron's hand tensed. We were twenty years old. We'd laugh about it later.

ELEVEN

I couldn't find my mother. I called out through the big house, hoping she'd hear me, hoping no one else was wandering around—a cleaning person, a gardener, an organic-delivery person—usually, people stayed outside the house: the front door was the separation between grounds and sanctuary, but occasionally people came inside, invited or presumptuous.

"Mom," I paged on the intercom, which my sisters and I had used to whisper commentary about our parents when we were teens—*she's dressing up again, he's coming home tonight, look at that ugly mole!* We must have kidded ourselves that they couldn't hear us or didn't have feelings.

"Mom? I thought I'd stop by—I, um, I got an A on my Chem final?" And Dad's an adulterer. And Olivia wishes him dead.

"I was wondering if you want to go shopping?" I said, but I really wanted to feel her out. Somehow, I suspected she knew. Somehow, this explained everything—except that they clearly loved each other. Except that Dad, upright, uptight, don't-you-ever-insult-your-mother Dad, had another wife.

"Mom?" I called, worrying for once about her, instead of him.

Shopping with my mother was very, very low on my list of

things to do. I preferred the dentist, the dermatologist for a mole check. And once again, Olivia wasn't answering my calls.

My mother was always slender and elegant, and I still felt sloppy in comparison, like an adolescent. My looking-glass self was decent, given an absence of thin, put-together people in the picture, but put Mom in the image with me, and I felt like a slouch, a louse, a lout, a mess. But I knew she knew by now—I'd called Odette, and Olivia had pointed out that it was public record, that Mom might as well know. Odette called Mom. Odette's report was that Mom was taking it in stride, which seemed dangerous to me. So I went to the big house and tried to coax out the hiding cat with a yarn ball of shopping.

"Mom?" I called into each room in turn. All the doors were shut, the chairs and tables gossiping among themselves in their privacy. I paused before my parents' bedroom door, still embarrassed by the king-size, wrought-iron bed that stood in the middle of the room like evidence. She wasn't in any room. I began imagining things, the way I had when Odette first told me Dad wasn't at rounds—that my mother had drowned herself in the pool, and I'd somehow missed the weedy hair billowing in the blue green. That Mom had driven her little Audi convertible into one of the sound walls on Route 1, that she'd downed a mass of her myriad sleeping pills—her cabinet, which I checked next, revealed all the newest kinds: Sonata, Ambien, Lunesta; and pills for anxiety, Xanax, Klonopin, lorazepam, Zoloft; most of them prescribed by my father. But most of them were full. No lumpen bleeding masses behind the shower curtain. No river of blood seeping from the base of a closet door.

He loved her. He wanted her to feel good. I knew this from

observation. For all my disgust about the Accounts and Diary, I had always envied the way they defended and supported each other. They had a physical relationship—they touched, they kissed, they were embarrassing and thrilling when we were little. We used to ask them to make a circle around the three of us with their arms. "Kiss Mom!" Odette would command us all, and Dad always made it first to her lips.

"Mom?" I called up the stairs toward the third floor, my former lair.

After I graduated from Oberlin, my mother had used her wasted talents to redecorate my room. I padded up the freshly carpeted stairs, with special-order bars to hold the runner in place, the new stained-glass custom-made for the landing—a version of my mother's Octavia rose; the knobby, white, designer bedspread and fat, mahogany leather Pottery Barn chair sat gathering dust for my mother's next cleaning rotation.

My father's office, I realized. Of course. In fact, as I approached the closed door to his only private space in the house, I heard a buzzing noise. Maybe she was electrocuting herself, I thought; maybe she had rigged up a fork in the socket, strapping it to her arm with duct tape so she wouldn't chicken out. Did duct tape conduct electricity?

Perhaps she knew long ago. Perhaps they had some sort of agreement. Maybe the other wife lived in Utah, though Odette was working with her own lawyer to find out. Perhaps what I was learning, most of all, is that I would never marry, at least not until I was sure I trusted everything about my mate.

"Mom?" I called, trying the door. It was locked. A surge of panic filled my arms, an ache of adrenaline.

"Mom!" I yelled, pounding on the door. The odd buzzing stopped.

"Just a minute, Clementine. Hold your horses," she said as if I were five. A clunking noise, a paper shuffling, and my mother unlocked the door. She looked at me briefly, then sat on the floor with the papers—papers she had torn from the sacred Accounts book—and started up the source of the buzzing noise once again: a paper shredder.

"I'm just cleaning up a few things," she said. I tried to catch her eyes, to see if they were bloodshot, to see if she was lost in grief, or simply angry. Her voice was remarkably calm. Not for the first time, I wished someone twinned with my mother; even if it was claustrophobic, someone could always hear you.

"Mom? Did you know?"

"What? Darling, I'm just tidying up. Your father's on a business trip, and he hasn't had a chance to clean up in here—"

What're you, out of your mind? I wanted to ask. But it occurred to me that she might be. That their closeness was a lie—that a part of me never wanted to know the intimate details of the way they kissed—but I'd seen it, I'd seen them holding hands under the dinner table; I'd seen him zip up the back of her raw silk sheath dress in a hotel room in Cambridge at Harvard graduation. I'd seen his hands lying.

"And I know. Your sister told me. I'm going to make a few changes, but, Clementine"—she paused and looked at me, her eyes a dangerous, watery blue, but tearless, huge, uncrying eyes— "you have to understand that this is a private matter."

"A private matter? Mom, he has another wife somewhere. He went to her. He's probably been supporting and visiting her for years." But our father was allowed to have a private life that didn't include us—that seemed as if Mom was betraying us, too. *I thought we were his private life,* I thought, *us, and you.*

"Yes," she said, feeding a page from 1985 into the machine. "I think I'm going to get a job," she said almost wistfully. "I also know he loves me."

I sat on the floor beside her and helped her rip out pages, wanting to call him a *fuckhead, bastard, asshole.* Wanting to swear revenge. Instead I fed pages into the machine, shredding common history.

That night we all had dinner at the big house, sitting out on the patio, as Olivia served us chicken cacciatore and broccoli rabe she'd picked up at the gourmet takeout near her office. I couldn't eat the chicken; it seemed disgusting, somehow, to consume flesh. It reminded me of a baby. It wasn't their pregnancies that drew them apart—tonight my sisters were odd together, mismatched in a way. Olivia and I had shared the secret exclusively for about a minute, and just that seemed like betrayal.

It was Dad's fault; he'd pressed his finger on a perfectly balanced scale. Or maybe he had wanted that. Maybe this was his sophisticated ruse to inspire individuation in my sisters. Sometimes when we were eight or nine, we'd play Scrabble with him— he'd always roll his eyes when our words were shorter than four or five letters. "You can do better than that," he'd say, and sometimes it felt like encouragement, and sometimes it felt like disappointment. Odette and Olivia would eye the same vowels on the board; they would intuit each other's letters and share. I felt it sometimes, too, knowing there would be Olivia's *quarter* on my father's *quiddity*, using the same *q*. It was competition and collaboration. I would use the *y* for *yule*, and Olivia would grin and add *tide*. It felt as if there was the quietest pleasure in understanding each other, in joining words like hands, better than Twister, and easier than conversation, somehow.

But Dad would have to think about us an awful lot to do that, and he seemed far too trapped in the small room of himself to venture into our halls of necessity. For a second, I recognized something about myself, but it passed as Jason poured wine.

Sometimes, we were a team of three, but sometimes, there was them and there was me. They'd shared a placenta and amniotic fluid, they saw together with four eyes when they emerged, and used eight limbs like a spider. They shared language and secrets without speaking, and when they finally spoke, it was in words only they understood. I was part of it, but not equal. Of course, this had changed over time, I thought, as I watched Olivia serve Jason a second helping of chicken. Her fingers were swollen with pregnancy; her giant pear-cut diamond ring wrapped her finger like a noose. I had never felt I could stand beside one sister, Odette or Olivia, without the other shadowing us both. Until now.

Maybe that's why I went to them each alone, maybe that's why I had been digging into the crack of the arch, digging, cleaning like a restoration, only instead of repairing, I pried at the keystone. Since I'd been home, I realized, they'd been different together, and different with our father, and now he was gone. Why now? Who was the other wife? For the first time, I imagined he might never come back. Maybe he left for her, I thought—or maybe he left because of me.

He was a coward. Now that we knew what he had done, he was gone. But part of me felt responsible, as though my incomplete adulthood could have shamed him into leaving. Or made him exhausted of this family—as if he had that right. I was living there like a child, depending despite my assertions of independence. Maybe my waffling drove him to departure.

"Kicking?" Odette's husband asked her, putting his hand on her belly.

"Not right now," she said.

"I've got kicking," Olivia said, smiling not at Odette, but at my mother.

"I saw the most amazing little Moses baskets in a catalog," my mother started, as if we were still at my sisters' extravagant shower.

"We have them," my sisters said in unison.

I almost laughed; it was like ringing a bell when they spoke together—even for me, the third sound. More, for me, than for anyone else—they resonated in my chest. I wanted all of us unified. We didn't need him. Look at us, four women and two men, perfectly happy in the house. I wanted to ask about the anniversary party because it surely had to be canceled soon—the caterers had required a deposit, and the tent, what useless decorations would be delivered to our house if we didn't cancel soon.

We needed him. We missed him. He was a hole in the floor. A hole in the conversation.

Odette interrupted Olivia's recitation of measurements of the nuchal fold from her last ultrasound, and Olivia looked sharply at her sister. For a second, I tried on schadenfreude, thinking that if there was some distance between them, maybe that was a space set aside for me. But, no, I realized, it was just sad. Sisters cleaving.

The way our cells had, growth and separation. It wasn't about room for me, it was simply additional distance.

When the doorbell rang, we all jumped. My mother had had the locks changed in the afternoon; I'd witnessed the locksmith with his portable key-honing machine grinding and drilling, set up at the front door as if he were camping for the day—the litter of soda cans and sub sandwiches cast about the porch. Maybe it was Dad.

Odette's husband, Evan, rose to answer, and we sat silently, chewing and chattering ceased, listening, while Alphabet licked at our fingers and let out an occasional bark to point out that he was on alert. Evan walked with a little bounce. He'd whispered to me in the kitchen, "I can't believe he did this—," but Mom came in before we could elevate our collaborative shock and disgust with the language of gossip and confidence. Ella slept on my mother's feet, complaining like an old woman whenever she stood.

Evan returned slowly, his voice ringing out in the tastefully decorated hall, bouncing off the clean white walls and recently polished hardwood floors. We all looked at the hallway, waiting. No one chewed.

"May I present Master Eli?" he asked.

"Whew," said Odette, digging into her food.

"I'm that exciting?" said Eli.

"You're not Dad," I whispered.

"He's better," said Olivia, raising her glass of ice water. She sent me a small shock of sweetness.

"Want to go to the movies, Clem?" Eli asked, touching a finger to the olive oil on my plate, gauchely tasting without washing first.

"Nothing would please me more," I replied, feeling released, if only for a moment. I couldn't wait to get into the cool darkness and watch someone else's story for a while.

The next morning I put in an application for paid summer work and then finished my shift at the shelter. I scrubbed down the cages while the dogs were outside—one by one, so no one would fight. I hosed out the muck in the corners with a hose blast, and my hands stank of bleach. No other dog had captured my heart since Pony left—it wasn't the same, even though the other animals needed the routine care.

I decided to appease my guilt for wanting my sisters to fight by going shopping for baby things. There was nothing else to do. I went through the day feeling shaky, as if I'd witnessed a violent crime.

"Anything special?" finished the woman at the boutique who had been following me as I touched the frilly dresses on the racks. We'd had one like these, I remembered, a "good" dress, from Me and Da, that one of us had worn at someone's event—a wedding, maybe? A bar mitzvah? I smiled to myself, and the woman looked at me as if I were daft. Was I allowed to smile when Dad was with his mistress? I just wanted normal back. Imperfect, irritating, normal, where my life was about my selfish self.

"Just browsing," I said.

The dress had roses and crinolines. We'd taken turns dancing around our Oakville room wearing it. Odette had smudged Magic Marker all over the trim, wiping her hands of purple without thinking, and she'd blamed me when Mom asked. Still, it was ours.

Now they would be mothers; I was going to be an aunt. I hadn't really thought about what that meant, until now, until I'd felt babies kicking at me, as if they were impatient to get out. Actual babies—and though I'd always contemptuously imagined baby nurses and nannies in my sisters' houses—Odette in her blue silk dressing gown, Olivia in pink, which made her skin look peachy and warm—neither of them had made the motions of hiring people. They were taking exceptionally brief maternity leaves; their husbands, Evan and Jason, were taking only a few days off. They'd still be up at night, at least—at least they'd have those small bodies needing everything from them when their hours overlapped. I recognized a strange tingling I hadn't expected, since I'd done everything in my power to never get pregnant, obsessively checking my diaphragm when Cameron and I slept together, insisting on condoms as well with anybody else—it was jealousy. I envied them their impending motherhood, just a little.

I found myself at Buy Buy Baby on Route 23, filling my cart with things from the registries. Things I couldn't afford but needed to be the one to provide. Developmental toys in black and white, matching color mobiles, soothing CDs, and two giant bears that made womb noises. I had never imagined either sister would go in for those, given their professions. And for Olivia, I picked out something not on the list, a frilly dress, less than half the price than the ones at the boutique, but still more than I should spend. I'd be paying interest on my credit card, which was a huge embarrassment to my father. And stupid, but I wasn't someone with a lot of options, at least right now.

Dad was paying for two wives, wherever he was. It wasn't enough to have two, but now I was sure he'd picked two who needed financial support—at least, that would explain the years of excessive frugality. I hated his disgusting Mercedes. His receding hair. I missed him.

Maybe Olivia knew something else we didn't—maybe he had said something to her, something other than the strutting speechifying he'd done at the family dinners, and at the shower, entering embarrassed by all the women, like a fat rooster peeking in at the chickens—and handing each daughter a bank book, for the accounts he'd opened in the names of baby Greeves and baby Arbor, their future children. I'd tasted a bit of bile then, but maybe the money wasn't what they'd wanted: maybe they'd wanted his approval just as I did. After all, he'd had babies, but there was no maternity leave for men back then—he'd never had to interrupt his career the way they would, he'd never had to settle for a lesser specialty.

As I was standing in line behind an enormously pregnant woman trying to keep screaming twin toddlers in the cart with all the swag she was buying—I watched the register blink over $200, and she wasn't half-finished—my cell phone rang. I imagined it was Eli. Who else called me, after all? Sometimes I missed talking with Lily, and sometimes I even missed Feet—Ferdinand—if only for the bodily company, for the fortitude of walking two together. I began to think I had a crush on Eli because he was really my only friend here—Pony, and Eli, and Pony was gone.

"I'm spending a ridiculous amount of money," I said as I flipped open the phone without checking the number. "My sisters have expensive taste."

"One of your sisters has gone into premature labor," said Olivia. "Three guesses which expensive-tasted sister that would be."

"Olivia?" I said because she'd startled me. Not that she never called, but lately I couldn't reach her, and I'd fully expected Eli, and until this call I'd always known when it was once of them, and I hadn't meant to say that about their taste and—

"No. This is Olivia. Odette is the one laboring as we speak. Her water broke while she was examining a patient. It's too late to stop it—this baby boy's coming early. And for some odd reason—maybe because Mom's acting like a headless chicken and I can't fit on the bed with her—she's asking for you."

TWELVE

The thing is, I'll never know how much I really loved him, whether we'd have survived outside the bubble of Oberlin, whether it was okay to fall in love young, whether I was really in love with Cameron or just so intent on coupling I'd chosen the most likely candidate and cast all my votes.

We went to our respective homes for spring break of sophomore year. My sisters overlapped with me by a day; they'd each lost their virginity, and we were discussing this, eating ice cream in town. A woman walking down the street stopped and stared, gripping her baby-belly swell.

"You two must be twins!" she said to Odette. Odette smiled.

"No," said Olivia, her face steady and humorless, despite the cone of chocolate dairy joy, coated with rainbow sprinkles, in her hand.

Odette laughed with her head back while her mocha almond melted down the cone and onto her fingers, and my mother came by in the big car, rolling down the window to call out to us on the sidewalk.

"Oh, Clementine," she called. "Clem!" She parked in the middle of the street and tore out of the car, her foundation smeared with tears. The pregnant woman walked on, cowed.

In the summer Cameron and I would both come back to Princeton—Cameron had a fellowship in a lab at Columbia Presbyterian, and I would work at my father's hospital, helping a colleague with his arthritis research. I was looking forward to bringing home my golden boy. Drew had just been practice. This was my other self. This was how my story ended and began. I was looking forward to being a pair in the face of so much matching.

Cars began to honk, almost immediately. My mother grabbed me, as if she were drowning, pulling on my clothes, almost pulling herself up toward my head.

"Your boyfriend died," she said quietly, into my ear, as I dropped my ice cream cone onto the ground.

After Cam died, Reed checked on me, calling weekly for a month or two, even when we had little to say to each other. When Cam's mother called, she needed something from me; she was brittle and broken, like the dazzling crystal Christmas globes Grandma Me had sent us the winter we were six. Odette's had shattered moments after she opened hers, and my mother had cursed her own mother in front of us.

Sometimes Reed would recount some story about Cam, as if my knowing might erase the loss. Sometimes we were quiet together on the phone, as if breath was enough.

It made no sense that he drowned. It made no sense because he was lifeguard-trained, because he was strong and lean. What did make sense was that Cameron had a sort of absence about him, what made him singular, what made him not exactly part of things growing up, even though he made the motions, even though girls attached themselves to him like leeches in a flesh-starved pond.

And when my mother told me Cameron was dead, my first thought was that someone had killed him. But he had been entirely alone in the backyard, supposedly swimming laps, no forensic evidence of a struggle, when he drowned. I thought his father had passed on something unbearable—unintentionally, of course—his father was never diagnosed with manic depression, but Cameron said he'd known that's what it was since he was in high school and took a psychology course. Or maybe all the pressure of freedom from his brother had caused them each to collapse like a pricked balloon over time. It was hard to imagine such need, and then such letting go. Cam looked different to me from the minute he was gone—before, he was golden, and afterward, he held dangerous energy under his skin. I wanted to be angry at someone, so I stopped talking to his mother. It was too much, anyway, her intonation like his, her loss allowed to be closer, even, than my own.

The night before he died, Cam and I had talked until 2:00 a.m. Back then, phone calls were still expensive enough to irritate my mother, who paid the phone bill from her allowance. I could care less. I'd found the other half of my pair, and no mother was going to stop me from practicing our attachment when we had to be apart. Neither family had been willing to let us go to the other's for spring break—or, rather, willing to pay for our airfare. Cam's mother had called me and said, "I wish I could do it, honey—I miss you so much!" and I knew she meant it, even though her words made my mouth feel prickly, as if I'd said something obscene.

My ticket to Newark was purchased six months before, and Cameron flew home for every break, even for the long Thanksgiving weekend.

"I miss you," I'd said, for the fourteenth time in twenty minutes.

"I miss you," he'd said back. "I wish Dad could relax—he's on some thing about building an arbor. And he keeps saying we should have brought you here, as if saying it could make it so. I miss that thing you do with your tongue—"

"You mean this?" I licked the receiver. It was disgusting, of course, but we were in love, and no one had ever been in love this way, and the germs on the phone were no match for the antibacterial superpowers of our love.

"He wants me to teach him violin. I just want to chill, but we started lessons anyway. And you know what? I don't hate teaching. He's a very eager student. But I have to say, I'm not sure about the fifth year for violin." Cameron, like Eli, was in the double-degree program. If it had been possible to finish two degrees in four years, Cameron would have done it, but too many credits were involved.

"We'll figure it out." I was so certain of our future, I'd already made plans for after we both finished school. He'd start med school, and I'd join him in San Francisco, or Boston, or Seattle. I might work for a while to support him, and then he could take his turn while I went to graduate school. We'd have a sunny second-floor walk-up and would feed each other strawberries at night on our futon, too tired to make dinner.

My own plans for med school were wavering, even as my sisters were taking practice MCATs and wandering Harvard Square with any one of their unserious boyfriends. They had a five-year plan: they'd date until the last year of medical school, because forming attachments before you know where you're going for residency was a bad idea. Then it would be okay to get serious. My answer to a five-year plan was imagining setting up an apartment off campus with Cameron. Imagining a job where I could pay for our rent and food and maybe even help Cameron as he played violin and studied medicine. I was that in love, or that deluded, and I'd never have a chance to find out, now that he'd drowned.

I drowned, too, just a little. My sisters tried to tell me things, tried to give me comfort, but I was closed—it was as though I'd lost that fourth dimension, and even the third. The world was flat. Music sounded like noise.

My sisters lay on either side of me as I tried to become part of the couch.

"Can you hear me?" Odette asked aloud. "I'm trying to sing you a song, silently."

"No," I said.

"How about a game?" asked Olivia.

"No," I said. I let their bodies rest again mine, but felt itchy, as though I ought to peel off my surfaces and pool into the earth, unfettered by skin.

They tried not to let me go, but it was spring break, and then it was the last semester, and my sisters went back to Harvard and I took a plane back to Ohio. The engine noise was a relief, a silence, a nulling of possible harmonies.

◆ ◆ ◆

I finished out my sophomore year and took a semester of leave, halfheartedly filling out applications for semester-abroad programs in France, Australia, the Netherlands. I slept in my bed at home for fourteen or fifteen hours, staying up late rereading the books of my childhood, *The Phantom Tollbooth, Anne of Green Gables, Black Beauty,* trying not to think of Cameron, but thinking of him just the same.

Dad checked on me when I was home; he'd come in every evening before he went to bed for a depression assessment. He referred me to the best psychiatrist he knew, who prescribed antidepressants. I filled the prescription and kept the pills in one of the makeup bags my mom got free when she bought her cosmetics—we three girls each had a dozen or more. I kept the bag in the file drawer of my desk after *Oberlin Application* and *Ohio Information.* O for *Only if absolutely necessary.* I never took them because I wanted the sadness, even if I were in a hole, at the bottom, no light and no chance of climbing up. I liked it in there, cool and lonely and dark.

Somehow, after my random selection of program applications, I wound up going to Australia, to a field studies program, studying the efficacy of several species of leeches—measuring their mouthparts and the amount of anticoagulant administered with each bite. It was hot; we lived on the outskirts of the rain forest, and the rainbows that covered dairy-farm fields like umbrellas after each day's rain disgusted me—so much sun and beauty, when Cameron was dead. I made a few friends, but mostly kept to myself and my leeches, walking to my study site each morning before breakfast, carrying two slices of bread and a hunk of cheese.

Never mind the beauty, I thought, for that semester. Never mind medical school. I collected regular postcards from Eli, letters from Lily, and Sophie and Mary, who were at Cornell and Michigan, respectively, studying religion and English literature. My father asked me to call once a week, though I had to go to the office and punch in a thousand numbers from his calling card to do it—this wasn't from Mom's allowance, this was from my father. It was the only time he gave me a lot of attention, and I was on the other side of the world, mourning and measuring leech mouths.

Australia was a rude shock—sun and company and humid heat.

I complied with Dad's weekly call mandate. It was a ritual like the bread and cheese. The calls were brief but I relished them despite myself.

"Dad," I'd say, standing in a phone booth in the tiny, eucalyptus-dusty town of Atherton.

"Clementine. How is the southern hemisphere?" Every time, habitual questions about my research and my measure of sadness.

The first call he established the routine, asking, "Okay, so how much does it hurt—scale of one to five?" I'd loved the post-op sense of that question, of his expertise, and I'd answered honestly with a five.

Toward the end of the semester he still asked the same questions, but our calls lengthened slightly, like sunlit minutes at the end of late-spring evenings.

"Do you love this sort of research?" he asked one night.

"I don't know yet."

"It's okay if you do. You know, I once thought I might find some other calling in science. Being a surgeon is rewarding, but there are other ways to apply your talents. It's okay."

It wasn't so much a lecture as an admission.

"Sometimes I sing when I'm alone in the field," I said because it occurred to me. Because I missed the confessional nature of loving Cameron.

"Me, too," my father chuckled. "You probably need to go," he offered, a small, polite gift. "Scale of one to five?"

"Fi—no. Four point eight five today."

"Good. Expect continued incremental improvements. I love you, Daughter."

He didn't pause for my reply; he hung up, and I didn't mind. Four point eight five. It was the truth between us.

I went back to Oberlin for the first half of senior year. Fall was glorious. I walked through the arboretum past the brain trees—I looked them up in a tree guide at the library when I was supposed to be finishing a chi-square project: Osage orange trees, they were called. I preferred to call them brain trees. They dropped giant sticky fruits that looked like brains. I thought of my father and his surgeries. I thought of Cameron every time I passed the conservatory, every time I passed our old dorm. Now the ache wasn't welcome. I wanted to move on, but I couldn't, not here. My freshman and sophomore year, I'd avoided the phone in my room, gleefully not returning my parents' calls, but now that I was back, I willed the phone to ring.

My weekly calls with Dad became biweekly, and he stopped asking for my pain assessment, as though he'd completed my post-op.

Still, he asked excellent questions—"Does your statistics class help you understand the tiny margins of research science?"

"It would, if I paid better attention," I admitted.

"You should pay better attention, then."

I wanted the pain scale. I wanted the balm of patienthood, but I didn't know how to ask.

Now that I was back, though, my father worried less. He seemed to think I was on the antidepressants, that things were back to normal, but there was no normal for me. I stopped eating for a month, tricking my body with water and celery, enjoying the light-headedness. My period stopped. Still, I wasn't exactly scrawny, so no one noticed. When I came home for winter break, my mom told me I looked great.

I had wanted my sisters to hear that sorrowful song—I longed for their crowding, but I had removed myself; I had chosen the quiet.

"Thank you," I said, secretly hating her.

"I mean, look at you—bloom of health! Do you want to go shopping while you're home? Do you have anything left in your budget?"

Of course, my father gave us each a budget to spend at school, for books, and for extras, such as movies, and clothes, and snacks, which I had none of, these days. If I'd ordered an Adjective Sandwich, it would have to be "empty."

I was probably hoping Mom would notice, and telling me I looked good made me furious.

"So skinny!" she said, looking at my legs. "Are you thinking about dating again?"

Of course I wasn't. I had Eli, who had become my best friend—though I had promised not to like him more than Cameron. I slept platonically in Eli's bed with him, in Oberlin fashion, once a week if he didn't have a girl there. I had two other friends who'd hung on through my melancholia, but most people were thinking about graduating, and I couldn't imagine anything worse. I'd have to move on. I'd have to admit that, having switched my major from premed to biology to environmental studies, finally landing on biology again, but only because I had the most applicable credits there, I wasn't ready to move on to anything. I still hadn't moved on from Cameron.

My sisters came home from Harvard and tried to jolly me out of my gloom. It was too soon and I stayed in my third-floor room, under the covers. I burrowed under a quilt I'd had since childhood, soft as skin, but it felt rough and stiff; I was a bruise. Olivia came inside with me, trying to get me to emerge.

"We can go to lunch," she said. "There's a new Thai place. We can do Party Trick to the waitstaff." *Come out,* she said silently.

"Not hungry," I said, trying not to listen.

"It's been too long," said Olivia, meaning both food and Party Trick.

Odette floated around the doorjamb like a moth. I couldn't hear her, but she was trying to tell me something in the ether. They were talking to each other. If I heard them, I couldn't be alone, so I was trying not to listen. If I don't look at you, you can't see me.

"I can't," I said, and I knew Odette knew this already. Olivia probably knew, too; she was trying to will me better with her pure and powerful force.

They brought me feasts and flashlights in bed and we tried to sit under the quilt-tent. They felt my sorrow; I could taste it in their sisterly kisses. They persevered and I stayed stuck as a barnacle to my bed and despair until they went back to school, to their hopeful fellowships and practice tests.

At the end of winter break, I'd started eating again because the food my mother cooked was tempting, and because I'd fainted twice in my room and hit my head on the metal screen in front of my fireplace—I'd explained the bruise away, but I didn't want to die, and I was tired of feeling partly dead. I stood in my room looking at the backpack full of things from school. I was going to live off campus in a group house and had only a few sets of clothes there and a thousand houseplants I'd inherited from the last occupants. My room at home was safe, and suddenly I couldn't go back.

"Mom?" I said, walking into her bedroom after a perfunctory knock. She was folding laundry on her big, king-size bed. She smelled of sandalwood salon shampoo.

"Clem," she said. "Ready to go to the airport?" Mom was going to drive me. Dad was away. He'd come home for Christmas dinner and had left before New Year's. I preferred the house when it was empty of him—he was a magnet when he was home, collecting all the attention and energy from my sisters, my mother, when what I wanted was to be noticed, to be rescued.

"No," I said.

"Can I help you pack?" she asked, looking up from the pair of my father's underwear she was folding. It was worn, and suddenly I was sad, because if my father's underwear was that old, he could be old. For all the money in the world, his underwear still sagged at the elastic waist. He wouldn't live forever, either.

"No," I said, welling up. "I can't go back. I miss him too much."

My mother dropped the underwear and folded me into her arms. "Honey. I was wondering. I mean, we all thought you were doing so well."

"Mom, I stopped eating, and no one noticed."

"I did—I mean, I said you looked great." She was stroking my hair now; it felt so lovely, but tender at the same time, as if my hair had nerve endings and was too sensitive to be touched.

"I didn't look great," I said. "I mean, I stopped eating—I fainted. I haven't had my period in two months—"

"You're not pregnant?" My mother's stroking hand froze.

"Of course not," I said, the tears stopping. "I'm just not going back." Why couldn't she just feel that? Why couldn't she just *know*?

"You can stay here as long as you like," my mother said.

My father disagreed. He and Mom rarely yelled, but I could hear his voice through the phone and my mother winced as she listened. It wasn't that he didn't want me at home; it was that no daughter of his would drop out of college a few credits shy of graduation. There was still a chance of medical school, he said, he knew several first-rate tutors in town who could help me with the MCAT. All this information was doled out in brief bursts via my mother, who spoke to him several times a day on the phone while he was away.

Then he came home, his bags deposited in the front hall by the cabdriver—though Dad could afford a limo, he chose the cab service from two towns over because it was cheapest—and was a demanding presence once again. Even if I had thought I could stay home before, once he was back, I knew I had to leave. Eli had a friend who was living in San Francisco and needed a roommate, and within two hours I had plans.

"I'm not paying for a plane ticket to San Francisco," said my father as I came downstairs with my backpack, having applied lip gloss for the first time in months. Maybe years.

"Dad, I'll finish college, just not right now. Maybe I'll take classes at UCSF—"

"Maybe isn't good enough. No daughter of mine—"

"Cut it out with that patriarchal crap," I said. My father stared at me as if I'd struck him. "Yes, crap. I appreciate that you're looking out for me. I appreciate the financial support—even if it comes with a spiderweb of strings attached—but, Dad, I'm getting over something, I can't go back right now, and I'm *going to San Francisco!*" I shouted this last bit for my own benefit as much as his.

"Clementine Lord," he said, taking deep breaths (I could almost hear him thinking, *Breathe one two three, breathe . . .*), "I have given you roof and education, clothes and care—and I insist you finish college. It's very, very important. More important than you know."

"Charles Lord." I wouldn't give up now. "I'm going to San Francisco. Mom already paid for my ticket. I'm going to get a job, and you are not going to stop me."

I cried in the car on the way to the airport, but then I refreshed my wiped-off lip gloss and marched into Newark Airport with a sense of purpose. I would get over it, all of it, and my father was, for once, not going to tell me how.

Two years and three jobs later (I worked at a health food store that reeked of patchouli and I was worried about maggots in the bulk grains but couldn't bring myself to say anything; I worked at a coffee shop and finally at a bookstore, which paid decently, and the owner contributed one dollar for every ten for courses I took at UCSF. It wasn't much, but it helped. Two loans got me through), Oberlin mailed me my diploma. I was a college graduate, and I had a great job in a bookstore, and the weather was glorious and my apartment had a view of the bay, if you stood on a step stool in the bathroom and craned your neck. My roommate, Liz, was a performance artist who worked at the coffeehouse where I'd been for six months, mixing up syrup-tinted drinks and making perfect *crema* on her cappuccinos.

Eli kept in touch, calling every week, or sending long letters from Kalamazoo, where he went for a master's in music before deciding his true passion was the pure science of biology and transferring to Princeton. Feeling very free from my father, I applied for doctorate programs in European history, in women's studies, and in ethnomusicology, but my heart wasn't in any of those, I just wanted to bother Dad. I lived in San Francisco for another year, waitressing, dating inappropriate men, and refusing to cash my father's checks, which I knew, from my sister's reports, were much smaller than the ones they collected. They finished med school, together, at Columbia.

Then I decided to apply to vet school, though my father was against that as well. Vets made small inroads into some of the world's injustices. People loved their animals, animals loved their people, and wasn't the wellness of those who couldn't heal themselves a small balm to a troubled planet? But with Dad, it was as if being a vet were some horrible betrayal, some pale imitation of doctorhood, though Mom had always encouraged us to be whatever we wanted to be. She also told us, don't forget to look for love, though; don't forget to look for love.

THIRTEEN

I had witnessed three births in my life—one dozen gerbils born at my friend Sophie's house—never mind that the mom ate four of them right away because she didn't have enough nipples, a tiny litter of two pups at a shelter (tiny, I thought, especially given that three of us had emerged from my mother's womb at once), and the thrilling viviparous birth of some snakes at the wildlife shelter north of San Francisco in Marin where I went to visit, though I never worked there. Snakes slithering out of a snake—I found it wondrous; Eli, who was visiting with Liz and me for a week, was repulsed. Eli reconciled with his father that year; they'd started to realize they could be friendly—Eli told me it was okay to have a father who had nothing exotic about him, that they could still talk about things. Ironically, I had tried to imagine having a parent with a whole family other than me.

Now I was standing beside my sister Odette, the ob-gyn, who could not yet have an epidural, and who said the contractions felt like hell.

"I'm dying," she croaked, crushing my hand and grimacing. She said it so calmly I almost believed her. Then the contraction stopped and her face became smooth. Smooth, but suffering.

"Okay," Olivia said, clapping her hands together as if she were about to make an announcement to a class of six-year-olds. "How're we doing? Breathing okay? Hanging in there until we can get you some relief?" *Get a damn epidural,* I heard her think.

"You're not my doctor," said Odette, waving her away. "And I heard that—I asked already."

"Fine," said Olivia, her lips crushed white. My mother came blustering in with two cups of coffee, one of which she promptly spilled on her jacket.

"Damn!" she said. "I'm sorry, girls, I didn't mean to say that. Is Evan here yet?"

He'd been to every Lamaze class, Odette had told me; he'd given his cell phone a designated ringtone for The Time, but he hadn't picked up the message yet.

"I'm dying, Clem, I'm dying," my sister said. Her face was pale, with red splotches that looked like some obscure disease. I wondered whether she could have contracted something in the lobby on the way in.

"You're fine," said Olivia.

"Fuck off!" screamed Odette, and I looked from one twin to the next, shocked.

"This always happens in childbirth," said Olivia calmly. "She knows. We're experts." She patted her own swollen belly as if she wasn't quite sure. No silent conversations ensued. It was eerie.

"Will you come with me?" my mother asked Olivia, probably just to get her out of the room. "I need to mop up." She pointed to her coffee-stained attire.

"Fine," said Olivia.

"I am *not fine,*" said Odette, crushing my arm this time.

"I just meant—," Olivia started, but my mother led her out of the room by the lapel of her doctor's coat.

"Now I am," Odette said. She appeared to be drowning or sunbathing, from minute to minute.

"Evan will be here soon, I'm sure," I said.

My sister scootched herself up on the hospital bed. She wiggled one leg, then the other. She breathed heavy breaths. The hospital was ridiculously cold and smelled of rubbing alcohol and bleach. Odette had a pile of blankets falling off her bed—I knew without discussion that she wanted her feet free and her considerable midsection covered, but she writhed so much during contractions the slippery synthetic things slid around the bed and onto the floor like tossed-off wrapping paper. The alcohol smell stung my nose, and the giant hospital gown my sister wore, covered in giant blue teddy bears, seemed ominous somehow. What if something was wrong? It wasn't that early, but still—I wanted everything to be okay, I willed it so hard I realized I was chewing the insides of my cheeks as I gently rubbed my sister's back, the bits I could reach around the bed.

It suddenly occurred to me that this pregnancy phase was about to be over. I would no longer have two pregnant sisters, they would no longer match; they would each have their own whole families without me, whole subsets of Lords—without the last name, and even though I overlapped, a Venn diagram of relationship, I didn't belong in the core. And they wouldn't belong so exclusively to each other, or to me. They'd belong to their babies. We all knew this. It was why she wanted me—it was what had allowed Olivia to hold Dad's secret for a whole week.

"I want her to call him," Odette said, grimacing, but not yet entering another bout of crushing pain—for her or my limbs.

"Evan? I can call again—" I reached for my cell phone, though I knew whom she meant.

"No, I want Olivia to call Dad. She has the number. I want Dad. I have Mom, and you, and O, of course, but I want Dad to see his first grandbaby right away. I want him here because he can make sure it all goes okay—you have no idea how many things can go . . . *wrong!*" This last word she screamed as she grabbed at my leg.

It occurred to me that there might have been just the tiniest bit of competition—a who will have the first grandbaby sort of thing—that I hadn't even considered before today. But Olivia was acting bizarre, and Odette had asked for me, not that I minded, but really, with Olivia there, she usually had all the expert witnesses she might need.

"Okay?" I said.

"Tell her," Odette said, coming down from the pain peak. It hurt under my belly button—I knew my own womb for just a second and wondered how anyone could bear such occupation.

"Why do I get the feeling you already did?"

"She said it's not an emergency. I was going to ask Mom—she has the lawyer's number, of course—but it didn't seem fair. But it is an emergency, O's being stubborn and mean. My baby's coming early. I need him here, and he gave her the number specifically for labor. And you—thank you for coming, Clem. You know I'm going to need a babysitter." She started to sit up, then lay back down.

"It's all about movement when you're not in this position. Move, and it won't *hurt so fucking much!*"

"I'm not leaving you in a contraction," I said, but at that minute Evan rushed in, his face wan, his cologne a lovely sort of sandalwood, his shoes scuffed in an endearing businessman-on-the-run way.

"I'm here! You okay?" He took Odette's hand from mine. This left me with relatively few options other than insisting Olivia fork over the number if she wasn't willing to call.

Evan waved me away, either protecting Odette or giving me a break, I wasn't sure. Part of me wanted to stay glued to her side; I wanted to be needed.

I ducked out of the hospital so I could use my cell phone— they weren't allowed inside.

"Dad?" I asked his useless voice mail. I was furious, but almost contrite. My hands hurt, my belly hurt, my eyes hurt from the light of the outdoors.

"You need to tell us how to reach you. Please. It's urgent." I sighed and dialed the next number.

"Eli?" I said, as if it would be someone else answering his phone.

"Clementine, my love."

"That's it. Sometimes I wonder about your love."

"Me, too," said Eli, and I felt as though I'd been kicked in the shin. Ow. What next?

"My sister's having her baby," I said. "She asked for me."

"Clementine! Are you in the room now? What is it like? You know Liz is pregnant, right? I mean, you two were roommates—"

Liz and I rarely kept in touch. Despite our living together, Eli had really been our only link. I had been a sourpuss when we'd lived together, and it wasn't her fault. I had temporarily forgotten how to be a friend. It would have been different if we'd met sooner, or later, and it hung in the back of my closet of guilt like a horrible, expensive dress. I didn't want to hear about Liz.

"*Right now*," I said. "It's wild. Don't tell me about Liz now, please."

"I just thought—"

"Don't think."

"So you didn't know about her?" Why was he so languorous, so casual? It was too important—this wasn't what I needed.

"I should probably get back," I said, wondering why I'd called him. I just felt as if Eli needed to know what was happening. Eli my lifeline, Eli with his too long lashes and creamy, almost-brown skin. Those chocolate eyes. And obnoxious calm.

"Do you want me?" Always the double entendre.

"Of course I want you," I said, wondering how I meant it. *Please don't like him more than me,* I heard Cameron whispering. "But here, I don't think they'd let you in. I'll call you later. It's early, you know. Not *too* early, but—" My mother and Olivia walked by the lobby, their bodies close, clearly exchanging confidences. My mother touched Olivia's back with a sweet sort of guidance.

"Gotta go," I said. Eli said something else, but I wasn't listening. The scales were all unbalanced, the new normal was impending, and Dad was still AWOL.

Something in the way my mother and sister walked together was a warning. I was wanting for something that wasn't about me; it was Odette who needed a full hand of family right now, and I could see order and reordering in the way people touched and separated. Triplets couldn't afford to have soft connections; triplets had electric poles—without a proper connection, we'd spin in space.

"Olivia," I said. "I'm just going to say it."

My mother donned her warning face, the one that said, *I don't like strife—don't you girls fight, no bickering, or I'm going to have to stop this car right now.*

"Yes?" Olivia said. "Since you're clearly the chosen one. Hey, what're you doing outside the room? I thought she needed to massacre your hand?"

"Evan's here," I said. "And don't feel left out—you get to do it, too." I cleared my throat. "Okay. I'll just say it: Odette wants you to call Dad—call that number he left. It isn't about him, it's about her, and she thinks it's enough of an emergency and so do I, and if you won't give me the number—"

"It is *not* an emergency," said Olivia, tight-lipped, clutching her belly as if otherwise her fetus might walk off.

"It is," I said. "Everything about his leaving is an emergency; everything about Dad is an emergency. Hurry up and wait. Do what I say, not what I do. You having the number is just his way of dividing us so we're not united against him."

"Enough!" said my mother. "I already called. He's on his way."

For a moment I wondered why my mom had the number—why she'd kept that to herself all along. Then everything was about the baby and Odette—their hearts' work recorded and amplified for everyone to hear. Urgency and miraculous exertion.

I was there for the rest of the labor, which lasted five hours, and the pushing. I stood at Odette's head as they decided to try for another ten minutes, or else it would be a C-section. She started to sob, but stopped for each contraction to hold her breath and grow red, then white. It was horrific, but also mesmerizing; I actually believed she could die, that having a baby was a huge deal after all. It wasn't a handful of stringy snakes wriggling out of a cloaca like a matter of fact. Odette was suffering, and she was strong. She'd had her epidural, but it wasn't too potent, so she was able to push, which meant that, according to Olivia, who came and went like the doctors and nurses, "It still hurts like hell."

Evan proved to be marvelous, bringing ice chips, performing foot rubs and back pressure with a tennis ball, which didn't seem to help, but certainly distracted everyone. "Here?" he asked. "Here?" while Odette just moaned.

"Love—nothing," he said, grinning soulfully at me.

Evan cracked jokes about ordering room service, about how terrific the drugs were, about how now she had some idea how her patients felt, which prompted Odette to kick him. But it was an excellent diversion. Sometimes Evan reminded me of a taller version of Eli—his kindness and intensity.

She might die, I kept thinking, watching her husband at the foot of the bed, staring into the inside of her body, where a baby was coming to and fro with her pushes—finally they realized the cord was around his neck. Odette's face was mottled with effort and blood vessels; her eyes were huge and bloodshot. Here I was, with my sister the obstetrician and my sister the pediatrician, and they were just as vulnerable as anyone else, performing this basic, primeval, dangerous feat of human childbirth.

"It's a . . . ?" prompted the doctor, handing the wailing mass at last to Evan.

"Boy?" gasped Evan, as if he hadn't known what to expect.

"Whew. He knows the difference," teased the nurse.

The baby was exquisite. He lay looking astonished on Odette's half-gowned chest for a moment, surprisingly quiet, and had nuzzled her, but wasn't ready to nurse. Odette stared at him as if she couldn't believe he'd happened; they were in concert, singing silent surprise. He was a little small, but they'd yelled out the normal Apgar before the nurse wrapped him up like a burrito and whisked him off to the NICU, where they'd double-check that everything was all right, since he was just under five pounds. Perhaps despite the obsessive planning of my highly organized sister, she'd gotten pregnant earlier than she estimated.

They delivered the placenta—an enormous and amazing organ—and then it had taken a little while to stop Odette's bleeding.

"Baby's fine," said the doctor, washing her hands and walking out as if something momentous hadn't just happened. She wasn't Odette's chosen doctor, who was still on vacation, she was just filling in, and she was perfectly fine, but not warm, not as heroic as I'd always imagined my sister would be at every birth. Odette had deserved more.

Mom and I stood in the room for an hour, holding Odette's hand as they ferried baby Adam away to be cleaned and measured.

Evan went along with the nurses so Adam wouldn't be left alone, and I gripped Odette's icy hand and tried to tuck the blankets in around her as she shivered violently.

Odette shivered and shivered and couldn't get warm.

"I'll get more blankets," said my mom, who looked a little ashen herself. "He's so beautiful, darling," she said, kissing my sister's head. Blood was smeared across Odette's cheek. "Wish number one!" Mom smiled. We were her three wishes, always.

"Performed like a pro," I said. Odette laughed a little. I licked my finger and wiped off the blood.

"Am I okay?" she asked me. Her eyes looked lost, as though she had witnessed something unbearable. I wished I knew. I wished I were a doctor, able to diagnose what was wrong with people, how to fix them. Oberlin made me crave purpose in the world, and even though I'd eschewed the authority and self-importance of becoming a *physician,* part of me knew they were necessary to make the kinds of calls my sisters made every day. I wondered how they could stand doing this sort of work—watching people's lives change daily and not collapsing from the sheer drama of it all.

"They left you alone—they wouldn't leave you alone with me if you weren't okay?" I said, but I wasn't sure myself.

"Can't get warm," said Odette.

And then, though we'd all forgotten, blissfully, for the past five hours, my father marched in the door like a king reclaiming his throne.

FOURTEEN

Although I love children, I have always been ambivalent about ever having my own, even when I was with Cameron. However, I had always wanted to be an aunt. My mother's sister was a fine example—adulthood without the burden of responsibility. She was *fun*.

When Eli and I were at Oberlin together for the fall of senior year, we volunteered to visit the Oberlin public schools as part of a college-town outreach project. Eli accompanied and coached a small group of students who were playing violin in the school orchestra; I did a science experiment with the third grade, collecting soil from sundry sites and testing it for pH, organic content such as worms, leaf matter, and insect larvae, and trying to sift out the mineral content. The kids were amazing; what looked like a bored bunch when I walked it, sitting slumped at their round tables holding their heads in scabby hands, turned out to be a group of amazing minds. They asked questions like "Are you married?" "Why do we need mosquitoes?" "How much money do you make?" and "Why did God put lava in the earth when it could squirt out and hurt people like it did in Italy a long, long, long time ago?" They wanted coaching, hand over hand, with the tests.

They wanted to know why and how, and they were willing to listen, even if their bodies were in perpetual motion.

After our third and final visit, Eli and I rode back to the library on our bicycles, our *Thank you, volunteer* certificates signed by the students rolled up in my basket so they wouldn't get crushed among biology and philosophy texts. His strong, sinewy body mottled by sunlight, Eli made up a song as he pushed the pedals.

"Kids are great, kids are good, and we thank them as we should, kids in the world, kids in the world, kids are swirled, kids, kids, kids!"

"Kids are swirled?" I howled, pumping hard on the ancient, one-speed upright I'd bought at the bike co-op, promising to sell it back after graduation—as it turned out, I never found out what happened to the bike because I left her on a rack outside Mudd, the main library, when I took my last shuttle to the airport, and never came back.

"Kids are burled! Those kids hurled!"

"They did not!" Eli's legs were longer than mine, and I had to stand and run on the pedals to keep up.

Eli stopped beneath a brain tree in the arb, and I almost ran into him, I was pedaling so hard. The old bike's brakes weren't exactly state-of-the-art.

"Clementine." He leaned over and picked a seed-gone dome of dandelion. It was October, and the arb looked like a painting, dazzling reds and yellows, the leaves shivering as if they expected the inevitable. A stone bridge crossed a river just ahead, and the sky was the sharp blue that cuts the world into earthbound and celestial properties. Eli's face was bright with exertion, his impossible lashes like fronds over his dark eyes. Eli's lips were perfect bows, doll-like, only somehow masculine, perhaps because they were wide and his smile showed no hesitation. He knew what he wanted from the world, and the way he looked at me as I stumbled to stop my bike made my cheeks hot with possibilities. I felt Cameron still. Eli and I had been friends before Cameron drowned; only it was a clandestine, unexplored, mutual admiration. An unexplored friendship that is, only seeing each other in classes, or with a pack of other friends. I was a small-group person, best one-on-one, and I would never have hurt Cam by spending too much time with Eli. After Cam left me by dying, I thought, he had less sway. Not none, but less guilt-mandated loyalty.

"Clem," said Eli. "We should get married. We would have beautiful kids. And we could teach them about science and music—" He blew the seeds off the dandelion, as if wishing.

I didn't say anything because he kidded about this all the time. I was Cameron's, even if Cam was gone. They'd been roommates—and even tape-divided roommates followed some sort of man code about not dating each other's girlfriends. I felt guilty holding Eli's friendship in my fist—too close for Cam—but it kept me from falling.

Eli was between girlfriends at the moment; he'd been with the voluptuous and gorgeous Guinivere, another double-degree student, studying voice and chemistry, a genius with dark blond, corkscrew curls and dimples when she sang, but a body like a mermaid's. Guinivere had graduated, and she and Eli knew he wouldn't follow her when she went to Juilliard for her master's (later she would become a food chemist and work for a large corporation that was trying to improve the nutritional value of its snack cakes—Guinivere would sing in a local opera company and marry an environmental activist and have five children and become even more voluptuous, as if that were possible), so they broke up.

"We could have two sets of twins." He grinned. "Boys and girls, one of each per set, and then we would only need to get one set of pink and blue overalls—"

"What makes you so sure I want kids?" I asked. "And twins. I'm not big on twins."

"But your sisters—" Eli was fascinated by my sisters. He flirted with them, and they often flirted back, though never in the presence of my father, or any of their respectable boyfriends. Or the unrespectable ones. Odette had dated a dramatically socially limited MIT graduate student who wore his hair in dreads—he called it a Jew-fro, and who was clearly so smart he should live on a more evolved planet. One where it was okay not to wash one's hair or clothing, one where it was okay to skip wearing shoes, even in winter, in favor of thick-soled feet covered with a hobbity sort of fur. He only lasted a month, but did succeed in worrying my father. My mother liked him because he fixed the icemaker, an air-conditioning vent, and the intercom system during his one brief visit on his way home to his parents' in Philadelphia.

"My sisters are my sisters. And we're triplets; they're not twins, even if it seems like they are, and you can just marry *them* if you think they're so fabulous." I picked up one of the brain-tree fruits, stumbling to keep my bicycle upright. It was sticky, green, and odd.

"No," he whispered. "It's you I want." Then he swung his leg over his bicycle and pedaled on to the library without looking back at me. I tossed the fruit in his path. My shirt got drips of brain-tree sap on the front, and like some kind of Super Glue, the wads of sap never washed out.

I always wondered what it would've been like to know Eli in high school, whether I would've loved him the same way. Or Cameron, for that matter, though for each boy I would've had to have had a whole different life to know them; until his mom died, Eli went to a private school in Manhattan and spent weekends at the Juilliard prep program with the other music geeks, playing first chair and talking about which summer programs had the best teachers, the best food, and the most comfortable living quarters. I had never known anything like what he described: a group with a sense of purpose and belonging, a group that was preprofessional at such a young age, but even more important, a place where everyone belonged, all talented; despite any pecking order, they were all musicians. They all had a particular talent (and most of them, like Eli, had more than one). It wasn't that I didn't fit in, in high school, it was that I never had that sense of belonging somewhere, the way my sisters belonged everywhere they went, owned a place, because they knew who they were and where they were going. You might think they would be the two out of the three of us who had trouble with differentiation, with individuation, but, no, I was the one who felt like a mateless shoe.

If I had known Cameron in high school, I would have been a California girl, and San Jose was nothing like Princeton.

When I first went back with Cameron, it was summer after freshman year, partly because of the cost of flying to California, partly because I had argued with my father every break when I came home, but I still felt obliged to be there, as if something might be lost if I didn't come back to check.

Cameron's family lived in a split-level on a cul-de-sac, a short brick-and-siding house that looked like the other houses. When we rode up in the SuperShuttle from San Francisco airport, I was surprised by how small it looked, how modest. The front yard was dry—it was a no-watering month—and a black mailbox was on a post by the curb, the kind frisky teens decapitated with a baseball bat from a car window in the movies.

"Oh," said Cameron's mother, a tall, frighteningly lean woman wearing coral lipstick and a polo dress. "*You* must be Clementine." She folded me into a brief, generous hug, leaning down as if I were a child. Then she held me back at arm's length and examined my face. I found it difficult to make direct eye contact; her eyes were the same color and shape as Cameron's. She shone; I wondered how her skin emanated warmth. *There must be something in the California air,* I thought. And then: *I wonder if I can ever live up to this.*

"I'm Alice. I have so much planned for us!" She swept my hair behind my ear—such an intimate gesture, I blushed. "You can come to my painting workshop? Unless you prefer shopping? And swimming—the girls can't wait to meet you? Did I tell you I'm in Master's Swim—nothing special, it's just fun. Do you swim?" Eye contact, more eye contact.

"Mom," said Cameron. "Remember me?" I knew he did it partly to give me respite.

THE ORPHAN SISTER

"She's never had a girl," said Cameron that night, sitting on my twin bed in the guest room. The house was deceptive on the outside; inside it rambled along, four bedrooms, a guest room, his mother's tiny sewing room, and constant little closets. You had to lean way in past their little doors to hang up your coat. I had unpacked into a dresser in the guest room, noticing the orange smell in every room, and then I noticed little sachets attached on hooks to the backs of each door.

"Clementine!" she called. "Oh, darling!" She wasn't daft, she was darling herself—a bit overwhelming, but darling nonetheless. "You must come make the salad dressing. All our guests make the salad dressing."

"She might not want to make salad dressing," said a huge voice.

He wasn't huge like his voice; he was a modest six feet tall with silver, boyish hair and a ridiculously boyish grin. If Cam looked like that when he was older, I'd have to work hard to compete. Maybe I'd have to swim a mile a day, like his mother. I was brave with my salad dressing and added six or seven different spices to the crushed garlic and green-yellow olive oil and the balsamic vinegar the Kites had brought back from their trip to Italy.

"It's so odd to be able to travel," his mother said. "All these years we've been home—and learned to love being home— Oh! You made the best dressing ever! We're going to have to keep you, Clementine!" She kissed my cheek. Then she looked into my eyes again. I couldn't decide whether I liked so much touching, or whether it made me nervous. Was I a prude? I asked Cam later, alone in his room.

— 173 —

"I'm not exactly exotic," I said. "And I'm sure you've had girl-friends home before."

"Not really," said Cameron, tucking my hair behind my ear—it was her gesture, I suddenly realized. Cam had learned it watching his mother, from infancy. I loved this man. I felt a surge of heat in my groin. Cameron could just look at me and I would want him. I'd wanted him on the plane; I'd wanted him as we held hands and walked across the airport; I'd wanted during dinner, when he ate his polenta and eggplant with tomato sauce and caught the tiniest bit at the corner of his mouth.

"She'll calm down. She just adores you."

"How come she glows, Cam?"

"Ha! I think it's probably some fancy skin cream. Or else all the swimming."

"I'm not sure I can ever live up to—"

"She's had a lot to deal with—my brother—," he said. "And now she has some *space*."

"Can we visit him?"

Cameron's autistic brother lived in a group house two towns over. His mother went almost every day, though Cameron said she didn't really need to. His brother had a job at the local grocery store and was taking art classes at the community school. Cameron talked to him every week on the phone, and once he'd put me on, and I'd asked his brother how he was, and he said, "You mean how tall? I'm six feet tall. I wear work shoes to work. How tall are you?" It hadn't been too odd, just formal, just the kind of conversation you might have with a shy and literal child, only he had Cameron's same deep voice and chuckle.

"Cam?" his mother turned the knob on my door. Cameron scootched away from me, as if sitting beside me were a sin.

"Oh," she said, looking at us, her eyes scanning the abbreviated distance between us. "Don't let me interrupt."

I was surprised she insisted on separate bedrooms, though I knew my parents would do the same when we went to Princeton, which I dreaded, and longed to do.

"Want some wine?" She beamed. "We're tasting."

It was too much, too wonderful.

"Well, I just wanted to say, your father wants to take you to the office tomorrow to see about something for the summer. Clementine, would you like to lunch with me and the ladies? And there's Master's Swim practice at the club—swim club."

I looked at Cameron; I'd assumed we'd spend all our time together.

"Okay," said Cameron, looking at his hands, then at me. "Clem, is it okay?"

"Fine," I said, trying to sound okay. I felt like crying. I felt like calling my sisters; for the first time since leaving for college, I really missed them. It was one thing to be gone during the school year, when life was filled with extraordinary musical performances, lectures, homework, raucous dining-hall dinners with the entire dormful of friends; it was another entirely to be on my own in a strange suburban house like a foster child with the most effusive mom on the planet. The truth was, I enjoyed being near her. She felt genuine, if overzealous. She was trying so hard I couldn't help liking her—though I didn't know how quickly I could love her, and that was clearly what she wanted, to be loved.

I went swimming with her the next day. The women, all in their fifties and sixties (and one was eighty-nine, Alice whispered to me, tilting her head toward a blur of speed and blue tank suit as it passed), only talked during the breaks. Their coach had them swimming in lanes divided by speed, and Cam's mom was only in the middle lanes, though trying to keep up with her in the guest lane, I was lapped twice in the first workout. My whole body burned with the heat of exertion. I was winded. These women still lived in their bodies, strong and calm. I wondered what Cam's mom—Alice—thought about while she was swimming, sound dun underwater, light in pieces from the sharp blue outdoors. Arms lifting—a slice of cooler air, a warm plunge. I thought about being alone with Cam. I thought about my sisters, how I could see them, years from now, swimming with me in a pool like this. I wanted to move to California. I wanted to bring them all. I wanted to bathe my mother in the pleasures of olive oils and wine tastings and swimming in the middle of the day.

In the evening, we dined again on fresh things from the organic grocery; Cam and his father talked about the day, and Cam rolled his eyes at me. We were waiting to be alone.

"I think we have jet lag," Cam said, yawning. "Clementine, are you ready for bed?"

We were in separate rooms, but Alice knew we weren't staying in separate beds at night. Cam took my hand and led me from the table.

"Don't worry, we'll wash up!" Was his mother being sarcastic? She almost seemed jealous—but still accepting, still deeply *kind*.

"Okay," said Cameron. He brought me into his room, shut the

door between us and his parents, and leaped onto the bed like a flying monkey. "Get your clothes off, fast. Young lady."

"Eek," I said, kissing his shoulder as I tugged off his shirt. His chest was golden, he smelled like Cameron, orange and sunlight. His body against mine was worth just about anything. I pulled my dress over my head.

"I'm going to deflower you."

"Too late," I said, but it wasn't. We were just beginning.

FIFTEEN

"Hello," said my father, his face bright with expectation and purpose. "Let me see the patients."

"Hi," murmured a barely awake Odette. "Baby Adam is in the NICU."

I expected an accusation, a complaint, something stronger than *hi*; only Odette had just completed her Herculean task—there was no fight left.

I would have to go first.

"And how are you?" Dad wasn't actually asking. He started reading her chart, pushing his glasses up his nose.

I couldn't bear it, the civilized voices, subtle discussion about the state of things; I couldn't do it.

I took a long breath, a guzzle of air like a diva about to sing, and hollered, "What the fuck, Dad?!"

"Clementine Lord," said Dad, holding up his hand like a traffic cop.

Odette covered her ears, hear no evil.

"Don't you dare," I said, lowering my voice slightly in deference to my sister. "You leave us all—you disappear, make us worry about you, make us think you're *dead*."

"I'm going to the NICU," said my father, replacing the chart at

the foot of the bed and tapping Odette on the shoulder almost lovingly. "I'll be back to check on you." He circumnavigated me as if
I were a simple island in the sea and started out the door.

I followed him. "Yo, buddy, explain yourself! You are a *bigamist.*" I couldn't let him go—I was full of steam, full of fury, weary
of carrying it all inside.

"Don't call me *buddy,*" he said without making eye contact.
"That's disrespectful."

"Would you prefer *asswipe*?"

"Ma'am?" said a nurse, blocking my path so my father, the
king, Charles Lord, could get away to rule another domain.

"You're upsetting the mothers and babies," she said, though
she didn't look convinced.

"Later," I threatened no one in particular, because my father
was gone. And I was suddenly deflated and empty. I thought of
the bridal portrait I'd just discovered, and the child's school
photograph—maybe I knew these people I didn't know at all better than I knew my own father.

"It never felt like he belonged to us," said Olivia, twisting her hospital ID around and around and around. I was sure she'd slice her
thumb on the plastic if she didn't stop. I wanted to put my hands
over hers, but I felt as if it were dangerous, somehow, to touch my
sister. She was all our anger embodied.

"Sure it did," I said, thinking of our phone calls. Of course,
that was me, just me, because I needed him then.

"No, you know what I mean—you of all of us, Clem. I've
always been jealous, you know, because you get to be special, you

get to be just you and not one of the pair. It's almost like he couldn't tell us apart. Which he couldn't for a while—Mom said." Olivia spoke as though this were ancient history. As though he were dead. A little dead to us, I supposed, though it didn't feel that permanent; it felt like a feet-across-the-carpet expected shock.

"But the truth is, he never had enough for everyone. He came and went at will—he never *fully committed.*" She gripped her babyful belly.

Our father was in the room with the baby and Evan—Dr. Dad to the rescue, as if we hadn't all been here doing just fine. Was he testing the baby's brain? Odette had started bleeding, though, and now she was getting another exam. She had looked so empty, pale, her breath short and shallow, and she'd felt so cold; I was suspicious that something was wrong. She couldn't just collapse so quickly, could she? Suddenly I didn't fully believe in science—some bad magic seemed to be at work here, even if Adam looked fine to them, "pinked up" as they said. Nothing was as it was supposed to be. And Odette had asked for Mom when they said just one visitor could stay with her. Mom had straightened her shoulders like a soldier and marched forth, nodding apologetically to me, though, honestly, I didn't mind relinquishing this particular duty. I was scared of what they might find.

And here I was in the waiting room with my other sister.

"You, jealous of me?" I said. "If you're trying to make me feel better because O wanted Mom, you don't have to, I don't mind. Though I am surprised it wasn't you."

"I'm not," said Olivia. "It's not like we're a set. I mean, we love each other, and we can finish each other's sentences, and neither of us likes peppers . . ." This speech I'd heard before; it was for new acquaintances, for the curiosity seekers who were fascinated by their identicalities. "But in some ways I'm more like you," she finished with something new.

"Again," I said, finally putting my hands over Olivia's on the ID to stop the fidgeting—her hands were cold, and a little clammy. She rested them, with mine, atop her belly, lest I forget there was still a baby to be born. Maybe this one would wait. I felt a kick and pulled my hand away. "I don't get it."

"I think being pregnant—him leaving—it changes my perspective. It's like the frame around the family portrait shifted, and I can see how separate we are. I sort of want something back, but I'm not sure what."

"It can't be the early childhood where we shared outfits," I said. I thought of Me and the puppy-ribbon dresses.

Olivia chuckled. "Maybe it is. Maybe I'm nostalgic for when I believed our parents were invincible. That Dad was a small god. That Mom was happy being a mom."

She was exhausting her breath and took in a deep draft.

"Is it still kicking you?"

"She," whispered Olivia. "We found out I'm having a she. Or at least I did. Jason didn't want to know, and he missed the last ultrasound, and I just changed my mind. I wanted to know. So I could exchange some of the yellow for pink. Frills. You should see what I have in her closet, though Jason isn't allowed to open the door. I wanted girls, Clementine. I don't think I can go through this again—" She waved her hand in the general direction of Odette's room. "And I haven't even done the hard part."

"You'll be fine." I wanted to know why she was jealous of me, but I didn't really want to ask. Things were charged enough already, and I'd felt her baby kick, and I'd held my nephew, Adam, and he was beautiful, so new, so extraordinary, a whole person, just like that, from a beating, kicking idea that lived inside my sister, now a person.

And Dad was here and had deflected my fury like wiping an easy frost off a window.

"I can't believe this whole thing with Dad," she said, wiping at her eyes and getting back on track. "I mean, I always felt like he was sort of closed—okay, really, really closed." She laughed at my raised eyebrows.

"Constipated," I said.

"Yeah." She laughed harder, her eyes starting to well. "And absolutely unwilling to let us really see him. But I thought that was a surgeon thing, or an old-father thing. Or something. I really never expected this. She's in Boston. His parents, I guess, didn't want anyone to know."

"Maybe she's poor and Hispanic."

"I didn't get any more information," said Olivia. "I mean, except that she lives in Boston. And it's not Lee." She smiled, rubbing away her laugh-tears. Her beeper buzzed and phone rang at the same time. She looked at one, then the other.

"Lee, wow. That was a long time ago."

"I need to see a patient," she said without picking up the phone. "Luckily, she's going to be admitted here. Do you think Odette—"

"She has us," I said, noticing, for the first time, how much weight my slim sister was carrying. It wasn't just her belly; it was her face, her legs, her clammy hands. She was a great vessel of baby, somehow much bigger than Odette was just hours ago, and she must feel very, very tired.

"I know. She might need me later," she said, confidant again, my sister again, because she was a doctor.

"Are we going to finish this conversation sometime?" I asked as she stood.

"Probably should. But in small doses. It'll be enough to face him." She flashed her professional smile and marched her huge, pregnant self down the corridor.

"Clem," said my mother, coming up the other hall. "We need to bank blood, just in case." She was carrying a spiral notebook and a ballpoint pen, brandishing one in each hand as if they would protect Odette, shield and sword.

"Crap—she's okay? Right? The baby's okay? Odette's okay?"

"She's bleeding a lot. They think they can stop it, but just in case she needs some—" My mother gripped my arm and led me toward the elevator.

As we stepped on, my father got off. His skin looked pocked in the terrible light. *Blight, gall,* I thought.

"Charles? We're going to bank blood for her," my mother said, looking at him, then stepping close enough so he could lean down and kiss her hello, which he did, as if he hadn't left her for another wife, without taking his cell phone, as if he'd never been gone. My mother's lips pursed—her kissy face for Dad; I hoped it was involuntary, that it was just habit. They were weird people, my parents, even weirder than I'd thought before. How could they be so stolid? I cried at weddings and at movies and even the occasional TV show, which Eli said was adorable. They fought, but everything was muted, blanketed in something. Money, I decided. Like insulation, money kept everything quieter.

"That's all?" I said. "He goes off, and that's all?"

"Now is not the time," Mom said.

"Right," said Dad.

Mom looked at him, a flash of despair in her face. "Wait," she said, stopping him from owning this minute, holding it like a rose, inspecting it for blight.

"You girls don't understand," she said, as if I were all three of us. "Your father was married before. He—"

"I'm widowed now," he interrupted.

My mother's face turned; it had held grief, sadness, but this was something else, a fury, a humor, almost relief. She turned to him, pen and notebook in hand. Had she been writing a note to a nurse? A gardener? To Dad? A lover? A note to herself?

"I don't understand either, Charles," she said. And then my calm, tamped-down, passion-held-only-in-her-marrow mother gripped the pen in her first and sank it into my father's shoulder, through his white button-down, through his old skin, like an inoculation, ballpoint poison. The elevator screamed at us—we stood in the doorway, all three.

"Christ, Octavia!" Dad grabbed his arm. The white shirt stayed white. He stuck his arm out to examine the wound, but there was just a tiny bull's-eye: black ink, a petite circle of blood. He stared at my mother with the strangest sympathy.

"Everything's fine, girls," he said. "I'll go to her room."

"Dad," I said because I could think of nothing else, as he stepped off and the doors closed.

"Not really," said my mother. "Not really fine." She sniffed like a knee-scraped child. She was recovering herself.

Half of me felt sorry for him, petulant, regretless. Half of me wished my mother had used something far more punishing than a pen—a scissors, a scalpel, a sword.

The elevator landed in the basement and we walked toward the blood bank.

"He can't just do that, leave and come back as if nothing happened."

"I always knew your father had more history than he offered. He is a good husband—not perfect, but he's learning. The sex has gotten better, actually—"

I covered my face. If you can't see me, I can't hear you. *Ick,* like a child.

"You didn't know this," she continued, "but his parents were very uptight people. Rich, but stingy. Did you know he wanted to go to grad school—but maybe not in medicine—and they cut him off? As if anything but med school were some diminutive kind of career—he really is very supportive of you, Clementine."

"Why are you saying this now? Why couldn't I know before, when I was feeling inferior? Why is he such a secretive asshole?"

"Don't say that about your father. He's not the only one with a history, with secrets. I took him, secrets and all. We are friends first—the sex is just glue. We managed to raise triplets, and we didn't only rely on family money—and I think you all turned out beautifully. Most of the time, I really respect your father."

"Most of the time?"

"Nothing's perfect. He will tell me everything, and he won't betray me," she said, confident, shoulders squared.

"He *did*," I insisted, but she stepped ahead of me, refusing to engage.

We filled out the necessary paperwork and sat side by side in the weird blood-donation desks—all cramped angles like the legs of a praying mantis—our arms tied with tourniquets. I winced as the phlebotomist coaxed the vein to the surface and pressed the needle in, but it didn't hurt that much.

"However," said my mother, when we were left alone to fill the bags of blood, "this allowance business is ridiculous. I was a fool to put up with it, and it's over." Her lips turned up just a bit. "That part wasn't such a great example for you girls. But I was so exhausted when you were born, and we wrote up a budget and it started from there. I had postpartum depression, Clementine. You might not remember, but I was hospitalized for a month. Nowadays I'd have been an outpatient, but then, it was total separation."

My free hand went to cover my mouth. A gesture just like hers.

"Why does everyone admit everything when a baby's born?" I sighed, trying to take it all in.

"Because it's all new again," said my mother, closing her eyes and leaning back in her chair. "And I didn't talk about this because I didn't want anyone to feel guilty—or to put off having children. We were always allied in giving you what you needed, Clementine, and many, many things you wanted."

"Who took care of us when you were in the hospital?"

"My mother—your Me—and my sister, and your father. They didn't even hire baby nurses."

It was a tender thought, that collaboration. For us, for her.

"He is married to someone else."

"Was." She waved it away. "She's dead now. That's why he left. Went. You know what I mean."

For the rest of the afternoon, I tried to avoid my father because I was afraid I'd call him out—and I was also afraid I wouldn't say a thing, that I'd fall back in line like a good girl. But I couldn't dodge from room to room forever. I saw him in the NICU, his huge hand cupping baby Adam's head as my nephew howled during a blood draw, but I didn't make eye contact through the glass and instead went downstairs to see my sister. She'd had to have one of her ovaries removed—a cyst ruptured and twisted the ovary during the delivery, which is why she'd started bleeding so much, why the pain was so intense. Now she had a single ovary, not that I knew whether she and Evan were planning to have more children—I realized I'd always assumed they'd have at least two or three, but I'd never asked. After Olivia's admission, I realized it wasn't easy, even for people such as my sisters, who looked so perfect on paper one couldn't imagine any complications. But complications weren't always on the surface.

"She's asleep," mouthed Evan, the more handsome of my two brothers-in-law, who was sitting beside my sister's head in her recovery room.

"Okay," I mouthed back. And then, because it had been so much, the whole day, the running from room to room, his sudden fatherhood and my sister, a mother—the amazing Adam, so small and clean and perfect, howling upstairs with his grandfather—I went over and knelt by the bed, taking Evan's hand in mine.

I don't think I'd ever held Evan's hand before. I'd stood close at the wedding; I'd seen him dive off the dock in Greensboro, his lilac swim trunks a silent joke between my sisters and me. "He's comfortable in his manhood," Olivia had said, giggling, as Evan and Odette swam across the lake together. Evan had been a diver in high school, and his body looked powerful and strangely smooth, like a single stretched muscle.

I'd been to Evan's father's funeral in Westport, Connecticut, the long line of black cars like ants in the sun. Events of sorrow and joy. Family conferences about my father most recently, but before that, parties, weddings, funerals, and swimming in our pool with his wife, still touching her as if he couldn't believe she existed. I was jealous, of course, of their couplehood. I was also not attracted to the man, but I loved him for loving her. I loved him for sitting by her head just now; I loved him because I knew he wouldn't leave her, wouldn't suddenly reveal a hidden wife like a magician's rabbit.

His hand was smooth and warm, much less hairy than the men's hands I'd held recently—Feet's huge paw, Eli's elegant musician fingers, long and tapered, with hair on every knuckle. Cameron's hands—strange square fingers, wide palms. I couldn't remember then as well as I could Eli's, or even Feet's. Evan held my hand back, squeezing a little too hard, but nothing like Odette's power grip during the delivery. It felt long ago, already, the event of it, the fear I'd held back like a wave of nausea suddenly coming forward, to the front of my head, blinding me, as I held Evan's hand and tried not to sob.

"Hey?" whispered Eli, standing in the doorway.

The nurse came up behind him, waving us out of the room.

"Too many visitors," she said in the hallway, after I'd kissed Evan good-bye—and he'd turned his head as I turned mine, so we'd inadvertently kissed on the lips, which was not unpleasant. A small assurance. He tasted like sprouts and avocado and smelled lemony, sweaty, and nervous. He was a daddy.

"Clementine," said Eli. "I've been instructed to take you home."

"Really? By whom?"

"Olivia called me. She said you'd done a long shift here, and that you needed to get to bed." Again, his face was enigmatic.

"What time is it?" I asked.

"One a.m."

"Really?" It occurred to me that I hadn't checked my e-mail or cell phone for hours. There could be news. But there was all the news I needed for one day: the baby, my sister, the other wife, my father.

"My father's here," I said.

"I know," said Eli. "She told me everything."

"I drove."

"I biked. Give me your keys and I'll put the bike in the trunk." We were holding hands, too, the way we often did, only it felt different. He was important; if I didn't hold on to him, I might drown in the ordinary weight of the world.

"It doesn't fit," I said. "Remember?"

"It will fit enough."

Eli escorted me to my own car. He propped his bike in the trunk, and we drove home in the breakdown lane, hazards clicking. I sat in the passenger seat, closing my eyes, but I kept seeing her, my sister, pale and crying with pain—such enormous pain. I was shaking by the time he pulled up by the carriage house.

"What, exactly, do you see in me?" I joked with Eli. "I'm always a wreck."

"Not always," said Eli, smiling seriously. "You've been quite sturdy when I was the one who needed a shoulder." I thought to the two Thanksgivings we'd spent together at Oberlin, makeshift meals with unmatched silverware, of Eli crying because his mother was "still dead." We'd both cried and laughed at "still dead." He'd tried to apply it once to Cam, but I was never ready. Until, perhaps, right now.

"Bring me home," I said.

"I'm going to put you to bed."

"I'm going to let you. She could have died," I let out, finally voicing what I'd been thinking, finally letting it dawn on me. "I can't lose my sisters." Now I was sobbing.

"It's okay," said Eli, settling me onto the couch. He held both of my hands and kissed them. And then I kissed his mouth, and then he pulled me to him, and it wasn't just comfort. I looked at him and wondered what it would be like to hear him the way I heard my sisters. It would make things easier, but there would also be no privacy.

"I'm not going to take advantage of you," he said, smiling, as we lay together on my bed, still fully clothed, but tousled and kissed and so aroused—at least in my case—the cloud of sleep and dread had vanished.

"Okay," I said, unbuttoning his jeans. "But I'm going to take advantage of you."

"I don't know if we should, Clem." But he didn't stop my hands, which were pulling off his shirt. "You're not yourself. I mean, of course I've wanted this forever—wanted you forever—"

"Excuse me?" I said, and Eli stopped talking and kissed me some more. It felt so exquisite I thought I might die. I wondered what the hell had taken us so long, and then I remembered—this was Eli, who'd seen me through losing Cam, this was Eli, who dated many beautiful women, who was so viscously sexy he couldn't meet me for lunch without collecting a few phone numbers. This was probably a bad idea.

"No," he said, as if divining my thoughts. "I can't—I have to tell you first—"

"What? What's wrong with me? Why can't you? What did I do? Is it my sisters? My—"

"Stop." He folded his hands together. Origami. Prayer. "The first week at Oberlin—remember? I saw you first, but Cameron said he did." Eli looked at me—the name, Cameron, like a poisonous gift. We usually said *he,* or *him,* and that was close enough.

"Excuse me; I'm not a tree dogs pee upon."

"No, I mean, I liked you right away—and I still liked him at that point—I wanted him to like me. He was so, well, everyone liked him. But he didn't like me. And I promised him."

"But you two fought all the time—were you in love with *Cameron*? Is that it?"

"No. Well, kind of. Not in love—I wanted to be like him, or be his best friend. That's what I wanted. But we fought, probably because we were both used to being alone, being in charge—"

"All those years you wouldn't—because of Cam—"

"I promised him, okay? And then he died, Clem—"

"That was a long time ago," I said, meaning it. "So please shut up."

I kissed his mouth closed. Then open again.

Relief, sweet, sweet relief. Eli was like a drug, only better. I was too far gone to think about side effects. I wanted this more than I wanted to get into vet school, more than I wanted to know for sure my sister would be okay, more than I wanted to punish my father; more than anything, I needed this fix. And it was better than I'd imagined, better than oblivion. Better, I thought, as we moved to the floor, blankets bunched around us like a frame, than it ever was with Cameron.

SIXTEEN

The summer after Cameron died I went up to Vermont with my mother before my sisters were freed from Harvard. They had summer internships in Cambridge and had rented an apartment together in Back Bay, courtesy of Dad, so I'd only see them for a few weeks before they were gone again.

First, it was just my mother and me padding around the wood-and-glass house, setting the table with cobalt-blue stoneware and bouquets of lupines and daisy fleabane from the wildflower garden. My mother was surprisingly quiet on the subject of my dead boyfriend, but she paid attention to me, something usually reserved for roses and my father.

We walked along the dusty road to town together with baskets for the general store—I felt like Laura Ingalls Wilder, having loved *Little House on the Prairie* in both book and TV versions. We picked black raspberries along the path up to the neighbor's sugarhouse, staining our fingertips and tongues with sweet deep purple. Vermont in the early summer smelled of mineral mud and timothy. Daisies watched us from fields, a thousand yellow eyes lashed in white, as my mother kicked pebbles like a child inventing a game.

Twice a week we volunteered at the Buffalo Mountain Food

Co-op in Hardwick. I was my mother's rehabilitation project: Save Clementine from the Depths of Despair, as if that were a place I might travel, packing my Tom's of Maine toothpaste and the short cotton skirts I'd made as part of a winter term project: learning to sew.

One week at the co-op we were transferring honey from huge tapped vats into labeled, sterilized jars. My mother held the jars with two hands and I pressed the spout open and tilted the vat, watching the viscous, amber liquid pour thickly into the glass, pooling like liquid energy, sunlight and certainty, the masticated product of a thousand worker bees, when the cowbell on the co-op door signaled a visitor. The co-op's one paid employee, a man named Dirk who had a thick, black beard and skinny runner's legs, was out for lunch, having baked the granola and stocked the bulk bins at dawn.

"Just a minute," called my mother, her voice lilting politely. I was embarrassed; my mother sounded rich. She sounded like a summer person, even as she stooped under a barrel of honey holding a jar. She was wearing chinos, of course, a neat little preppy, whale-embroidered belt, and her signature hair scarf, which, I had to admit, always made her eyes look large and her hair neat. It was her rustic look, just for the Green Mountain State. Never mind the platinum cards and embarrassing yellow Audi convertible parked in the dirt lot over by the bike store.

"Hello?" called a male voice. It was familiar. I almost thought it was Cameron, or my father.

"*Just a minute,*" my mother enunciated again, capping the honey before I turned off the spout, so honey spilled down my thigh. I cupped the rest of the lost gold as I put the barrel upright.

My mother was wiping off her incomplete jar with a wet rag, preparing her smile. It was the same face she made in a mirror before a dinner party, and, I realized with a green shoot of sadness unfurling under the skin of my chest like a time-lapse sunflower seed sprouting, the same face she made when she heard my father coming.

"You poured honey all over me," I said, but I wasn't really mad, I was sad. Always, that summer. Sadness like a layer of skin under my own. Sadness as thick as the honey and almost as sweet. I could cry for an hour, sitting on the damp dock, smelling the algae and hot lichen smell of the lake, or I could sit for the same hour unable to cry or speak. This was why my mother was rescuing me, why I needed her, why I didn't mind the honey all over my thigh, the handful I could think of nothing to do but to taste.

"Clover!" I said to my mother. "It says rose hips and lavender, but it tastes like clover!" My mouth was messy and sweet and my mother was talking to someone at the cash register, palming a Buffalo Mountain Food Co-op T-shirt like a good waitress explaining the dessert tray.

"Hello?" I said, and he looked up. Grey Munro. After all this time, Grey, my Sky Masterson. I breathed in the scent he brought with him, mud and diesel. He cradled a motorcycle helmet under his arm, which, I had to notice, was tan and firm. He wasn't as beautiful a man as he'd been as a child, but there was the too straight red hair, the wide blue eyes slightly smudged around the corners by early laugh lines in the freckled, tan face.

"Are you Clementine?" he asked as I stood with a face and hands full of honey, thinking I should go wash up, but if I went to the sink, the mirage might disappear.

"Grey?" I asked, but of course it was he.

"Here," said my mother, abandoning the shirt for the wet cloth, which she used to mop my hands, as if I were three and the victim of an ice cream disaster.

"I can do it, Mom," I said, though really I hadn't minded.

"Grey. How are you? Are you living *here*?" Last I'd heard through the grapevine, he'd started and left Emerson, then UVM, though I wasn't sure my source, Sophie, had reported correctly what her mother had heard from Grey's mother at the tennis round-robin.

"I'm just up for the weekend," he said, though it was a Thursday. "I'm going back down to school next week." He looked at me almost the same way he had in our school play, before we fake-kissed. Before the flowers.

"School?" I asked.

"You're at Oberlin, right?"

"Sort of," I said, feeling Cameron's pulse under mine, his thin, pale skin. His soft angel hair, his heart still doing the work of circulating his blood. I could almost taste his mouth, apricots; I could almost feel his hand on the small of my back, bringing my body into his.

"I'm at UVM," said Grey. "I came up on my bike because my mom wanted me to open the house." He opened his hands, offering them, or opening the air the way he'd open the house. My parents usually had the fireman-dog-catcher-teacher-milkman open the house for them, but Mom and I came up without warning and did it ourselves, following a list the fireman-etc. made for us. Open taps. Turn on water. Check furnace pilot light. Check fuse box. It had felt like an adventure. It had also reminded me that my mother had once been an independent entity. Maybe she even knew how to change a tire, something I'd learned at Oberlin in the experimental college in Car Repair for Women, something I would use later to help Eli out of a half dozen flats in his grease mobile.

"Okay," I said, staring at him. Had I been in love with this person? What was love when you were twelve years old? He was still in there, the boy who twirled in the first snow with such pure enchantment, the boy who'd helped me start the rope climb by offering his back. Chapped lips and scabs and all. He wasn't as tall as I'd imagined, and he had a smudge of dust on his cheek, which I longed to wipe off, and which I would leave. He was a stranger. Beloved stranger. Not that I was up for loving anyone right now, but I realized I'd never let it go, that unrequited adulation. I would never let it go entirely, I would never relinquish each love— would I let go of each wound? Or any of them?

"Studying engineering." He grinned.

"Okay." If I said more than a sentence or two at a time, I might cry. Best to keep everything short.

"Just wanted to pick up a T-shirt for my girlfriend." He grinned at my mother. The same wide grin, offering everything.

"Okay," I said again, starting to feel stupid. My mother had rung up the shirt and folded it, offering a reused plastic sack. Grey nodded no, and Mom came back to attend to me, swabbing at my face and thighs, still sticky with honey.

"Nice to see you," said Grey, holding up the shirt, then tossing his head and popping the helmet on the way someone might pull a lollipop from his mouth to hear the hollow sound. Pure boy. And then he was gone.

I never wanted to go home. I wanted to stay in the warm belly of the Vermont house, where I was only responsible for my own sleep and food. I wanted the small noises of outside to matter; I didn't want to share the world with my sisters, like having extra eyes, extra limbs, but no great brain, so I focused in one direction at a time, couldn't walk with any preferred gait.

With Grey there, I could be in elementary school again. With Grey there, I could accept the flowers from my idea of love, and from my father, and keep them both. I would never have to meet Cameron Kite and stitch myself to him, then rip away when he left me, leaving thread and wounds and unfinished edges.

For a while, I did think about ways to die. It wasn't purposeful; it was almost like a hobby, a distraction. The pain of losing Cameron came and went like sweet sips of iced tea. I almost liked the pain—when I wasn't feeling it, I was numb, my feelings asleep, like a pincushioned limb. My mother took me twice to a psychiatrist in Burlington, and I enjoyed the ride in her convertible, the top down, our hair snarled and battered, the rolling green dotted with bright red barns and copses of trees, deeper green. Cows wandered the fields, purposeful in their simple chewing. I could unbuckle quietly, open the door now, and let myself fall out. I could swallow the pills my mother kept in her Estée Lauder free-with-purchase bag, festively flowered, filled with Valium and Xanax and things I'd never heard of. I had looked a few up before we left Princeton, using the library to search suicide websites, so no one could trace it back to our home network. Not that I planned on doing it. I didn't plan anything; I just let time tick on and hoped I'd feel something other than hurt once in a while.

The psychiatrist asked me to tell her why I was there. She wore a velvet wrap over a neat wrap dress. All wrapped up. She had colossal dark eyes and parentheses of kind wrinkles around her mouth. She sipped tea while we talked, and her lipstick stained the mug, a subtle kiss. I told her Cameron died, how he died, how I felt close to his family but couldn't stay close anymore—another loss. I told her how his brother had held my hand at the funeral and laughed, inappropriately, at the grave site. How I hated cemeteries and wanted to be cremated and thrown in the ocean.

"Why do you feel you should be in the ocean?" she asked me.

"Because we all came from the ocean, right?" I improvised. Really, I just didn't like the idea of graveyards. "Or maybe Caspian Lake, I mean, it's named after a sea."

"Have you been thinking about your own death?" she asked, sip, sip, sip.

"No. I haven't really been thinking about anything."

Then my sisters came.

There was always this moment after not seeing my sisters—whether for a day or a month—that felt like looking in a mirror: surprise, recognition, awareness of things I'd forgotten. Even though I was nonidentical, it was as if I'd forgotten the shape of my own eyes in the corners of theirs, as if I thought of the lashes as lighter, when really they were cast dark webs against the pale skin. I loved Olivia in this moment of seeing her as I loved no one else, and partly as I loved myself. As long as they were in the world, I couldn't miss enough pieces to be the sort of puzzle you have to cast aside, disgusted.

Sometimes, I had felt almost that way about Cameron. Sometimes, after he died, I still found myself wanting to remember what he looked like, that sweet surprise. Like opening a gift you picked out yourself. I had pictures, of course, but I also lugged some other things in a box: an answering machine he'd attached to his dorm room phone, cables and cords connecting the clandestine apparatus before there was campus-wide voice mail. And cell phones. If Cameron had carried a cell phone, I would have kept it if I could. But he didn't so I had this shoebox-size machine with his outgoing message on a tape I never played because, if I did, it would be stretched and grow brittle and no longer reassure me.

With my sisters, there was no box, or I was the box. We kept our own voices, but there was some of Odette's voice in mine, some of Olivia's. There was a disastrous confluence about us, a we-ness that sometimes preempted individuality, even when we lived with the distance of the continent between us. It crippled me, sometimes, wanting to look in the mirror and see my sisters. And sometimes my differentness made me stronger than they were, and sometimes it made me feel as though something were always missing.

"Stop moping" was the first thing Odette said when she saw me.

"We're going to have fun," said Olivia, though her face was worried.

"Nice," I said, hugging them both. I was moping, but still felt

I had every right. I had found my *bashert,* my destiny, as Eli said, my other, my pair, and now he was dead, and I didn't want to look for anything new, or even look. I wanted to close off my senses to the green and the buzzing of flies trapped between window and screen.

My sisters took me swimming every day. Took me, because Odette picked out my suit and led me to my room to change. Olivia held my hand when we walked down to the dock. And to jump in, they stood on either side of me and counted. Brittle, cold mornings, the occasional steamy afternoon, we jumped into the blue-green Caspian Lake, all three holding hands. When we hit the water, we let go, three maidens in the water. I belonged with them; I made them whole. They would never let me extinguish myself.

And then I started to get better. I longed to talk with Cameron's mother. We'd held hands at the funeral—she'd invited me to stay with them, but I felt as though I couldn't keep them without Cameron. She wanted to be my friend—I couldn't have her that close now that he was gone. On the phone she most often cried. She asked me once, "Do you believe he's in heaven? Or reincarnated?" The conversation was too close—her loss would always dwarf mine. We both stopped calling. I was still angry with God, if there was a God, for giving me such a beautiful boy, then taking him away, but I liked the taste of iced tea again, liked the chocolate ice cream I churned with my sisters on the deck, after shucking corn, watching the lake lap against the glacial erratics that made smooth, gray cliffs by the shore. We had a hand-crank ice cream maker and needed to churn for about an hour, though one's arms grew exhausted after about three or four minutes. So we rotated. Mom was driving to Burlington to meet some friends from Princeton.

"So," said Olivia, churning. "What's it really like?"

"What?" I tortured her, rubbing my sore wrist. "Sex? You're still a virgin?" I knew she wasn't. I knew both sisters had lost their virginity to their matching MBA boyfriends sophomore year, that neither had enjoyed it all that much, but both were proud. They'd broken up with the boyfriends a few months—and a lot of sex— later, realizing sex actually mattered. I'd heard about it in conference phone calls and over winter break, but I hadn't really listened; I'd been in my Cameron haze.

"Love," said Odette, who was lying on a towel with her eyes closed. She wore a sweatshirt because it was cold out, and her legs were chicken-skin cold—I saw hers and felt it on my own. There was still that, physical empathy. *Love,* she said again, without speaking.

"Oh," I said, hurting as if she'd stabbed me with a rapier. "I don't know because I am having my heart surgically removed. Really, it's an extra organ. I figure I can get some kind of motor to circulate the blood. . . ."

"You actually felt it in your heart? Not just your head? Can you feel love in your heart? I don't even know if your heart has much in the way of nerves, being a muscle and all—"

Odette sat up. She sent me not a word, but a feeling, an electric current, a buzzing from my shoulders to my palms.

"She can make a metaphor once in a while, don't you think?" Olivia stopped churning.

"My chest," I said, shaking out my arms. "I felt it in my chest, and my nose, and my eyes, and my fingernails, my dead-matter fingernails. I felt him everywhere. Probably the way you two feel each other—almost the way we three do—only different, of course."

"Of course," they said, in unison, which made us all laugh.

"You don't think you've been in love?" I asked both of them at once.

"No," they said, unison again. *Maybe,* said Olivia, but just to me. She was trying to give me something, an exclusivity.

"Your turn," said Olivia, handing me the churn.

"I just went," I said.

"I know," she said. "Go again."

It was perfect, the jumping into the lake, over and over, holding hands, then letting go. Sometimes I let myself sink without moving, then let my body rise slowly. I might have scared them sometimes, underwater for a minute, maybe even two. The silky waterweeds had made us scream like the children we hadn't finished being. There were fish if I opened my eyes—trout, minnows, and shadows that meant nothing, unidentified things of the lake, which made me imagine, made me want to be eleven again, made me want to feel as if I could do anything.

Then my sisters left, in tandem. They took the internal dialogue that left me revealed. They drove to Boston in Odette's Porsche, a grudgingly accepted graduation gift. Olivia had refused a matching car, insisting that she would consent to a car when she didn't live in Boston. But I knew they drove the car to the beach, to Walden Pond, home and back again, up to Vermont. They drove the Porsche and Odette let it gather door dings and the pits and cracks from gravel roads, without fuss. She appreciated the car, she told our disapproving Dad, but she wouldn't spend all her time worrying about it. It was transportation. They drove off, waving to Mom and me, and I felt the sadness slip under my skin again.

"Dad's coming up for the week," said my mother. She sounded so joyful, like a girl anticipating her birthday party. I didn't really want to see my father. When he was there, Mom worried about dinner; when he wasn't, we ate ice cream and pie, or noodles from a pot. I convinced her we didn't always need to set the table, and she indulged me, letting me cook food co-op recipes with ingredients from Buffalo Mountain—chickpea and feta salad, three-bean chili, which left us gassy and uncomfortable, but tasted really delicious with loads of cheddar cheese, cracked-wheat tabbouleh and marinated tofu. Making it reminded me of Oberlin, and Oberlin reminded me of Cameron, but I was getting better. I was thinking about going back, or moving on, finishing up somewhere else, getting a job, becoming a cowgirl on a Western ranch. I reread the books of my childhood that sat on the knotty-pine, built-in shelf in my room, over the narrow brass bed and pilly white bedspread with fringe from the 1970s. *Black Beauty, Anne of Green Gables,* and books brought from college, the eager first year's *Pilgrim at Tinker Creek,* and *Gödel, Escher, Bach.* I reread a hardbound copy of *Walden* from the Greensboro library, its cover thick cloth, an occasional pink or wood violet pressed between the pages by another thoughtful soul. Maybe Grey had read it, I thought, maybe he sat out on the rocks by his summerhouse, tearing flowers from the cracked lips of the boulders, thinking of what he would become.

I was going to change things. I was going to change myself. I wasn't going to care so much what other people thought, even if it made my father angry, even if it disappointed him. I was going to remake myself, so I could start again.

SEVENTEEN

It wasn't an ordinary morning—the sky was thickly gray, the light-filtering shades my mother had ordered custom for the two front windows of the carriage house were battering their frames with the ambivalent wind's exhalations. I'd walked the dogs and given Cheese a frozen chicken neck. Someone was knocking at my carriage house door, and I guessed, by the shape and slice of blue button-down I could see through the glass, that it was my father.

"It's open," I muttered, clearing my throat.

It wasn't open, which meant he had to turn the knob and push, then try again, in his stubborn, certain manner—unwilling to give up on the information presented to him.

He knocked again.

I was leaning on the counter trying not to spill the coffee beans as I filled the grinder. Eli was asleep in my bed, and my voice-mail light was blinking, and I had a sore spot on my neck, quite possibly a hickey. The last time I'd had a hickey was the day I broke up with Feet, who seemed to like sucking my neck, my fingers, and even my toes—hence the nickname.

"Fine," I said, turning the dead bolt, but not opening the door.

"Hello, Clementine," said my father, walking into the cottage as if he hadn't been gone for a week and a half, as if he didn't arrive in the twelfth hour, thirteenth, really, just in time to oversee the repairs to his daughter's reproductive organs. The only cadential change was that he'd knocked on my door instead of entering unannounced, using his key, which I suppose was a minor act of deference. I'd take that, but I expected a hell of a lot more. I'd meant it when I called him *asswipe,* but I'd lost some of my steam since then—seeing my sister slip on the dangerous ice, sleeping with Eli.

"Hello," I said. "So, I hear you have another wife." I went to my desk and slid the bridal portrait out of the Chaucer.

"Clem?" Eli called from the bedroom.

My father raised his eyebrows at me. "Sleepover?" The corners of his mouth revealed his amusement. Historically, I'd take umbrage because his approval of my sex life wasn't something I cared about. Or I did, which was why I bothered to be bothered. But not today.

"Don't change the subject," I said.

"Everything okay?" Eli called.

"It's just my father," I said. I could hear Eli clearing his throat. "Is this her?" I waved the photo.

"Want company?" called Eli.

I did, I wanted him here to protect me from this familiar stranger, the way I wanted my mother to come into the classroom every day with me in first grade, even though there were only two first grades, so I was in Olivia's class. I had wanted her to leave something of herself, even just her breath, in the room, before it was safe for me. Like a blessing. I had loved my mother so much, I thought, feeling melancholy for his betrayal of her.

"That's okay," I called to Eli.

"Snake in the bed," he called back.

"Eli! My dad's here. That's kind of—"

"No. Skinny. He's out of his cage again."

I wanted to laugh, but I couldn't.

"Never mind," said Eli. "I can put him back."

I heard Eli shuffle into the bathroom, turn on the shower, and shut the door. He was giving us privacy. I had slept with Eli. At last. I wouldn't think about this now, I couldn't.

I brandished the portrait.

"Clementine," my father started. Still gripping the portrait in one hand, I turned on the coffee grinder so he was inaudible. My anger was fierce, but my desire to know everything was winning the arm-wrestling contest with fury. I couldn't look at his eyes or I'd know something I wasn't ready to know. I poured water into the coffeemaker, poured the fresh grounds into the gold filter. My mother liked surfaces clean, so I wiped the counter, tossing the extra crumbs of coffee grounds onto the floor. I'd sweep later. I still couldn't look at him.

"Clementine," he started again. "Yes. That was her." He made a hurt face. Boy expecting sympathy for his boo-boos. I hated him for lying.

"It's more complicated than you might think. We all make mistakes—"

"Mistakes? Bigamy is a mistake?"

"It was supposed to be annulled," he said.

"Mmm, so that explains away years of betrayal. *Supposed to be annulled?* What does that mean?" The weave of my dish towel was fascinating. My mother's dish towel. I wondered whether she'd detailed this expense in that horrible Accounts ledger, whether she'd sacrificed something she might have wanted—to go to a movie, to buy some seedlings for the greenhouse—to buy dish towels for the carriage house. I hated everything about my father—his bossiness, his control of everything, his obsession with money—because all of these things were orchestrated to keep his secret from us. He wanted to have more than everyone else—more information, more power, more money, maybe, it occurred to me like a breath of skunk air, more children than anyone knew about. Maybe he had more children, somewhere else.

"My parents told me it was over—they'd take care of it. But it wasn't technically over; it wasn't a Catholic wedding, so even though they had the Church's okay, we weren't actually divorced. I was too upset to investigate, Clementine, I know I should have made it official, but—Clementine—"

I was fidgeting with the bridal portrait, and he yanked it from my hands. There was a quick tear, and I held a scalloped corner, while he had the rest.

"Don't take my things." He recovered himself, as if remembering he was the father. "Please."

"Does she know about us?"

"Look, Clementine; I want to tell you the whole story, but you have to be willing to listen." Dad stood and put his hand over mine on the dish towel. There was a rustle from Cheese's cage—he was probably watching again.

"Fine," I said, looking up. He looked old. He needed a haircut, and his belt was too tight on his belly.

"She's dead," he said, face screwed into someone's idea of sorrow. He just looked odd to me, as though he'd cracked his tooth on a walnut shell. Bitter and pain, great together. "She asked me to come when she was dying. And to the service just two days ago. I went without my usual . . . planning . . . because she died."

Eli's shower was running; I could smell the steam and the hotel shampoo my mother stocked in there—a soft, milky, almost sweet, clean smell.

"It was something that happened right after college—really, it started in college. We were babies," my father said, twisting the dish towel. For once, he didn't sound like an authority on the subject, as if he were testing out a new lecture for the first time.

"You were never a baby. You were born an old man." I was digging in, trying to make a red mark somewhere, because as much as I needed to hear this story, I didn't want to.

"Anyway, Clementine"—he held up his hands, I give up—"whatever you want to call it, we were young. She was in my theater class at Harvard. We had scenes together."

"You took *theater*? Really?"

"Clem, I loved all kinds of things—I still do. Music, theater. My parents may've been uptight WASPs, but they appreciated a variety of things. I was allowed to dabble in the arts, as long as I became a doctor, as planned."

"Was your father a doctor?"

He looked at me, puzzled, his head tilted like that of a dog listening to food rattling a bowl. "My father was a businessman," he said, still quizzical. "You don't know all this?"

"How would I know if you never told me? Did you sleep with her and Mom in the same day?"

Outside, there was lightning and a rumble of thunder, but no rain. I was wearing only a sleep T, bright purple, too festive for this occasion. I hugged myself, wanting something. I heard the shower stop. Eli would smell amazing, and his face would be clean-shaved, and I didn't know what we had done, though it had been incredible, like scratching an itch when the cast came off, like cracking open a coconut for the sweet, thin milk and oily, delicious meat.

"He sold auto parts," said my father, ignoring my questions. "It was his father's business, and it was lucrative, and he hated it. Three generations back, a Lord started selling carriage parts on the streets of Philadelphia, and after fifty years they had a city-block-size auto-parts store downtown. It's gone now—everyone sold out. I thought you knew this?"

"Again."

"Will you be mad at me forever?" he queried, a little aggressive, a little contrite.

"Yes. Grandpa."

"He's magnificent," said Dad, getting almost misty-eyed. "And, Clementine, I love your mother."

"He's going to be okay—they both are, right?" Suddenly I didn't want to go back, I wanted to go on, I wanted to divorce his first wife from our family, but I still needed to know everything.

But Dad wasn't listening; he was still involved in his personal narrative. "I was supposed to be a doctor because it was the right thing to be. After my brother died, there was so much pressure."

"Your brother?"

"He had leukemia," said my father, a stranger, this man.

"Jesus—is there a reason you pretended you didn't have any family, that you didn't tell us we had an uncle who *died*?" How did

I get to be almost thirty without knowing all this? I mean, most families don't keep so much to themselves.

"I was angry at my parents. I wanted to make my own choices, but after Adam died—"

"*Adam?* Your brother was an Adam? Does Odette know this?"

"I told her about my brother. Honestly, I thought I'd told you, too."

"Odette and Olivia are the ones you're supposed to mix up. I'm the different one."

"Which is why it's more important for you to understand," he said.

I thought of Me and Da, their clean faces. How Me always had makeup on and wore a corset. How when we stayed with them, she let us help put on the cold cream to "take off her face." Unlike my mother's parents, I never knew these Lords at all, never had a chance to make up my own mind about them.

"I wanted to do something different after he died, Clementine—maybe research, maybe something else. But they wanted me to be a doctor; they'd planned my life for me, and when I said I wanted to change course—when I fell in love with Amelia—"

"Amelia? Her name is Amelia?"

"Her name *was* Amelia Cohen," he said, sighing. "She's gone, Clementine, that's why this is all coming out now. She's gone. Amelia Cohen Lord, only of course she dropped the Lord when we had it annulled—when . . ." He was actually misty-eyed. He wanted my sympathy for his dead extra wife. I couldn't help it—I was a little sorry for him.

"*You* married a Jew?" I said. "So it isn't possible to annul a *mixed marriage*?" This all seemed like theater of the absurd. I heard Eli coughing in the bedroom. He made a loud show of emerging.

"That's why I thought we weren't married—a technicality. I didn't know about my daughter for several years—"

"Dr. Lord!" Eli proclaimed as if he hadn't been listening all along. "I have to get to work," he said, leaning in toward me. "The mushroom study is really heating up. You may be using boletus in your operating room someday, Dr, Lord."

"Need me to interrupt?" Eli whispered, leaning in, having appeased the bear in his need for small talk. I shook my head, *No, thanks. "I need to handle it on my own,"* I whispered back.

"Call?" Eli held his hand to his cheek like a phone. He kissed me, but I turned my head, so he made contact with my cheek, not my lips. Still, I felt it everywhere, his kiss, in my belly, in my arms and breasts, between my legs, absurdly electric and good. I shouldn't feel this now.

"Okay," I said to the door, but he was already gone.

My father was quiet for a minute, then went to the cabinet and selected a mug—my favorite mug, because unlike all the perfect second-home mugs with their blue flowers and smooth rims, it was stolen from the cobalt casual set in the kitchen of the big house. I had dropped it on the brick patio and chipped the lip, so it would've been rejected anyway, culled from the perfect crop inside. I was surprised to see him choose that one, so clearly not a part of his flawless life. He didn't have Alzheimer's—he had a horrific case of narcissism. And fallibility.

"How serious is this with—" He paused as if he'd forgotten my best friend's name. He used to do that with Sophie and Mary, act as if he mixed them up, as if they weren't as important as they really were. I used to think it was a social ploy, but after seeing my father from a distance, I thought it was a mild social impairment. He just forgot, for a moment, couldn't access his inner perfect memory, didn't read the face as anything other than Clem's friend what's her name.

"Don't change the subject." I replaced the coffee beans and slammed the freezer door. "Don't do that. This is about you—like just about everything in my life—about you. Just tell me everything and get it over with."

I winced, feeling the way I felt before a blood draw, embarrassed to be nervous, embarrassed to be bothered by something so clearly necessary, a fear so ordinary. We were not supposed to be ordinary. But then, we were not supposed to be applying to vet school, we were not supposed to have dead boyfriends and uncles named Adam, we were not supposed to learn our father had been married before Mom—to dead Amelias.

"Okay," he said slowly, drawing it out. If it was going to be on my terms, he was still going to have some control. "I married Amelia Cohen just before college graduation. I loved her. My parents didn't approve—because she was Jewish, and because I wanted to crap out on med school and not *become a doctor*—and Amelia and I were married for three months and my parents wrote me out of their will. I found a job in a construction company— your father built houses for a few months, Clementine." He paused and looked at his hands as if this were impossible. He was smug, narcissistic, and I wanted to call him on it, but that would prolong the Band-Aid removal that was his slow reveal. I wanted to see what was beneath the bandage. I wanted it over.

"And then I realized I actually *wanted* to be a doctor, that I had done all this to rebel, to prove I wasn't going to just be the son they wanted. My father hit me, you know, Clementine. I never laid a hand on any of you."

I wanted to gasp and say I was sorry, maybe I was supposed to, but I knew if I interrupted, I'd never get the whole story, so I just looked down at the counter, counting the silvery flecks in the stone. Fifteen, sixteen . . .

"Anyway . . ." He heaved a huge sigh. I looked up and saw his eyebrows needed trimming. They were more gray than reddish brown. His nose hairs were too long, too, and his pores looked enormous, up close. I was about two feet from my father, standing in the kitchen of my carriage house, his carriage house.

"Amelia and I split up before I knew she was pregnant. My parents had it annulled, or at least they said they did. I loved her, but my love was entwined with my rebellion, and when I decided to attend medical school after all, she disapproved. She said I was sacrificing my own life to make my parents happy. I was, but it wasn't only that." He spilled a little coffee on the counter, taking a noisy sip. His fingernails needed trimming. The man was a veritable wreck, considering his usual impeccable grooming.

"It was also for me." He poured another cup. I could feel the acid in my own belly. No milk, my father never drank his coffee with milk. He had ulcers; he had a hernia and diverticulitis and acid reflux and, generally, "weak guts." His words, not mine. It was a joke that he could take everything in, it just ate him from inside. And right now, that seemed truer than ever. He was just a man, after all, and no longer young. I wouldn't relinquish my fury, though.

"We fought a lot," he continued. "It wasn't playful after a little while—we were both just growing up at the same time, but neither of us was willing to make space—oh, it's complicated."

I snorted. Obviously complicated. She had a kid—*she* must have made plenty of space.

"Anyway, she never told me she was pregnant. I found out when I had a two-year-old daughter, but I only saw her every few months or so. I never told my parents—Amelia wanted nothing of them. Now I have a grandson. He's ten and lives with his mother in San Francisco."

San Francisco. I could've met my own half sister there. I could've met my half nephew and never known it. I thought of all the people I'd known there, scanning faces in my memory— the women who worked at the co-op, the Mexican-cooking class I'd taken in the Haight, the used bookstore on Twenty-Fourth Street.

"And she died, Amelia. She just died of breast cancer." His eyes were watery, rheumy. Either he was old or sorrowful; either way, it was more than I could bear. I was wishing bitterly, ridiculously, that I could meet her. I *was* sorry for him, and I was surely sorry for this dead wife, but I couldn't say so. Sorry, so sorry that he didn't think I was important enough to know these things about his life. So sorry I wasn't entirely convinced I was that important, either. Were there just so many women around him, constellations of women, that he didn't focus on the individual stars? Or was I too dull, too far from his gravitational pull to matter? I wanted to matter.

"And that's it," he said.

"No. The money. You were giving her money." This was a stretch on my part, but it only made sense, piecing together what Olivia had told me, and thinking about Mom, shredding the Accounts. All those years of counting and measuring. Years of being more careful than she had to be, because of his mistakes. But we had plenty; we always had enough, and sometimes more than enough. The principle of it was what infuriated me—why keep it a secret? We didn't live in the 1950s. But then, he had.

"Yes," he sighed. "I sent her money. But I didn't know at first about the child. It was just part of what my parents arranged. I didn't want it to get complicated, that's why I kept track of everything so carefully—"

"*You?* You kept track of everything? No, Dad, Mom kept track of everything. Mom is the one who had an allowance, like a child, Dad, you treated her like a child. I don't know why she put up with it, and I don't know why you think that's a good example for anyone. You have three daughters—" I stopped. "No, you have *four* daughters. And you've taught them to cover up their secrets and treat the people they love with suspicion and—"

"Now, Clementine," said my father, trying to put his hand on my shoulder.

"No. You told me enough. Now get out of my house." I pointed at the door. I was evil; I was uncaring. This woman he had loved had just died. I didn't have anything against youthful mistakes, just colossal lies of omission. *Mom never knew he still saw her. Or did she?*

My father raised his eyebrows at me. *Your house is really mine,* his face said. *It's all mine, you're just borrowing it.* He clenched the ripped portrait and picked up the Chaucer.

I wanted to push him out the door, but couldn't bring myself to touch him. Instead, I went into my bedroom, where I started packing. I wasn't sure where I planned to go, but I knew I had to get out, do something. I imagined taking Mom with me, accidentally backing over Dad in the driveway as we made our getaway. He'd have crushed legs, but would live to suffer with them, and his guilt. I could see the sinews exposed, the blood filtering through the gravel like water draining out of a potted plant. Or else he'd be uninjured, but would run after us, calling toward the car like a lost lamb.

I stopped packing and got dressed instead. When I came out of the bedroom, he was gone. I made cinnamon toast because the world is more bearable with butter and cinnamon. My cell phone rang.

"Clem?" said Odette. "Are you coming in to see me?"

Of course, I thought. Leave it to Dad to get me to forget all about my sister and her new baby and her stitches and missing ovary. Then I sighed. That part was all me. I was the one who'd slept with Eli, I was the one whose life was a total disaster.

"Of course," I said. "On my way. How is he? How are you?"

"Gotta go. We have lactation consultancy."

We have Mars liftoff, I thought. My sister, the maker of milk. I shivered.

"Okay. Be there soon," I said.

I was about to leave, keys in hand, sunglasses atop my head, cinnamon toast in hand, when I realized I hadn't checked my e-mail since yesterday. I logged in to the multiple-application site and checked my status. Three were pending, and three, though I actually touched the screen, not believing the all-cap green words, were ACCEPTED. I'd got into vet school. In Iowa, Wisconsin, and Davis, California. I was going, going, gone. And the first thing that occurred to me was that I wanted to tell my father. I wanted him, after all, to be proud of me.

EIGHTEEN

Twins—and triplets, for that matter—understand each other in ways other people can't. When Odette came to visit me in San Francisco without Olivia, the first time I'd seen one sister alone in years, I kept looking and listening for Olivia, who was stuck at home at work, and so did Odette. It was almost as though Odette were missing a limb, and we both felt its absence. When we were little and played duck-duck-goose, three of us enough to make games fun—no need for schoolmates, we were a class all by ourselves—Odette and Olivia knew whom they would goose, when even I didn't know which sister I'd pick to chase me in the circle, put me in the pot. In a way, my own secret language with my sisters was to see their couplehood in a way no one else could. It didn't seem fair that my gift was related to their relationship, when their gifts were related to each other. No one was my doppelgänger.

I'd been in San Francisco for six months, and I was dating a man named Marston, who had grown up in the cranberry bogs of Cape Cod. He actually had pictures of the family, grainy little Marston and his three younger brothers, his wide mother and tall, skinny father, wearing waders in the pink bog. He had the impaired *r*'s of a Bostonian, and dark, curly hair, fierce blue eyes, and a candid smile. If I hadn't been in love with a ghost, we might've stuck together longer, though Marston was only interested in traditional, missionary-style sex, and at the same time every evening, so if we'd stayed out late at a movie at the Pacific, we'd have to wait until the next night to make love. I liked the smell of him, green and minty, a bit like outside, and a bit like spearmint gum. He worked a job in construction and a job in air-conditioning sales and was finishing his bachelor's a few credits at a time.

Every weekend for my first few months, my roommate Liz invited me on outings—a hike in Marin, a cooking class in the Castro. I said no every time and felt vaguely uncomfortable, as if I were ditching a suitable suitor. But I wasn't ready to have a new friend, a confidant; I wasn't ready even to like myself. Instead, I found Marston at a café.

I wrote letters to Sophie, who had graduated from Michigan and was giving two years to the Peace Corp in Guatemala. She invited me to visit and offered to visit me, but somehow I never let it happen. I wouldn't lose her; she was my longest-lasting friend, but I couldn't bring anyone closer right now.

Once I picked up the phone, innocently, to call Marston, and overheard Liz complaining about me to Eli.

"She's just so cold," she said.

"No," said Eli. "She's not cold at all, just injured. But I'm sorry you can't be my proxy. You're a good friend, Liz." It was true—I couldn't let her be my friend, and she'd have been a wonderful one. I thought of my mother, and her inevitable distances—was I becoming my mother, so soon?

I'd hung up as quietly as possible.

✦ ✦
✦

I had Marston sleep over on Odette's first night, probably to prove something to Odette, who had taken off three days from her oncology rotation to come out to see me. Liz was on vacation in Hawaii with her boyfriend, an anesthesiologist. My joke with Eli was that Liz would marry him so she could shield herself from pain. It wasn't really fair; like most people, Liz had enough pain in her life, she deserved some unjudged pleasure. But Eli had humored me and laughed.

On Odette's first morning, Marston was sleeping. The sun spread across my living room like an egg in a pan. San Francisco was too bright for me, sometimes. I plucked my sunglasses from the shelf by the door and sat beside Odette on the futon couch where she'd slept.

"Mmm," said Odette. "I don't have to work today."

"It's Saturday. Would you have to work on Saturday?"

"Yep." She shaded her eyes. "I have to work whenever my attending writes my name on the whiteboard. I hate his handwriting—it's illegible, and he always leaves out one of the *t*'s."

"You're awfully perky this morning," I said because, I suppose, I wanted to pick a fight. The night before we'd talked about Dad's checks, and about how he came to visit her at work, and how she was getting serious with her boyfriend, and fancy that, so was Olivia, with hers. I'd pictured a double wedding, and spleen spread inside me like stomach acid.

"East Coast time," she said. "And I don't have to work. I feel like I never come up for air."

"You're a good little fishy," I said, appeasing. "Dr. Odette."

"That's what Evan calls me." She grinned. *Marriage,* she let slip without saying it. I didn't think she even knew, even remembered what I could hear. "I might as well tell you." She smiled again, then pulled the flowered sheet—one I'd stolen from home— over her head.

"You're getting married," I said because I couldn't let her say it.

"Hey." Odette punched my arm. "You didn't let me have my moment."

"Nope. Don't tell me Olivia's marrying her Jason, okay? I don't want to hear it."

"Okay. I won't." Odette pouted. *She is.* "I thought you'd be happy for us."

"Which us? You and Olivia, or you and Evan?" I'd met Evan exactly three times. He seemed nice enough. He had a long nose and light blue eyes, and he shook my hand with an almost campy enthusiasm, but he clearly cared about my sister.

"All of us," she sighed. "Why do you have to be mad? We want you as double best girl. None of this matron crap—you're best girl."

"How about best woman?" I asked, my Oberlin training showing.

"I know you probably meant to marry Cameron," she said, holding the sheet over her mouth so I couldn't see her full expression. "I know you're not over him."

"Hey, Marston's in there." I pointed toward the door and stood to get coffee started. It hurt, a wedge of sharp heat in my throat. She would have to know that would bloody me. I pretended it didn't; maybe she could feel it, too. Maybe I could will my pain across the amniotic ocean, wash her in the red tide.

"You're not serious about Marston," she chirped. "He's cute, and you've entirely outmatched him. He's not half as smart as you are. Nice guy and everything, but c'mon, Clem, he's no intellectual match." *Do-de-doh,* she thought. She couldn't help herself.

"Why do people have to match intellectually? And are you hoping he'll hear your insults?" I asked, extracting three eggs from the fridge, balancing them in one hand, the way Eli would, the way Cameron would—he could juggle balls, eggs, pins, oranges—eggs, without accident. He could keep eggs intact, but not his perfect, invisibly fragile self. I dug in the crisper drawer with the other hand, realizing my roommate had thrown out my mostly rotten parsley. I'd planned to use the still vaguely green parts, so I slammed the fridge closed and dropped an egg on the floor. It cracked, but oddly the contents stayed inside. I picked it up and looked at the cracked surface. *These come out of chickens,* I thought, to keep myself from crying. It almost worked.

"We were too young anyway," I said to the wall.

"Duh, it isn't meant as an insult. But you do need a match," said Odette.

"Jesus. How is insulting his intelligence not an insult?"

"I just said you don't match." She actually thought she was being rational.

"See how far collective brilliance got Mom and Dad?" I said, my nose stuffy with the oncoming sob. "Mom's frittering away her talents and genius on window treatments and folding Dad's clothing with algebraic precision."

"Algebra's not always precise," said Odette, getting up. Her body always surprised me, so much like Olivia's—so long and lean compared to me, beautiful in a childlike way. I was jealous, every time I saw her, though I wasn't sure whether I was jealous of her mild beauty, or simply of the space she took up in the world, being my sister—something leftover from living together in the womb.

"Why didn't Olivia call to tell me?" I was sobbing now.

"Because I told her to let me tell you in person."

"If you're married"—I was choking now, coughing and spluttering, my nose and eyes leaking. I felt disgusting and relieved— "you won't live together. You won't care as much about me—"

Now I was wailing. I wanted her here so much, wanted someone to will me back into the triad, someone to make me feel that I was needed. As if I had a home. Olivia had sent Odette alone— though Olivia was on a rotation she couldn't leave, still, I had wanted both of them, even if I'd asked for no one. Didn't they read that in our phone calls? I should be grateful for the visit, but I just felt more desolate. If everyone else was married, where did that leave me? Of course I'd always known I was distinct, of course I'd always enjoyed the privacy of not being twinned, and I'd always wished to be part at the same time, but this was unbearable. I was losing everyone.

"Hey," said Marston, stretching his tan body, wearing only boxers and scratching his head in the doorway. "What's up, Clementine? You okay?"

I could see the tiniest bit of his penis peeking out of the boxers, and I looked at Odette; she could see it, too. She raised her eyebrows, thinking, *Nice,* and I started laughing. Marston and my sister both hugged me, and I surreptitiously adjusted his underwear. I was one in three, as usual. I stopped crying and laughing and kissed them both. I think, for a minute, Marston considered what it might be like to sleep with both of us, the twin fantasy incarnate, even if we didn't exactly match. But of course it wasn't sex time. It was time for breakfast, for walking on the Presidio, for me to start the long division of letting Cameron go, letting my sisters go, letting my anger and loss go, as much as I could let it go without emptying myself entirely into the sea.

Odette stayed for every possible minute of her time off. She would have to shorten her honeymoon by a day because she postponed her flight and took extra vacation days she couldn't afford to be with me. We walked the city, taking the Muni to the Mission to shop Mexican shops for Ibarra chocolate and the world's best burritos and embroidered blouses (matching but different, blue, green, and white, for Olivia, Odette, and me). We walked in companionable silence, something I missed, something Liz couldn't give me, or else I never let her try, through a little park at the top of Kite Hill in the Castro. The little outcropping of rock and dwarfed conifers was a tiny mountain, lavender blooming, the city stretched out like a white model of itself, the sea part of the blue distance. I hadn't been seeing San Francisco, even though I lived there. I'd let my despair dull the beauty of the place and let the exquisite pain dull as well.

We sat in the apartment eating strawberries while I fed Cheese the corncob Marston saved for me after he scraped the kernels into soup.

"I have to be honest," said Odette, watching Cheese gnaw the cob. "I think ferrets are disgusting."

"Thank you," I said. "Don't listen, Cheese-head."

"When are you coming back?" she asked, looking out the window at the sharp blue sky.

"I don't know."

Cheese was watching. He'd always been a watcher—Marston had noticed he sat silent in his cage while we were making love, but his eyes were wide, even if he was curled in his fur-silky shape. He dropped his cob on the floor and bounded down; Odette yelped.

"I miss you," she whispered.

We went to Golden Gate Park and rented a rowboat—I rowed Odette out onto Stow Lake, like a suitor. She leaned back in the bow, wearing a too thin cotton dress and one of my heavy sweaters, with a street-purchased baseball cap she gripped like a royal damsel holding her tiara.

"Shit!" she yelled suddenly as I tried to steer the boat past some grebes that were congregating like churchwomen after a sermon.

"Excuse me?" I said. "I'm doing my best." All day we'd explored in relative silence, and for once I felt like a sister, a partial match, because we'd made decisions easily; she'd followed my lead when I steered her past the wax museum and out to watch the sea lions on Fisherman's Wharf.

"No, I just got my butt wet." Odette giggled. "I now have your sweater, this corny cap, and a wet ass! I'm utterly gorgeous." She started laughing, and I laughed, too, dropping one of the oars into the water.

"Shit!" I yelled, realizing I sounded exactly like my sister.

"I got it!" Odette leaned over and dropped her cap into the water, but retrieved the oar. She put it back in the oarlock and tried in vain to row with one while I used the other.

"You girls okay?" yelled the boat attendant through an old-fashioned cone-megaphone.

"Fine!" Odette howled with laughter. "I can row!" she said to me, standing up.

"Never stand up in a rowboat," I said, laughing harder.

We managed to switch places, and I slid back on the bench, immediately dunking my own jean-clad bottom into the puddle.

"We wet our pants," I said, now semihysterical.

"What will Mom say?" howled Odette.

It was freeing to only speak aloud.

By the time we were on the bus home, having given the buffalo enclosure only a perfunctory look because we were freezing our asses off, we were both uncomfortable and happy. I felt young, I remembered how when we went into town in Vermont, Odette would scan the big posting wall just outside the Willey's store with me, looking at WOOD FOR SALE signs and HORSEBACK RIDING LESSONS and SHEEP (two ewes, one sound ram). We'd discovered the barn dances that way; we'd once ridden our bikes, the three of us, to visit some puppies for sale, even though we knew our mother would never let us have a shepherd-Lab mix that was good with goats.

"Wow!" said the guy whom I saw almost every time I was on the bus. He wore striped pants, suspenders, a fake beard, and an UNCLE SAM WANTS YOU! high hat.

"You two must be twins!" he said to Odette. She startled, shivered, and held my hand.

"Yes," she said. "As a matter of fact, we are."

It took me another month to break up with Marston. I was thinking about what it would be like to bring him home, as we walked through the park, and he laughed when I told him the names of the flowers. He made up his own names for them, monkey-butt, bad-breath, mushroomy thing. It was wonderful, watching him. His face was youthful, the eyes bright and innocent, and I knew we would never really love each other, because as funny as his jokes were, I couldn't help thinking he was joking about the flowers because he didn't actually want to learn their names. I couldn't help thinking how embarrassing it would be when he met my father, who would instantly notice, as Odette had, that he was not an intellectual match. I remembered when Dad met Cameron, when he'd told us to remember we weren't the only two people in the world. Cameron had made my father fidgety with his ease and quietude. Unlike Marston, unlike anyone else I knew, Cameron could stand quiet, throbbing long minutes of quiet, which other people would interrupt with chatter for fear of the silence.

"I think this is my stop," I said to Marston, as the bus pulled up to Twenty-Fourth Street.

I had been thinking about how I'd stopped seeing San Francisco—or maybe, when I arrived, I hadn't been ready to see it, the foreign, extravagant landscape. The hills shaped my vision, foreshortening the ocean, cutting up the world into blue sky, white buildings, and sea rising up into the horizon like a glassful of blue. I hadn't noticed how those foreign flowers—and all their real names—filled space between the succulents and green smears of grass. How everything was sharper in the sun, how the fog, when it came in, was like an eraser smudging the edges. My edges were smudged. I needed the clean lines of the East, hills that took their time, buildings that rose from stacked foundations instead of the sharp cheekbones of sudden hills. It was like a glorious experiment, the city in the hills, an experiment or a beautiful mistake.

"I was going to come over," said Marston, pouting.

"I think we're done," I said, looking at my shoe.

"You're tired? You'd rather crash at my place?"

"No, I mean, I really like you, but I think we should break up."

"Really?" Marston looked shocked. His eyes were almost turquoise in the blue and yellow light of California afternoon. I hugged him, but he stood limp.

"I'm sorry," I said, climbing down from the bus. The last step was always longer from bus to ground than I expected, and as I stepped down, my ankle twisted, so I looked up at the bus from a heap on the curb, as Marston waved good-bye, slow and sad and even, like the queen.

I came home for two weeks after my first San Francisco summer. My father sent me a plane ticket a month in advance in a FedEx envelope delivered to my job at an upscale restaurant near the Castro. I hadn't put in for vacation, but I also hadn't decided anything—how long I was staying, whether I even liked my roommate, whether I wanted to live in San Francisco, whether I should have broken up with Marston, which shoes to wear. One morning I wore one loafer and one ballet flat, just to see if anyone would notice, which they did not, until I came home and Liz answered the door as I turned the key in the lock. She was kind, and welcoming, and I was a wreck.

"Eli called!" she said, smiling. "Why are you wearing two different shoes? Want to come to cooking class with me tonight? It's chicken in a phyllo crust with pomegranate reduction. Which sounds very complicated to me."

"What did he say?" I asked, because I couldn't bear all that welcoming. I missed my sisters.

"He asked if you were going to Princeton this summer. What's Princeton like—is it all ivy on columns and preppy coeds?"

"Not where my parents live. It's big houses with big lawns. And horses."

"We've lived together for eleven months and you've never told me what Princeton's like," said Liz, a little plaintive. I was a jerk.

Sorry, I thought, but of course she'd never hear me. "I'm sorry," I started. The phone rang, and I was relieved of making a real apology.

NINETEEN

Clearly too many things were happening at once, so I decided to go with the most important: I went to visit Odette and baby Adam. Adam was out of the NICU, and Odette was lying on her side in her hospital bed, watching him as he slept in a little translucent bassinet, which looked like a produce drawer.

I wanted to be furious with Dad, I was, but I was also tangled in the strange net this baby cast, making me soft, making me dream I was producing milk, that I was pregnant, that Eli was my twin. Maybe Dad thought I felt sorry for him now—maybe I did; but it all felt unreal, the hatching of this other wife, her brief life in his words, her death.

I sat on the guest chair and watched Odette watching Adam for a while. Neither of us spoke, and I didn't really know what she was thinking or feeling, but I could tell it was a big, suck-you-under, wavelike feeling. I could tell without speaking that she was as close to laughter as tears.

I could feel it, a tearing, a stitch-by-stitch division of our seams. It was as though Dad's secret had sewn us together, three girls, and Mom, a tight fabric of family. And all along we'd been peopled by these others we didn't know—this other wife, her daughter. All along the seams had been so tight to keep us from wandering off, to keep us from wandering off into the world that held other people—Other Women.

I thought about this woman, about how her days were filled. Did she tear her salad from the head, the way we did, or did she slice through romaine, making too neat pieces? Of course, it didn't matter. It didn't matter because she was dead, and it didn't matter because it wasn't anything we could change.

Babies, I thought, meant separation for my sisters—but it was a chance for me to provide a catalyst. Finally I could be between them, in a way, not just because of my own needs and woes, but as a bit of family glue. Lord knows Charles Lord wasn't great as family glue. Or maybe his fingers were too sticky to keep but one family.

Finally Odette whispered to me, "Sit here." She patted her bed, and I sat, though she winced.

"What hurts?" I whispered back.

"Everything." She laughed. "Especially when I laugh, smile, pee, hold the baby, nurse him, or cry."

I felt a thin thread of her pain. "But there's nothing to cry about," I said, knowing otherwise. All of this was too intense, too out of control for my sister. She liked knowing what was going to happen next. She liked being the one in charge, the doctor, the orchestrator of events and lecturer. I thought of my father's awkward way of taking over a room with his ponderous, informative speeches and realized Odette was more like him than I'd noticed before. Though just now she was clearly of the body, not the mind.

"Where's O?" I asked, not to make a point, but really wondering. "Where's everyone?"

"Olivia's at work. Evan's at work. He gets two days when I come home and wants to save them. Mom's at home, sleeping. She stayed last night—I convinced them to let her."

This felt bad. I should've been here, instead of, well, sleeping with Eli. I rubbed my hands together, thinking about his fingers on my collarbone, his sweet mouth.

"How long have you been sleeping with Eli?" she asked, grinning, but still reclining. "Ow." Obviously the grin was enough to hurt.

"So sorry I made you hurt yourself," I said. "And how did you know? I didn't think out loud. One night."

"You know I know these things."

"So, Dad's home."

"Honestly," said Odette, raising her eyebrows at my avoidance tactic, "I care a lot less about what Dad's doing than I did, say, yesterday."

"That good, huh?"

"I guess his big mistake, his big secret, is less important to me than this little guy being born. I guess I'm tired of always putting Dad in front of everything, of worrying about how he'll react to things, worrying about how much he likes Evan, whether he thinks I'm as good a doctor as he is."

This particular professional jealousy hadn't occurred to me. It always seemed they were so satisfactory, so fulfilling as daughters, they didn't have much to worry about. No, of course that wasn't true. Evan tolerated my father, but I knew from his body language—and from Odette—that Evan thought my father was pompous. Of course, he was. Of course, when she'd told me, several years ago, I'd felt loyal to Dad and irritated that Evan pretended to be deferential. Now I was proud of Evan for pointing out a truth. I wouldn't want to be Dad's son-in-law.

I had been so occupied by feeling sorry for myself I hadn't bothered to live up to my triplet part of the bargain—worrying for them, feeling sympathy from time to time, not for myself, but for those other objects of my shadow.

"It wasn't really a competition, was it?"

"Sort of." She reached over the bassinet and touched the tuft of hair on Adam's head. It looked like a single pinfeather, the tiniest fluff. I could smell him, and I wanted to pick him up, wanted to hold my nephew, wanted to feel his weight against my arms, but I wouldn't ask, not yet.

"I can't lift him," said Odette, still stroking her son with exquisite gentleness.

"Yes." I grinned, leaning in to pick him up for her without hearing the question aloud.

I lifted my nephew from the bassinet and breathed in his smell, milk and new skin, like nothing else, animal and impossible not to breathe in, deeper, more. I held him close and his tiny hand gripped my hair. The giant gray eyes opened, and I inspected the little white bumps on his nose, the tiny pink bow of lips. Maybe someday I would have my own. Maybe I should skip vet school and just get pregnant—sacrilege and biology made me think this. Eli and I could have lovely babies—I allowed myself to conjure a tiny house on the outskirts of Princeton, matching cradles made by hand, and Eli preparing a feast of biryani and Moroccan chicken, putting raisins in my mouth—then I stopped. This was not in the plan. I was going to vet school.

"Can you help me get him into position to nurse?" Odette asked. I cradled Adam as she opened a non-hospital-issue nursing gown and shifted, making involuntary sounds of agony.

"You're not on pain medications?" I asked, because she wasn't groggy and looked as if she felt every bruise, stitch, and battered internal organ.

"No. Just ibuprofen, or I can't nurse him."

"You're kidding. There must be something."

"There is, but it all goes into the milk, and I can't risk doping him up, he's too small, not quite five pounds is—ow!" she said as the baby latched onto her nipple. I realized my hand was up against her shoulder, the other holding the baby to her.

"Stay like that. Sorry, I can't do it myself."

"Don't be sorry." This was more important than anything, than Eli, than vet school, than our idiotic father, though I couldn't stop imagining him with some other woman, with his first wife, his first child.

"He was always holding back," said Odette. I thought she meant Dad. "Now that he's a father, he's a big wobbly mess of feeling." She grinned. She meant Evan. I wanted that. I wanted other people to be so much more important that I wouldn't be bothered by my father's thirty-year betrayal of his family. Of Mom.

"Who, me?" asked Evan, standing by the door with a giant bouquet of balloons and a bag from Gymboree.

"Who, me?" echoed Odette. *See?* she told me.

I took the cue and left the room to check my cell phone for messages from Eli. Nothing from Eli, but there was a message from the shelter, telling me I hadn't gotten the administrative job, and could I come in for an extra shift or two on the weekend?

Thank you very much, I thought. I didn't mind bleaching down the cages—I did mind loving and letting go. Plus, I needed money. Everything was always about money. It would be Starbucks for the summer, or waitressing. There was actually competition for Starbucks jobs. Friendly's, I thought, feeling unfriendly. I imagined what it would feel like to wear brown polyester, a little apron, to fish pathetic tips out of the bottom of sundae glasses, and I sighed.

"Hi," said someone, touching my hip. I leaped and brushed the hand off—autonomic response. I knew who it was.

"What are you doing here?" I asked, turning to Eli, those unmistakable laugh lines, the long, strong fingers.

"What do you think?" he asked, kissing me like a starving man.

"I have no idea." Then I looked around—anyone could be here, my sister, my mother, my wayward father. Was I making a huge mistake kissing my best friend? It felt blissful, better than anything. Better than horseback riding, chocolate, better than kissing Cameron, even if my memory of kissing Cameron was the mark against which I measured all kisses, so impossibly good nothing could match it, or I didn't want anything to match it. Who remembered kisses all that well? Who knew what it felt like when you were no longer doing it? Like a kid, kissing a pillow, imagining the give of another mouth.

"Um," I said, retreating, sitting with my arms crossed as if I wanted distance between us. I was inexplicably nervous. This was what my body wanted—this was what I wanted. But could I trust him with this the way I could trust him with friendship?

"They hired someone else for the shelter job," I said. "I can't believe it. Of course, he can type, and I can't, not really. I guess it's Starbucks for me this summer. Which is fine, really, I—"

"You got in, didn't you," he said, looking concerned.

"Yes. Which means I'm not staying here. Not that I ever planned to stay here—"

"Congratulations, Clem." He leaned over my folded arms and kissed me.

"Thanks."

"Why so miserable?"

"Ah, the lovebirds," said my father. That man, for whom we'd searched morgues and hospitals, who'd made us phone his lawyer to inform him of rapidly impending grandfatherhood—not his first time, it turned out—was now ubiquitous. Like a mosquito in August. I wanted him to stop popping up everywhere, commenting. I wanted him just to go away again so I could decide how I felt about him, whether I even liked the man.

"Dr. Lord!" Eli shook my father's hand as if he hadn't just seen him this morning in my little house. "So. Adam. He's gorgeous, the little guy."

"I hope *you're* not planning anything," said my father, still gripping Eli's hand. "I've had enough additions to the family for a while."

"Dad!" I said, pulling Eli away from him, an unnecessary rescue.

"I've paid for enough weddings for a while," he continued.

Cameron's face came to me, Dad telling us not to get married. I wondered if he even remembered.

"Hm," said Eli. "I hear that fourth daughter was a surprise to some of the other people in your family."

My father's face turned pink. Blotched, the way mine does. He hated being challenged in any way, even now. I noticed how deep the circles were beneath his eyes, how his hair was so thin you could see the freckles on his scalp. His big hands had age spots.

"Touché," said my father. "Actually, she was the first daughter. But I meant what I said." He stalked off, smiling his Big Important Doctor smile, slightly wry. He couldn't fool me—things actually bothered the man. I was glad. I didn't want him to have a heart attack. I didn't want him to drive into the guardrail of the Garden State, but I did want him to be bothered, to think about what he'd done to us. Of course, I had to decide what that really was.

"So did I," said Eli, to my father's turned back. He kissed me and said, so quietly I almost didn't hear him, "I love you. I am in love with you."

Then he stretched, readying himself for a race. "I have a meeting with my adviser in an hour. Can I take you to lunch afterward? Or for a swim? Or anywhere?" That grin. I knew he meant back to bed. I didn't know about him, but I felt as though I'd been starving for years and had just now discovered the fruits and vegetables of my appetite.

"Sure," I said, wondering whether I should have said I love you, too, and what that meant. I was going to vet school. Would we shack up for the summer, only to part in the fall? Would he continue to flirt with waitresses, baristas, the buxom woman who checked our IDs at the pool?

✦ ✦
✦

I went back to Odette. She was propped up in her bed with a lunch tray. Adam was nestled in her lap, and she tried to fork salad in her mouth while holding him.

"He's going to get an early taste of dressing," she said. "I'm famished. Can't wait. Can you hold him?"

Carefully circumnavigating my sister's IV line, I took my nephew for the second time. The weight and warmth of him felt important. His face was screwed up in sleep. He yawned, a perfect O of mouth, and let loose a loud fart. Then his sleeping face relaxed.

"Did you hear that?" I asked my sister, but Odette was shoveling white cake into her mouth, starving. We were all starving for something.

"Mmm," she said. Adam fussed and I settled him back on her blankets.

"So, I got into vet school. Three of them. Still waiting on others. And I was rejected by the shelter for the administrative job of my dreams. Or nightmares. I just hoped I could work with animals for the summer. Instead of waitressing. Maybe one of those posh restaurants would—"

"I could use some help," interrupted Odette, trying to lift her arms with Adam in them.

"Oh, okay." I took him from her again. We were Marx Brothers, physical comedy, pass the baby. She started swigging the apple juice that came with her lunch in a little plastic cup. She spilled a thin river down her neck.

"No," she said, swallowing, then smiling at me. "I mean, I'm going back to work sooner than humanly possible. I could use some help—you know, a sort of nanny. But aunt-nanny, which would be better. I'd pay well." She grinned. Cheshire grin.

I couldn't tell who felt luckier. I couldn't imagine a better way to spend my days—getting to know this impossible creature, my nephew. Hanging out by Odette's pool feeding him rice cereal. Not that I knew when he'd start rice cereal. Maybe it would just be bottles. So now I could spend the summer falling completely in love with two guys I'd have to leave. I wondered about Cornell— not so far. I imagined driving down the Hudson, arms hungry. I wondered whether Eli had heard about any of the fellowship programs where he'd applied. I wondered whether I remembered, from my babysitting days, how to change diapers.

"Of course," I said. "My summer job. I'm going to tell Olivia," I said, picking up the hospital phone.

"I'm busy, Clementine," said Olivia. "Do you need something?"

"What do you think it accomplishes, not talking to him?" I could hear Odette in my question to Olivia. *Accomplishes.* I'd meant to tell her I was going to take care of Adam this summer. That I had been admitted to vet school, but she was so closed, I felt the need to pry at the seam, like wresting open an oyster for the good meat.

"I don't care," she said. "I have my family, and I can't talk to him. No one should treat a wife like that. No one should be so foul and deceptive and—" I could hear her pager beeping. "The point is, I don't need the anger in my life, and we can't pass it on to the babies in the breast milk."

"You really think that's possible?"

"Sure, when you're angry, you produce certain stress hormones—fight-or-flight . . ." Olivia continued her mild lecture, and I looked across the room at Odette, who was pretending not to watch me.

"Okay, O," I said.

"Odette should know it doesn't mean I'm not talking to her," she divined.

"She knows, I know."

"She should know I don't think she should talk to him, but if she does—"

"Christ, O," I said. I carried the phone over to Odette and Adam. "Talk to her yourself," I said to the air.

"Olivia?" Odette said, sounding so strangely cautious I held my breath. "She already hung up," she said, sorrow like a joke around the corners of her mouth. "But it's really okay, Clem, you don't have to broker peace. I'm not mad. She's mad."

"I'm mad," I said. "We're all mad as hatters!" I took Adam tenderly from her arms and started dancing him around the room.

TWENTY

Eli was invited to my sisters' wedding, and he brought a date, a flutist, about three inches taller than him—six inches in her heels—who sported a rim of blue eyeliner around her big brown eyes. She wore her hair cropped short, and it fell in smooth lines like an artist's pencil sketch around her face. I was busy that day, holding up trains and buttoning a thousand buttons at Odette's back. The dresses didn't match, and the vows were all individual, but everything about the twinned rest of it irritated me, scraped at my skin like a rough wood floor under bare feet.

My father was late for the ceremony. I was with my sisters in the Room of Preparations, or the Brides' Room, as indicated by my mother's girlish, round handwriting on a cream-colored card on the door. I should have seen it then; he wasn't busy, he was hiding something. He had another family—who else did that? I didn't know that then, I just knew that Olivia started chewing on her nails, which she had stopped in second grade by painting them with a bitter polish. She'd had me lick it just to see how disgusting it was, and I'd thrown up my after-school snack of about thirty Ritz crackers spread with great wads of Deaf Smith healthy peanut butter.

"Don't," Odette said to Olivia, putting her hand over her sister's. "They're so beautiful, we don't want to chew them."

"Why do weddings have to look perfect, anyway?" asked Olivia, holding one hand in the other as if to keep it from straying toward her mouth. "I think we should skip the portraits and pomp and let Aunt Lydia sit near Dr. Horace, even if he's clearly afraid of her because she might be a lesbian. I think we should forget about the place cards and just let people sit wherever they want. Where is he?"

"You're babbling," I said to Olivia. "Calm down, he'll be here." Of course, my own heart hurt for worrying about when he'd arrive. My familiar, potent, liquid wash of fear for my father—it wasn't rational, and I wouldn't admit to it, but it returned like a cold sore at times of stress. He had been at the rehearsal dinner the previous night, which was held aboard a borrowed yacht in the Hudson. When we'd all tripped off the gangplank at midnight, tipsy and alive with nerves and the pleasure of having completed an important ritual, Dad had waved good-bye and crossed over to a heliport on the other side of the West Side Highway. I'd watched his shadowy form waiting at the stoplight, his hunched shoulders. I'd wondered how often he took helicopters; I'd never been in a helicopter. Mom had already left with the parents of the grooms, who were staying the night at a hotel in Princeton. She was settling them in, she said, which really just meant she wanted company in the limo on the way back.

"He said it was just a quick appearance at a conference," said Odette. "He'll be here soon—if he can take a helicopter to—where did he say he was going?" She adjusted her hair, taking out one of the four hundred thousand bobby pins the stylist had used to give her pin curls a boost.

"Boston," I said.

"Maryland," said Olivia, at the same time.

Someone knocked at the door.

"May I come in?" said my mother, her voice almost shy.

"Mom, is he here yet?" Odette asked, opening the door at once.

My mother's face flashed something strange, a dark expression, but not anger, something more like grief. Then she gave us her composed smile. "He called from the limo; he's almost here. Are you girls ready?"

"Yes," said my sisters in unison. I wasn't. I wasn't ready to give them up.

Of course all was forgiven once he arrived. We were too busy with the details, all the details—the boutonnieres, the wrist corsages for all the mothers. The last-minute realization that the Octavia roses had been left out of the centerpieces, but no one minded, least of all Mom. After all, she may have seemed to care about the roses, but what she cared about most was seeing us off to more open lives than her own. What had she done to deserve this? I didn't notice then. Instead, I noticed how Eli's date threw her head back when she danced, how her neck was long, and white, almost swanlike, and strange, holding her head back. I didn't like her, but not because she wasn't nice—she was plenty nice. She hugged me when she said good-bye, and Eli just punched my shoulder, as if we were sports buddies.

✦ ✦
✦

Eli was in Princeton when I came home to visit from San Francisco, which is why I decided to use the ticket Dad had sent. For two days I woke up late, still on California time, and sat by the pool wearing jeans despite the heat, dangling my feet in the water and reading some of the novels I'd bought at the used-book shop on Twenty-Fourth Street. I had a few fantasy books in my to-be-read pile—dragons and magic—stuff I'd never been all that interested in before, but which looked soothing when I was shopping, along with a field guide to butterflies and an ancient copy of *What Color Is Your Parachute?*

My parachute was blue green and looked like a pool in New Jersey. I'd called Eli fifteen times and he hadn't answered. My sisters were still in Cambridge. My mouth tasted of sour airplane air, three days later. The dogs, slightly wild after their sedated journey in the pressurized baggage (in the cabin, I thought of them every minute with guilt and a little jealousy—I would've liked sedation), started barking; Ella ran in furious, ridiculous circles around herself, and of course it was Eli who came over to the pool and pushed me in. Then he jumped in, too. I wasn't sure I was up for the roughhousing, but I climbed on him, my legs around his waist, my arms on his shoulders, and pretended to dunk him. He stood, holding me, and beamed. I couldn't stand so much touching, even though we were wearing clothing in the pool, and I extracted myself and climbed out, collected towels from the pool house.

"Hello," he said, shedding his soaked polo shirt. I almost cried again, watching his sinewy shoulders tug the wet cotton away from his chest.

"Jerk," I said, but I didn't mean it. Everything about him reminded me of Oberlin—the openness of his face, that he was different here in the land of sameness, the grin that reminded me how we'd biked through the brain trees, how he'd teased me about the hickeys Cameron left on my neck, how he'd pretended to wrestle over my honor with Cameron—suddenly it didn't seem as if he'd been a brotherly figure, suddenly all the complications of his love life seemed invented to compete with mine. I didn't need another competitor: I had my sisters. I wasn't sure I needed a brother, either, but I clearly needed Eli, and that was the relationship we'd established.

"Got any naked brunch?" he asked me as we changed in the pool house, separated by the Japanese screens my mother had set up to maximize changing space.

"Sounds good," I said, and ducked, naked, around the screen. Eli was toweling off his privates, and he blushed a cinnamon color when he saw me, then snapped his towel in my direction.

"Come to Vermont with me," I said, realizing I needed the deep green, the cold dip of the lake, the quiet and lupines.

"Okay," said Eli. "I'll check my social schedule."

"Now."

"Okay. I'll drive."

We packed backpacks: a few clothes, a lot of snacks—Eli baked us snacking granola with cashews and flaxseed—and bathing suits. No one was home in the big house, and it suited me to only leave a note. Home had the wrong kind of silence. I was surprised how much I missed the stark blue and white lines of San Francisco, brightly colored houses tilting into the horizon, the way the sea cut off the sky, the way, if you were headed downhill near the Presidio, the green of the lawns and brown buildings seemed to stand atop the water, mingling with the sailboats and tankers coming in under the bridge.

I sat in the passenger seat and cried while Eli drove. It felt as though I'd saved a year's worth of tears, as if I'd been holding everything inside, though I'd been sad for long enough that I should've exhausted my sadness and moved on into another stage of grief by then.

"Stages of grief," Eli said, grinning, always grinning, as if things such as grief could be a joke if we willed them to be.

"Flatulence, pissed-offed-ness, night tremors, nocturnal emissions, and the last, most excellent: extreme thirst. Can you pass me a soda? I want one of the pomegranate ones."

He'd stocked a cooler with exotic sodas, with juices and fresh cheeses from the farmers' market—his fridge, as usual, was full of beautiful things. He'd told me once that when his mother returned from a tour of Asia, filming for her new show on the Food Channel, her scent had changed. She'd left with one combination ("Think patchouli softened by citrus and made richer by a combination of musk and vanilla bean—not vanilla extract . . ." Eli grew rapturous when he talked about scents, though he often also grew melancholy, thinking about his mother, missing her) and come home with new elements—a little passion fruit, a little lemongrass. Eli's cooler smelled like bergamot and lemongrass, like Eli's apartment, a little like Eli himself.

"I think I'm stuck at flatulence," I said, handing him the soda and zipping up the cooler. I sniffled and started crying again. It felt great. I'd long since emptied the first box of tissues, and now I was sniveling and sobbing into Eli's bandana. I wasn't feeling sorrow, though; I felt relief.

"Oh, no," he said. "Not you, never my sweet petunia Clementine."

I cried a little longer, watching the sharp, rocky profiles of New Hampshire open and close like the pages of a book as we drove north.

"You need to open this for me," said Eli, handing back the soda. "Here." He handed me a Swiss army knife. It was something Cameron would have had. Cameron actually brought his Eagle Scout manual to Oberlin, and his tent. We'd taken a weekend trip together, hiking through cornfields and along dusty roads, stopping to camp by the Black River in the Indian Hollow Reservation, the outcrop of rock and silver mica in the river such distinctively different colors from New Jersey I felt as if I'd moved to another country. The aspens were yellow, and Cameron found a walking stick clinging to the tent in the morning, a stubborn bug, hanging on to the tent fly as if he'd found a mate in the rip-stop nylon. Finally, Cameron had extracted the insect, but it left one of its legs behind. The whole hike home, we'd made up prayers for the walking stick, songs of mourning for the walking stick, hymns of walking-stick thankfulness. I wished, now, that Cameron had lost a leg. I could've dealt with that—I could've stuck by him—I could have made him even more mine for suffering through it together, but instead, he'd left me for death.

"Clem?" said Eli, interrupting my sobs. "I'm really thirsty."

+ + +

We were alone in Vermont for two days. We played house, unpacking staples from the storage pantry, with Eli's commentary on the brands and how they measured up. He loved going to the Willey's store, picking out the best cuts of meat—cut fresh for him, though I had a hard time not thinking of the cows that watched from the timothy fields, their innocent giant eyes, and the sheep. Goat I didn't mind as much—they seemed tough and uninterested in pleasing anyone. Eli chatted with Charity, the woman who wore the bloody butcher's apron and taught swimming at the town beach when she finished work.

We swam twice a day, like a ritual, first in the morning when the cold water hurt, so we had to race out to the raft. I was a better swimmer than Eli, but I didn't want to beat him every time, so I lingered with each stroke, letting him touch the slimy wood before me. In the early evening, our swims were more comfortable, the raft dry and warm, the surface of the water clear and almost warm enough not to clear the breath from my body on impact.

We had a schedule—Eli made plans for us each day, even after my mother arrived, then my father, then my sisters. I felt cared for—letting him make all the decisions—horseback riding at the stable where I'd taken lessons, a trail ride up into the farmland and preserve on Barr Hill. Eli hadn't ridden much, and his horse knew it and trotted when he wanted her to canter. We stopped at the top of the hill, and the horses ate early apples from the trees, though I knew it would make a mess of their tack. I'd clean it when we returned; I still knew the woman who ran the stable.

We drove out to Cabot creamery, where they gave us curds if we asked, letting us have them for free, because they were unpasturized and not salable. They tasted delicious, creamy, warm, and squeaked against my teeth. We took the factory tour and bought six kinds of cheese, which Eli would use for frittatas, foccacia, a magnificent veggie open taco he prepared for all the women of my family, but mostly, I knew, for me.

Then, the last day of my sisters' stay, he started flirting with them. It was subtle, and not unprecedented, but it felt like the end of the reverie, the end of his singularly dedicated friendship, which had almost felt like courtship, only mostly chaste. I say mostly, because he'd kissed my hand twice during the week, and my forehead, and my shoulder, once on the raft, not that I was counting.

That last day, we all raced to the raft. My sisters, taller, less practiced, and as usual luckier than I, stretched past us both and tied at the raft. They looked like girls almost, long and lean in their matching blue-and-white, sailor-themed bikinis. Of course, I just wore a functional Speedo, red and plain. They lay out on the towels Odette had ferried out on the kayak so we could sunbathe the way we had when we were kids. She'd also brought sunscreen, but no one wanted to use it. We wanted to take a risk. And apparently, so did Eli.

"Girls!" he called, climbing up after them, dripping on their already sun-warmed bodies. It was midday. Usually we had plans, but Eli hadn't said anything, he'd just lazed around the house with the rest of us, reading the leftover weekend *Boston Globe* and watching everyone. I'd even made breakfast—blueberry pancakes—serving them to my sisters, who ate six apiece, doused with wads of the fresh butter we'd picked up at the farm, and so much syrup their plates almost overflowed. I never loved blueberry pancakes, preferring my fruit and pancakes separate, but I made them for my sisters, for my mother, who was sleeping late or hiding in her room up the knotty-pine stairs, for Eli, a tiny gesture of thanks.

"Hey!" shrieked Odette as Eli lay his wet body across my sister's already towel-and-sun-dried legs. It wasn't an angry *hey*; it was charmed, it was sexual. *Cute,* she thought. *And delightfully firm.* It was appalling to hear her.

"Cut it out," said Olivia, but she rolled over so Eli was practically in her lap.

"You left me no alternative," said my fickle friend, gracing them with his most charming smile. "There's no room on the raft, and your four legs looked so warm—"

"Flirt," said Odette, but she made no move to push him off. *You're right, O,* she told us both. If nothing else, college had made my sisters assertive, sure of themselves, able to stand up to men in any realm. Or so I thought.

"There's plenty of room over here," I said, disappointed in myself for playing the game.

Eli didn't seem to hear me. He was shaking his head, showering my sisters, who squealed obligingly.

I'd finished toweling myself off, and there was no way I could stay for this. Of course he'd never actually make a pass at either of them, but the Eli I knew and loved would be the charming, sinewy shoulders, the touchy guest and cuddly friend I knew with other women. My sisters, in particular, who had no need of a new man, who wouldn't be interested, but who wouldn't mind taking him away from me for a while.

"Fine," I said, and dived back into the water, pulling through the cold underbelly of the lake, away from the house. I swam to the middle of the lake, not looking back. I was chilly now, despite the sun. I rotated: ten strokes of crawl, ten backstroke, ten breast. Finally I stopped and floated, feeling the momentous work of my heart. I looked back toward the raft and could see three forms standing. Maybe they were looking toward me, maybe they were wrestling. Whatever the case, I knew better than to need Eli so completely anymore.

That night, I came into my room to find my sisters sitting on my bed.

"We're worried," they said. Their eyes, four animal eyes, four eyes that wouldn't let me be invisible, and I was angry with them, and with Eli, and with everything. Then I noticed that Odette held something neatly in her lap, her manicured fingers resting on my journal. My journal—the fourth, perhaps, in a month. I'd bought the plain, short, stocky spiral notebook at Willey's store while Eli chatted up Charity the butcher. I'd expected sometimes they read my journal before, but now, I thought they were too caught up in the English fence of their cojoined lives to care about what I wrote to myself.

"You said you didn't think it was worth living," said Olivia, gesturing toward the book. *Wallowing, or really?*

I stood at the edge of my bed, a double, staring at their hands. Who knows what I'd written? I hoped I hadn't written something as clichéd as *I don't think it's worth living,* but I knew I confided in my book more than anything, that it was where I could say whatever I wanted and not be judged.

My chest hurt; it was difficult to breathe. I felt as though I'd swallowed great gulps of the green lake water; I felt as though I were drowning. As though maybe I wanted to.

"We want you to know we're here," said Odette. "And also that you can't kill yourself. It's selfish and mean and we won't let you."

"And we're here," said Olivia, her voice slightly softer. "And we can get you whatever help you need."

"You must be twins," said Odette, holding my hand too tight.

"Yes," said Olivia. "You are twins and so are we. The transitive property. The triple math of doubling." *Give me some of the pain,* she thought.

I gasped. *Can't.*

I couldn't say anything. They had no right. They had every right.

Sometimes I dreamed I was in the womb with my sisters. Of course, I'm sure I invented all the details rather than relying on any sort of memory. But when I woke, I missed the jousting of elbows, the beating of two other hearts. I was forever a puppy on my first night away from the litter, howling for that collective warmth. When we were born, we were slow to warm on our own, slow, but it was not impossible that we'd find our distinct internal suns.

"Okay," I said, though I was thinking all sorts of other things, unkind things, jealous and hurtful things. "Okay," I said again, because they meant well, and because I would always need them.

And that was the end of wallowing—if not the end of sorrow.

TWENTY-ONE

I walked beside Odette in her wheelchair. I knew hospital rules stipulated that I couldn't push the chair, but I wished I could—I wished I could be the one to roll her out of here, to rescue her from the constant lights and noises, the perpetual noon of the hospital. All these years they'd worked in places like this—white coats and bright fluorescent lights, the desks separating the nurses and support staff with their hidden novels and knitting from the sick, the patients, the people who didn't carry their wallets or wear their jewelry, who were tagged by the wrist.

Of course, hospitals help people get better. That's why they'd chosen them, for the science of it: figuring out the puzzles of the body, diagnosis. I'd always loved this part of having three doctors in the family: the discussions, the dinner-table games of Clue about patients and their symptoms and possibilities. But of course one sister was more concerned with the out-of-the-hospital things—quality of lives, immediate needs of pediatrics, and the other with the performances that were labor and delivery.

But Odette had been more than a simple theater, delivery and home. She'd actually been at risk, and despite the owls protecting her; the body itself was unpredictable, dramatic, difficult. And pain. She'd been in pain. And miracle—Adam himself. And now they were going home, and I wanted to be a facilitator. I felt closer to my sister than I had in years, even though Olivia would match her soon in motherhood. I had been able to sit by Odette's bed, where she was not a person of power, but a person in need of help and healing. Okay, so it wasn't that simple, it wasn't just that I liked my sisters better when they were sick—I didn't. It was that she'd actually wanted me there. And now, we were off into the unknown of after.

Eli had come back to my house; we'd slept together for three nights, and on the third we just slept, no sex, hardly any talking, just lying in the same bed as if we'd been doing so for years. He was exhausted from a fourteen-hour day at the lab, and I had spent the day assembling a crib, setting up a mobile, putting together a changing table, which involved a power drill, measuring table, a lot of swearing under my breath, and Evan bringing me iced tea at dinnertime and asking whether I'd made dinner. I laughed. Evan laughed. I could tell this nanny gig would not be without challenges.

"Um, I'm not a cook," I said, smiling as seriously as possible.

"Oh! I just thought . . ."

"No thinking allowed. Unless you're very good at it."

Evan frowned, but we ordered takeout from the Lebanese place and drove together in companionable quiet to pick it up in his perfect-skinned, midnight-blue BMW. I was ready for my sister to come back to take over her own life.

I didn't know, though, what we expected to happen next. I was going away, though I hadn't chosen where just yet, and Eli was planning, as far as I knew, on another postdoc year here at

Princeton. It was so good, so obvious, but I didn't dare talk about the end of the summer for fear of ruining the now.

"Your chariot, madame," I said to Odette. "And monsieur," I said to Adam, helping my sister buckle him into his car seat for the first time. She was no more expert than I, and I felt a sense of propriety because I was going to care for this boy—he was going to be both my job and my nephew. As if he knew what I was thinking, Adam spat up a little white blob of partly-digested milk and gurgled. I cleaned him off with my sleeve and didn't mind at all. This would be one satisfaction. Of course, I'd have to leave him, too.

"Are you Clementine?" asked a tall woman with curly, salt-and-pepper hair, familiar eyes, and freckles across her nose. Maybe she was an off-duty nurse; I knew her from somewhere.

"Yes?" I stood up from the car, readying to walk back to my own.

"I'm afraid your other sister needs you—um, Olivia? She's just been admitted."

"Is she okay? Olivia? Are you from maternity?"

"She's in maternity, and she's asking for you."

"And we thought we were done with that place!" called Odette, unbuckling.

Evan put his hand on her soft, recently full lap. "You are coming home," he said. "She has Clem, and your mother, and your father. You need to rest at home."

"But I'm an expert," said Odette.

"Yes, and your breasts are required. We can't offer Adam a homecoming and then renege on our offer."

"You kids work this out," I said, following the tall woman,

noticing how her legs were longer than her torso. "I think Evan's right, for the record."

"She's almost term?" said Odette, looking miserable.

"Go home," I said, turning one more time to blow kisses. "Go home and you can visit later."

I followed the woman back into the hospital, thinking she didn't look like a patient, or a nurse, wondering how she knew who I was, and wondering, even more, if everything was all right.

"She's okay, right?" I asked.

"She's okay," said the woman. Not-unlovely laugh lines bracketed her eyes. They were green and widely spaced. Her hair was rusty ringlets, though silver strands ran through them like mineral veins.

"You're not a doctor here? A nurse?" *A baby thief?* I'd heard of those and felt protective of my new nephew.

"Well, now's not really the time," she said as we both took the stairs two at a time instead of waiting for the elevator I'd just ridden down with Odette and her family. Her family. Separate from my family. It was a little unnerving and very wonderful.

"Excuse me?"

"Your father thought we should meet now. My father, too." She looked as though she might not be breathing, her face wax-smooth. "I know it's kind of an awkward time, but I only have until tomorrow. I'm your half sister, Claudette. But go." She patted my arm. "I'll find you later."

I wanted to ask a million questions. I also wanted, quite secretly, not to like her. I wanted to resent her. But Olivia was in labor. So I told Claudette perhaps we could talk later and went to repeat a new version of the drama of four days ago. Olivia refused an epidural, which was shocking. I was sure she'd know she didn't want quite so much pain. In the next room, a woman screamed out "Bastard! *Bastard!*" and we looked at each other and giggled. My mother fell asleep in a chair; Olivia was so quiet in her laboring.

"It hurts like hell," she said calmly. She was sweating. And then, after only twenty minutes, she was ready to push. *Give me some of your pain.*

"Ooops," said the ob nurse, wiping off my sister's behind. "Nothing to worry about."

"You'd think," gasped Olivia, crushing my hand on one side and Jason's on the other, "that I wouldn't be embarrassed." She gasped and bore down hard. *I think I can do it,* she thought to me, *but thank you.*

"Not too fast," said the nurse.

"I can't help—," said Olivia, pushing again.

"Breathe, mama, breathe," said the nurse.

"By a little involuntary bowel movement," finished Olivia, laughing now. Her eyes were leaking tears. Her legs shook with effort, and her forehead belied the agony, but she was doing it, drugless, delivering her baby.

"They're coming," said the nurse. She hollered out the door, and the gynecologist flew in like a white bird. Under her lab coat, I noticed, she was wearing a fancy blue silk dress.

"Who?" I asked Jason.

"The babies," he said.

"Excuse me? More than one baby? How is that possible? I thought you were having a girl."

"We are. Two of them. As for possibilities—well, you can ask your sister about probability and fertility if you want."

I looked at Olivia, her eyes closed, her head and neck lifted off the bed as she bore down. I looked up at the door, expecting my father to appear, as he liked to do, at the moment of truth, at the end of greatest effort, the way he appeared at my mother's grand dinner parties for their friends—or his colleagues—fresh and ready to partake of other people's efforts. To be master of all, the rooster strutting among chickens. Instead, standing outside was the half sister, Claudette. What did it mean, another sister in the world? Another nephew? Everything and nothing.

"Two babies?" I asked Jason.

"We just wanted to keep it to ourselves—they'll be public interest soon enough. Olivia and Odette knew all about that."

"Sure thing," I said, raising my eyebrows.

"And you, too, of course."

"Twins, not triplets?"

"Just two." He looked smug for a second, then frowned. I didn't always like Jason. "We weren't sure they'd both survive. The pregnancy was vulnerable—"

"*Shut up,*" said Olivia, as the doctor gestured for Jason to come cut the cord.

"And here she comes, number two!" said the doctor. "Nice timing! I can still make my cousin's wedding."

"We aim to please," said my sister, whose body started to shake. *Two, really two,* she thought to me.

"Just another push for the second placenta," said the doctor. I noticed a fleck of blood had touched the neckline of her dress, and it gave me a strange pleasure to see she wouldn't depart untouched by the events at hand.

Two girls, lucky you. Then I said it aloud. "Two girls."

Olivia held one; Jason held the other.

"Jasmine," said Jason.

"And Chloe," said Olivia. *I like C names.*

Will they hear each other? Some twins did and some did not. Would they share a puppy and fight over the best dress? All new; all unwritten book. All my sister's new kingdom, her new home.

My half sister was somewhere in the hospital. I wandered the halls of maternity looking for silvery-spun ringlets. I had no number, no information other than a sketchy memory of her walk and her name—Claudette. My hands were tired from my sister's crushing grip as I dialed my father's cell phone. Voice mail, of course. Gusts of warm air entered the lobby with patients—the hot breath of outside.

"So," I asked his voice mail, "is this supposed to be a grand reunion? Or union, I guess?" I paused, but couldn't come up with anything else to say.

I stopped back in to hold each of my nieces while Olivia sobbed with pleasure and relief, and Jason stared at the babies as if he thought they might disappear if he didn't keep watching. I settled them back with their parents and chose that moment to exit at last.

Eli was chopping in my kitchen again. Mirepoix: onions, carrots, celery; precise, tiny cubes that looked like children's toys. Children on my mind.

"Hi," I said.

"I hear it's a girl! And it's a girl!" said Eli, looking up from his cutting board. His hands kept chopping.

"Why did you flirt with my sisters?" I asked, because it had been brewing since we slept together, before that—since Vermont after Cameron died. It came out hard and accusing. "Why do you flirt with so many women?" Because I realized all the way home I'd been imagining what it would be like to be the new mother, finished with that gruesome and impossible work, ready for new work at hand. I thought about what it would be like to be married, to know I was with one person and didn't need to waste my time with people like poor, incompatible Ferdinand, what it would've been like—for the first time, I let the idea flicker in my mind like an old movie: I thought of Eli, if I'd married Eli, instead of Cameron.

"Excuse me? I'm chopping herbs, not flirting." Eli scraped the mirepoix into a bowl and started on something else. The scent of cilantro spread from his board across the room, a big, green smear.

"I just wondered," I said, softening my voice. The anger wasn't meant for Eli, but for my father. "Sorry, I'm not mad. I just wondered why you flirted with my sisters—back when we were in Vermont, and you came up—after Cameron died—and why you flirt with women so much. I'm not asking you to change, Eli, I'm just wondering, now that we've started—whatever this is?" I wanted to be able to trust this man—not just as a friend. I wanted to be able to trust someone. I wanted to be able to trust myself.

"Shit!" yelled Eli. He held up his hand, the knuckle scraped by the knife. In all the years I'd known Eli, as long as I'd seen him chopping vegetables, stirring a roux, folding batter, flipping pan breads with his hands—I'd never seen him injured by cooking. There wasn't much blood, but Eli crouched down on the floor as if he'd been stabbed.

"Is it that bad?"

"Of course not," he said, his face pale.

"Let me see," I said, since he was swaddling his hand with the other. "Not bad," I diagnosed. "A scrape. It'll stop bleeding soon."

"I did it because of you. Because I've been in love with you forever, and I was insecure and jealous." He said this with a wince, as if his hand really, really hurt. I couldn't imagine it was that bad.

"You're blaming me?"

"No, I'm blaming me. I was insecure and jealous."

"Of Feet? Of Marston? Really?"

"Of Cameron. Always of Cameron. None of my girlfriends were ever serious—not even Guinivere, really—I was always wait-ing for you." He said this grimacing at the towel as if it were blood-drenched, but really, he had just a scrape.

"Really?"

"Quit milking it."

I did what any other confused girl would do. I kissed him. Then I administered antibiotic ointment and a Band-Aid, turned off all the burners, and took him to bed.

"So what's the deal with this sister?" I asked Odette, when she called.

She was nursing the baby; I could hear his suckling noises and her little gasps of pain. "Just like that. Don't suck that part, little boy, it just hurts!"

"Can you talk now, or would later be better?" I asked.

I'd noticed a rental car parked at my mother's house, but I didn't want to go in. It wasn't that I didn't want to see her, it was that I wanted to know how I was supposed to approach all this. Claudette. A name to match mine—if I'd had a twin.

"Yes," Odette said.

The phone was quiet for a good twenty seconds.

"So," I said. "We have a sister. Dad betrayed us, all that."

Odette sighed. "I guess I don't really think it's about us."

"Okay, about Mom, then."

"That's the thing—Olivia seems to think it's about us, and Mom is off in outer space somewhere, but she'll land, and it doesn't matter, really, what we think, does it?"

"Sure it does," I said.

"Ow, that hurts!" The baby started to cry, a sweet, fussy noise. "I mean, we're grown-ups. I'm a mom, Clementine. Sure, I'm surprised Dad had this secret other life, and sure it's upsetting, but I'm not willing to let it dominate *my* life. Ow! The boy insists on nursing too hard. Hold on."

I wanted to hold him. It was going to be my job, and I was impatient, but Odette had said she wanted a few days of quiet before we all came over. I had other things to worry about—whether I would be living here anymore, whether I would become a vet, whether I would have purpose in this world, and of course I could worry about Eli.

Eli was sleeping, and I was trying to finish his cooking. It looked like a curry soup. I cradled the phone, cramping my shoulder, while I waited for Odette to return to the call. I opened the can of coconut milk and spooned rice out of his rice cooker into my pot. There was never a recipe with Eli.

"They were still married," I said as soon as I heard her fumbling to retrieve the receiver.

"Yeah, sort of, I guess, but she passed away, Clem."

"Our dad the bigamist," I said, thinking maybe marriage wasn't such a great idea after all. And babies. It was too complicated. Animals were much easier to understand. Then I thought of my vulnerable-looking father in the light of the hospital, of how mortal he was, how I'd been terrified he had Alzheimer's, how he could still get Alzheimer's, how maybe Mom would have to care for him in dotage after he ran around sowing seeds until his other wife died.

"Sort of," Odette said. "But now he's sort of a widower. A remarried widower."

I knew it was a played-out drum, but I still felt it and asked, "Aren't you furious? You sound so calm."

"We all make mistakes. I slept with O's boyfriend once."

"Yikes! You slept with Jason?"

"God no, not Jason. Just some guy in college—he was a jerk, and he never even guessed I wasn't her. I suppose I wanted to prove I could do it."

"How perverse."

"I didn't say I was proud of it," said Odette. I thought of how they looked together, how I'd always assumed they leaned lovingly, but perhaps the competition for light, for nutrients, made them as dangerous to each other as superfluous seedlings.

The baby started crying again, a full-force baby wail. It sounded urgent and also cute—babies were so much like other animals. The problem was when we began talking.

"I have to go, Clem. I'm too busy right now to be mad. I'll save that for later—maybe eighteen years?" Odette's voice escalated over the wail. "I might need you for an intervention, though."

"Um? O? Who's the alcoholic? Why not throw in some anorexia, some drug addiction, while we're at it?"

"No alcoholism—yet, anyway." My sister laughed. I loved how loose she was in her self—like limbs relaxed in their joints. Motherhood suited her. "I just mean that Olivia says she's never speaking to him again."

"Seriously?"

"Seriously. I see no reason not to move on—or, at least, I'm too distracted to make this any bigger a drama than it is already—okay, baby Adam, okay, honey." She put down the phone. So, wishing I could help soothe my nephew, and seething about my father at the same time, did I.

Seething wasn't useful, though I could see Olivia's point. I wasn't sure how I felt yet. I wasn't sure how much it mattered right now, anyway. I lifted the family portrait I'd put facedown on the desk when Dad had first disappeared—I'd been afraid to look at his face, in case he was dead. Now I stared at him and realized, through the haze of my own self-framed vision, through my own griefs and agonies and pleasures, that I knew little about my father. All along he was mysterious. And mystery makes us desirable. We all wanted to know him, and at the same time we were intimidated, afraid. The closest I'd come was our fights—that was when he revealed himself the most. Part of me, all along, and part of my sisters, because we were a team, a three-against-two with my parents, fighting for separation, fighting with them to belong to them, to matter—part of us always knew our father lived somewhere else—if we knew it metaphorically, and it was literal.

My job now was to let go a little—and to kiss Eli for every time I'd missed that opportunity. I wanted to love without mistake, to love without pretending it matters what anyone else thinks, anyone except the people I respected, anyone, regardless of their ability to betray me. My sisters matched me more than ever before, even as we each took to our own invented families while leaving the one into which we were born.

She was at my door, my other sister, her hair a halo, and though I'd left the door unlocked, she knocked politely.

"Clementine?" she said when I let her in, as if I could possibly be someone else.

"So, you're my half a sister," I said, walking to the sink to wash my already-clean hands.

"Ha!" She grinned. "If I go on a big diet, maybe." She worried a curl with one long finger. One familiar finger—her hands looked just like O&O's.

It was going to be difficult to dislike her.

"So," I said, sighing. "Do you want to stay for dinner?"

"No, thank you. This is new to me. It's kind of a lot—and I have to get back to my son—my mom just died," she said as if I didn't know, as if this weren't a keystone in the fallen arch of my own family.

And we just found out about you. And my sisters just had three babies, I thought, but of course she could hear none of it. I pitied her—never having this.

"I just wanted to say I'd like to get to know you if you feel comfortable. We could e-mail, or call, or visit—or not. This is new to me. I didn't know I had a sister—let alone three. I knew I had a traveling dad—he was so hilarious when he was with us, so much fun. My dad—your dad—" She paused and tugged harder at her hair. This must feel bad for her, I thought, at least as awkward as it was for me. She didn't know either, she wasn't complicit, she was as much a victim as I was.

Hilarious? I was incredulous. But then, I could almost envision it.

"Whatever," I said. "That's okay, go on. I didn't know—that you didn't know."

"We saw him once or twice a month. He had clothes, a dresser drawer. He brought birthday gifts—unless he missed my birthday. And he was almost always there for Hanukkah—except when it overlapped with Christmas, which was always a puzzle."

"Hanukkah!"

"We're Jewish?" she said, putting her arms around herself. "Sometimes we didn't see him for a few months—so of course I knew there was something—at least, I really knew by the time he missed my wedding. But Mom never explained, except to say that we should enjoy his company when we had it and not fuss when we didn't."

"Wow." My fingers smelled of garlic; it would take forever to fade. I wanted to return to not knowing. I wished I could unknow, but the closest I would get for now was to meet the other victims—

my halfs. If he missed her wedding, he wasn't one and the other—
he was himself in two places. How could he lie like that?

Claudette had already backed toward the door again. She'd
never fully committed to the room.

"Um, are you sure you don't want to stay?"

"No, but thanks." She handed me a wrinkled slip of paper
with her name and phone number and started to go. "Oh, and I'm
going to wait to meet your sisters until they're not immediately
postpartum." *She sounds like Dad,* I thought.

"Claudette?" I said, feeling that I had to take a few steps onto
the bridge between us.

"Clementine?"

I stepped forward and hugged her. It was a gangly hug, not
quite comfortable, but neither terrible. Claudette blushed. She
smelled sweet, and minty. She had maps of laughter at the corners
of her eyes. I wasn't sure I could bear being so close to her, to the
product of my father's betrayal. But then, she was a person in her
own right, not just a product. As were we—the three of us, people
in our own rights. I longed to hear my sisters thinking something
to me, but this way, I could let the news of this woman dwell in my
unedited self for just a while.

"I could actually, if you don't mind, I have to go to the bathroom."

"Of course," I said.

In the carriage house, you had to do something when someone was in the bathroom so you wouldn't hear them, but I couldn't
think of anything I needed to do, anything I could do, besides
wait. I heard Claudette shuffle, I heard her pee, and I heard her

sigh. Then she screamed: a short, controlled burst of fearful sound.

"Um, Clementine?" she asked without opening the door.

"Are you okay?" I pictured blood. She'd cut herself on Eli's razor. She would bleed out in my bathroom.

"You have a boa constrictor in here." Her voice was steady. She flushed. The sink water ran. Claudette was wiping her hands on her own sleeves when she opened the door. There was Skinny, coiled under the radiator in a patch of buttery sunlight.

"Skinny!"

"Thank you," she said.

"Ha! Do you like snakes?"

"Not particularly," she said, shrugging endearingly. She gave my hand an extraneous shake and left my carriage house. Someday I might know her, but not yet.

I had a bit of a workout, getting Skinny back in his tank, then went out to find my mother. This time, I wouldn't accuse her of anything. She must have known all along, the way we did—only more explicitly. What inspired her to stay with Dad? Did she think that little of herself, or did she like being left alone? I didn't know this woman, either. I thought of something Cameron said to me once in bed. We were lying across his futon, the damp Ohio light revealing every stain and bit of lint and dust mote that filled the scruffy room.

"So, I guess this is a little too soon to be in love."

"Excuse me?" We'd professed love, we'd dissected love, we'd

invented love, so I knew there had to be something of great theoretical complexity following this statement.

"Well, I always felt one has to know himself—or herself—really well first. Then you can get to know another person really well. Then you can be in love."

"Can't you do all three at once, Professor Kite?" I chuckled, because his language was so plain, but made so much sense.

"Maybe. Or maybe number three can lead you to number one."

"What makes you think I don't know myself?"

"It's me I'm worried about," he said, and for a minute he sounded entirely serious.

"I'm not worried at all," I said, kissing his warm, smooth stomach. He smelled of oranges and I wanted to burrow into him, to be as much his flesh as his flesh. I changed the subject with my body instead of words.

My mother wasn't in her house. I went out to look around the pool, my heart hurting. Would I forever be afraid of losing the people I loved? I didn't trust her not to take herself away from me, I realized, as I found an empty pool and let some of the pain in my chest fall away.

"Mom?" I called out to the grounds. The sprinklers were hissing, wasting water to the late-afternoon heat. Even I knew you should water in the still of the night.

"Clementine!" my mother called. "Over here! It's marvelous!"

My mother was lying in the lawn. Her white eyelet dress was

grass-stained, as though she'd just been rolling down the hill. Her makeup was a smudge of slightly smoother flesh tone across half her face; her eyes were raccooned and somehow young. She looked like a rock-star groupie, and she was watching the sprinkler cast its spray over her, she was part of the lawn—a robin, a grasshopper, a mourning dove crying its hollow longing, only she was laughing.

"Mom?"

My mother reached up and pulled me down beside her. I lay on the grass, shading my eyes from the spray.

"A rainbow!" she said like a child.

"Are you losing it, Mom? I just need to know if I should call someone."

"Not losing it, Clementine, finding it. There's a rainbow—I learned how to turn on the system today because the grass looked dry—but it's still a rainbow. A fine thing. I want to appreciate fine things. I want to look at rainbows with my little girl. One wish."

"Okay."

We lay there for a minute while the lawn hissed and water seeped into the back of my shirt. The air smelled green, and I noticed my mother's hand, still in mine, felt vulnerable, as though it might crush under the weight of the water.

"I'm a grandmother."

I grasped her hand. Maybe she felt left out sometimes, too—I could sense my sisters even now, a thin gold vein, warm exhaustion.

"Okay," she said, getting up and wiping her hands on her dress. "Time to change and get this dress to the cleaner." She turned her lips up politely. "We lost the deposit on the New Black

Eagles, so they're still coming. Want to come over for a very small anniversary party next week? I canceled everything else."

"Yes," I said, watching her pick grass from her clothes.

"Thanks for indulging me, Clementine. I think becoming a grandmother is even more momentous than I'd imagined. More momentous, maybe, than the granting of my three wishes." She held her hand out to me, and I felt like one equal part in three. Isn't the last wish always to have a million more wishes?

"Becoming a grandmother? That's what's pushing you into the deep end? Not your husband—"

"Shush."

And with that, I let something go, cut the kite string, let my mother's mistakes and sorrows float into the sky. I could watch rainbows with her, but I couldn't protect her from her own heart.

"See you later?"

"Yes. Oh, and could you check the mail for me? I'm off on vacation with Lydia until the party. I'll see you when I get back."

"But what about O and O and the babies?"

"They don't need me right now," my mother said, and I knew this was wrong, but again, I couldn't get the kite back.

"Okay." I sat up and watched my grass-stained mother walk her crooked walk, so much like my own, back to the house.

"So," said Eli as we washed the dishes. It had been a chicken curry soup, and I hadn't ruined it. Eli had also made pan bread, carrot cake, and three pans of lasagna—one for each sister and one for my mother. All this after a two-hour nap.

We ate and cleaned up, and the house was so quiet, it sounded as though the crickets in the bougainvillea were screaming, the silverware clanked like percussion.

"Fireflies," said Eli, looking out the window.

"So much at once," I said.

"I'm going to add to that." Eli took his hands out of the suds and put them, wet, on my hips, turning me toward him. "First of all, I got the money. My mother's money. It won't change much, but I just wanted to tell you. I've invested it, and I did buy something."

"Oh, Eli, that's great—now you can get a reasonable car," I said, knowing full well he didn't want a reasonable car. "Or a reasonable—I don't know—what exactly do you need? What did you buy?"

"That's what I wanted to talk to you about." He was examining something on the side of my neck.

"What's there?" I asked, fully distracted. "A nasty mole? Am I growing another head?"

"You're fine," he sighed. "I know it's a lot right now, but I've waited long enough. First, what do you think we should do tomorrow? It's Saturday, and I'm done at the lab for at least a day and a half, and you don't have any hospital visits, right? I was thinking we could go for a trip somewhere—the shore? Pennsylvania? Romania?"

He was running this all together, as if he was nervous. I watched his face, his smart jaw, the chocolate of his eyes, impossible lashes. Then he pulled a box out of his pocket—a jewelry box, a ring box, and actually bent on one knee, opening it. I think it was a black opal—it had a thousand colors—but I couldn't look at it for the glory of his face.

"And will you live with me forever, Clem? I know it's weird with your father and everything, but I just got this fellowship for the mushroom paper—and I have two years I can go anywhere that has a lab, and I can't let you go to vet school without taking me, too, so what do you say?"

Now he looked away, back to the dishes. He took his hands off me and put them back in the sudsy water. Then he looked back.

"Marry you?"

Alphabet padded over and snuffled Eli's feet, then mine.

"Live with me, and someday, when you're ready, marry me. It's not as though we'd just met. I've been waiting forever, and I'm not letting you go—"

"You're not?"

"Stop torturing me."

I'm sorry, Cam, I thought. *You're gone, and I love him.* Please don't like him more than me. *Not more; just a different like, a different love. I'm sorry, Cameron. Forgive me.* I think I might be able to forgive you.

"Yes," I said, surprising myself. I said yes.

EPILOGUE

Adam's first birthday party was at Odette's house, and Odette invited Dad, but he had told her he was pretty sure he had to have a root canal instead. I passed this information on to Eli, and he invented a little song.

"Ah, the loneliness of the American dentist," sang Eli, packing up his chocolate ganache in the cooler. He was the cake master, but Mom insisted on a division of entrées and appetizers.

"Never mind the lavish scuba vacations; it has to feel awful to be so feared and despised and simultaneously necessary," he finished, speaking.

"Did you hear that piece on NPR about how people are loyal to their dentists, and yet dentists are the ones very likely to find pretend cavities in X-rays?" I asked.

"It's all a matter of interpretation. Shadows."

"And trust," I answered.

My cell phone rang, and I almost dropped Skinny, who I was exercising before he'd be in his tank for the weekend.

"Just let me put down the snake," I said to my sister, setting the phone on the floor.

"Proctologists!" Eli continued. "Gastroenterologists! You know, I like my dentist."

I could hear Adam wailing as I recovered the phone.

"Forget guts," said Odette. "Teeth are agony."

"Did you hear us talking about dentists?"

"Adam's teething," she said.

"He still hasn't called back, has he?" I asked.

"We're better off without Olivia's fury," said Odette.

Eli raised his eyebrows at me and began taking his goodies out to the car.

"But Mom is bringing a date," she said.

I didn't want to be surprised, but I felt as though I'd fallen hard on the ground—no wind in my lungs.

"Don't panic," said Odette. "It's not that serious. He's just some guy from her art class."

Adam's wail crescendoed—Odette was lifting him and allowing him to gnaw on her fingers. I'd experienced this firsthand a few months ago when I drove up to help Mom clean out the last of her things from the big house. They weren't divorced—or annulled—just yet, but she'd sold the house and moved into a condominium with walls in three shades of soothing green, less than a mile from my sisters.

I missed the big house—and missed Dad, though we texted several times a week, sharing more details of our days and ways than we had in years. Or ever. It was an embarrassment of riches, his attention. Embarrassment, as well. He was diminished, less powerful; he'd admitted all sorts of health problems—back, prostate, even his heart, and somehow this made me want to forgive him. I didn't want Mom to forgive him, though. She donated all the furniture and most of his belongings to a women's shelter in Trenton and the Vietnam Vets.

She'd set Dad's office out on the lawn like a yard sale—papers, photos in pewter frames, the $3,000 custom chair, the heavy-footed oak desk, his extraordinary pen collection, and an incongruous gravy boat atop his disc-wiped computer—with a TAKE ME sign—the afternoon before bulk-refuse day. The mail carrier politely removed the computer and the gravy boat; the rest was hauled off after dusk.

"Let's go," said Eli, to me and to Alphabet, the only pet allowed at Odette's house. Our neighbor's fifteen-year-old would come care for everyone else while we were gone.

"Let's go see our babies," I said to my dog, who wagged obligingly. I missed everyone for a moment, the way you can only miss those you've held and let go. Then I settled into the driver's seat of the grease mobile and turned the key.

Acknowledgments

Many thank-yous to friends and champions at Gallery Books, including the creative, insightful, and indefatigable Kara Cesare, her talented assistant, Emilia Pisani, publisher Louise Burke, editor-in-chief Jen Bergstrom, Sally Franklin, Stephanie DeLuca, and John Paul Jones. To my agent, the amazing and incredible Jennifer Carlson, and the staff at Dunow, Carlson & Lerner. Thank you to Ma'ayan Plaut, who provided recipes, enthusiasm, and a reminder of Oberlin fortitude.

Hugs and thanks to friends and students including (but not limited to) my brilliant fiction group: Joanne Nesi, Maria Oskwarek, Annie Cami, Phyllis Rosenthal, Cindy Starr, and Suzanne Samuels (you are all my favorites); Lisa Williamson, Lisa Roe, the poets and mom-writers, fabulous book groups, and the collective talents of Just Writers. To Huckleberry Finn for podiatric affection. To Peggy and to Dad, who is not at all like Dr. Charles Lord except for the MD. To Mom and Tom and to Harry, too.

And, most of all, thank you to my fathomlessly beloved home: Josh, Jacob, and Carina Rosenberg.

Notes

Lester Trimble wrote *Four Fragments from the Canterbury Tales* for soprano, harpsichord, clarinet, and flute. Published by Edition Peters (PE.P66068).

Adjective Sandwiches are a real thing—invented by the multitalented Ma'ayan Plaut (Oberlin '10) at the DeCafé. Visit her blog for more: http://thelittlegirlsguidetosugarand spice.blogspot.com/.

For more on Stanley Greenspan's Floortime method: http://www.icdl.com/dirFloortime/overview/index.shtml.

THE
ORPHAN SISTER

GWENDOLEN GROSS

INTRODUCTION

For as long as she can remember, Clementine Lord has always felt like the odd one out—"the unmated shoe"—when it comes to her relationship with her sisters. Although they are triplets, fraternal Clementine is not just genetically removed from the identical Olivia and Odette, but also different in every way imaginable: while Olivia and Odette manage bustling medical practices and prepare for motherhood, Clemetine struggles with her applications to veterinarian school and lives in her parents' carriage house. But when a family secret threatens to unhinge the bonds that have been forged over the years, Clementine learns not only how deeply connected she truly is to her family, but also the changes she must make to break free from a tragedy in her past and move forward with her life and her relationships. In this story of sisterhood and sibling rivalry, of betrayal and unadulterated love, Gwendolen Gross has created an enduring novel that speaks to the complications and the pleasures of growing up, adapting to shifting relationships, and finding yourself along the way.

TOPICS AND QUESTIONS FOR DISCUSSION

1. The Lord triplets communicate in a number of complex ways that are often immutable to those outside of their bond, and even to Clementine herself at times. Describe the various methods of communication—both verbal and nonverbal—that the sisters employ throughout the novel. Which methods are more effective and why? When does Clementine feel left out of the dialogue, and how does this make her feel?

2. Clementine comes from a family of doctors, yet she decides to attend veterinarian school and chooses to surround herself with animals. Why doesn't Clementine choose to join the family profession, and how does her decision impact the family and her role within it? Why does she gravitate toward healing animals versus humans?

3. Clementine's thoughts and memories are largely dominated by Cameron. Why is it so difficult for her to move on? How does Cameron's suicide affect her life ten years later? To what extent does Clementine use Cameron and his death as an excuse to hide from relationships with men?

4. Until her grandparents passed away, the Lords lived a comfortable but modest life. How does their newfound wealth impact their lives and relationships with one another? What is the significance of "The Accounts"? Why does Dr. Lord need to control the household finances of the family in such an authoritarian fashion? Especially considering the fact that money is no longer an issue for the family?

5. Clementine repeatedly accuses her father of being paternalistic and overly controlling of the women in the family. Describe Clementine's father's view of women, thinking about his relationships with his wives and each of his daughters. Why does he act this way, and how do his actions, secrets, and behaviors affect the family? What does "The Diary" symbolize, and why does Clementine choose to remove herself from it when she leaves for college?

6. Odette and Olivia have both become doctors who care for babies and children; they both are married to responsible and successful men and become pregnant at the same time. Do you think Odette and Olivia are so similar because they share an identical gene pool, or for other reasons? Can Clementine's deviation from her sisters' nearly indistinguishable paths be attributed to the fact that she has a different set of genes, to the events of her life (including the tragedy of Cameron's death), or to something else entirely?

7. Olivia is the first to know about her father's infidelities and secrets, yet she repeatedly refuses to tell Clementine and Odette about why their father has disappeared. Why does Olivia keep her father's secret, even though it means essentially betraying her sisters?

8. Clementine spends much of her free time volunteering at an animal shelter and is the owner of two adopted dogs, as well as a ferret she took in when she was a still a student at Oberlin and a boa constrictor she rescued from a sewer. Why does Clementine feel such empathy toward creatures that need to be saved? Does her need to rescue others apply also to her relationships with her parents, her sisters, Cameron, or Eli? Why or why not?

9. Clementine's mother's reaction to her husband's secret life is to essentially carry on as if nothing has happened. Why and how is she able to maintain such a calm facade when her world is crumbling around her? What explains her stubborn loyalty? When do we see the cracks in her armor? Has her character evolved by the end of the novel? If so, in what ways?

10. How is Clementine's relationship with Eli different from her relationship with Cameron? Why does it take Clementine and Eli so long to act on their feelings?

11. While her sisters slave over college applications and eventually leave the rarified world of Princeton to attend the equally prestigious Harvard University, Clementine attends the more experimental Oberlin College and later moves to San Francisco, where she works on-and-off at a health food store and a bookstore. Why isn't an Ivy League education important to Clementine? How does she feel about not conforming to the standards set by her father and sisters?

12. Who is the "orphan sister" and why? How does your impression of this term change over the course of the novel? Is there more than one character that could be given this title? Why or why not?

13. How do the births of Olivia and Odette's babies toward the end of the novel help with healing the Lord family's relationships? Did Clementine's powerful emotional reaction to the newborn babies and her sisters' new roles as mothers surprise you at all, and why?

14. The names that the author chose for the Lord sisters of the novel are not accidental. If Odette and Olivia are doubles, has Clementine found her double in her half-sister Claudette? Why or why not? Is there anyone else in the novel who you would consider to be Clementine's double?

ENHANCE YOUR BOOK CLUB

1. Clementine and her sisters play a game called "Party Trick," where each speaks one word in turn to form a sentence "with the fluidity and natural cadence of a single person speaking." Try to play Party Trick with your book club and see how long you can keep it going!

2. Spend the afternoon volunteering at an animal shelter near you, or host a fundraiser event and donate the proceeds to an animal rescue agency in your area.

3. Stock up your kitchen and make "Adjective Sandwiches"! Assign an adjective to each person (try manic, melancholy, gleeful, narcoleptic, whirlwind, ponderous, sublime, and confusing, if you need some ideas). Have a tasting and award a prize to the person whose sandwich best fits their adjective.

A CONVERSATION WITH GWENDOLEN GROSS

Where did you get the idea to create characters who were polyzygotic triplets? How would the story have been different if the Lord triplets were identical, or all fraternal?

I have always been fascinated by the internal lives of multiples—my grandmother had triplet uncles. There's a family story about the theft of one of the three at a train station when the family was emigrating from Poland. The woman who snatched and ran with one baby screamed "it's not fair; she has three and I have none!" and I've always thought of that as a seed for a story. Maybe the next one. Meanwhile, there were triplet boys in one of my neighborhoods—they were French, and older, which made them deeply enigmatic.

One day I asked my friend Cindy (a writer with a medical background—and mother of twins) whether it would be possible to have two matching triplets, and one fraternal. She said yes, they'd be polyzygotic, and also that she knew a set just like that.

What a thing to be born not-alone, but to be alone!

I knew I'd have to write the story from Clementine's point of view—that triplets who were all the same or each different, genetically, wouldn't present the same layers of sameness and difference. I wanted Clementine's voice to have the influences of her sisters' and the strengths and lonelinesses of a self.

Did you always know you would tell the story from Clementine's perspective? How did you make that decision?

I did know—point of view is a crucial decision in the foundation of a novel (in the workshops I lead this is fascinating—how we can move closer to a character, how what we know about her changes with point of view); I love exploring proximity and distance. It's something you can do in fiction, in music, in art—but it's much harder in real life. In close third person, you can see outside your narrators—with first you are too close to see everything—you have to use dialogue and exposition and internal monologue to reveal your characters' positions in the world. It's all about the looking-glass self. With Clem, she has twin funhouse mirrors—she has a closer link to two others than most of us will ever have. (Only a first-person narrator can reveal how the one sees and feels within the three.)

The book is dedicated to your sisters and a "sister in words." How did your relationships with your own sisters influence you when you were working on the book? Do you ever communicate with them in nonverbal ways?

My sisters each have their own extraordinary strengths and talents— my older sister, Claudia, was the first ocean swimmer to cross the Sitka (Alaska) Sound. My younger sister, Rebecca, seems to learn languages like learning colors. My youngest (half) sister, Samantha, is in law school now—she was the first baby I fell in love with; I thought of her when I wrote about Adam's birth.

Each of my sisters and I seem to know some small things together in a way no one else can know them—perhaps only the next line of an obscure melody, or how to true a bike wheel (okay, I'm really rusty) or how to tie a bowline. When our mother had a dramatic and terrible bike accident on my twelfth birthday, my older sister Claudia and I knew to turn back our bikes—we were at least a mile ahead of the rest of the family on a Vermont road—and even though we had energetically sought the lead and distance, we stopped and turned together. We knew together something was wrong, and I don't know how we knew.

My friend Cindy and I have a running narrative of messages; somehow we also seem to know what sentence comes next in the ether. Sometimes we write simultaneous matching messages, even though the topic at hand could be a knitting pattern or the history of the cell. Everyone should have friends like that, who understand your oddities without elaboration.

Clementine spends much of her time with her rescue animals and volunteering at a shelter. Are you an animal lover yourself? Have you ever owned a ferret, or a snake like Clementine does?

Oh yes, in addition to writer, composer, and scientist, vet was on my grow-up list when I was little. I never had a ferret or a snake, though I almost adopted someone's ferret at Oberlin. I've had dogs since my tenth birthday (currently we have a corgi named Huck Finn), and they are always adept at knowing human habits better than we know ourselves.

When I was in college I applied for a job at the Boston Museum of Science as a live animal and physical science demonstrator. I wanted a summer job, and even though they wanted someone permanent, they gave me a try. Mostly, I believe, because when they asked me how I felt about snakes, I said, "Fine!" *Fine* meant holding twenty pounds of active snake (unless they'd just been fed) while standing on stage in a lab coat, answering questions about venom and habitat. I learned to love holding the big old constrictors and helping them shed. We had rescued possums (*fifty teeth in a possum's mouth—more than any other North American land mammal* still trips off the tongue) and kinkajous and a porcupine (porcupine rash burns!), and I learned demonstrations with them all. I felt like an ambassador, and I also felt honored to understand each of them just enough to show them off onstage and help care for them.

***The Orphan Sister** and your previous novel **The Other Mother** tackles suburban life and the relationships between family members. Why do you think these topics provide such rich fodder for fiction? Do you draw on your relationships with your own family when writing your novels?*

Ooo! Sneaky question. Fiction is a chance to frame your truths in more interesting facts than you have yourself, or by selecting only the juiciest fact-berries from life. We want to read about ourselves, only made more interesting. I also love the almost magical element of how the triplets can hear each other—much in the way a dog hears you thinking about a walk and looks at the leash on the hook before you even know what you're thinking.

Family secrets play a huge role in the novel. Do you think that family members should keep secrets from one another? Under what circumstances is keeping a secret necessary? Was Clementine's father right to keep his secret for so long?

No. Yes. Maybe. I think secrets become habits. Between adults, most secrets are about fear or power—and often that power or fear is expanded or diluted in the telling. I think, as a parent, that sometimes you forget that you had a whole narrative of life before your kids were born; you don't necessarily have a right time to tell them everything. On the other hand, it's our job as parents to tell all the important things.

I'm not sure when Dr. Charles Lord could have just come out and said, "and by the way, I have another wife and daughter," to his kids. I also think his wife knew (except, probably, about the fact that the marriage was never officially dissolved); I believe he may have told her, and felt, in his controlling way, that the best way to raise his children was to have them do what he said and not what he did. If they knew about all his mistakes, they might be wont to repeat them, or at least not to idolize him. He wants to be idolized. He also was too selfish to realize how not taking control of the one thing that had been purely his choice (the first marriage, and its dissolution) made him absurdly culpable. He wanted to keep everything—even if he was flooding the boat with his chattel.

So maybe. Or probably: no.

Like Clementine, you went to Oberlin College. How did you draw on your experience there to make Clementine the character that she is? Why was it so important for her to attend that school versus her sisters at Harvard?

Oberlin was an incredible place—college really was about learning to learn, for me. I was in the college (majoring in science writing) and the conservatory (like Cameron and Eli, but I studied voice) and was in awe of so many musicians around me. I sang in composition majors' recitals and experimental microtonal operas; I went to master classes; I took Rocks for Jocks and danced wildly in the 'Sco. I taught a course with a friend named Karen Silberman—about Women and Body Image. We'd seen so many gorgeous young women striding toward the dining hall giving bitter voice to body disgust, and the class taught me how to teach. I also met my husband there, but not until senior year (he was a math and religion major). There is so much freedom in that time of life, and also a deceptive sense of immortality. Just like any transitive time, not everyone makes it through.

Clementine doesn't want to be the same, even though she wants to be understood and known. Watching her sisters speak in tandem, choose in tandem, makes her want difference that much more. But she's also seeking a same that makes her feel like the other half of a whole. I think in a way her time at Oberlin was really as much about her work— about how she learned what kinds of connections she wanted in the world—as it was about meeting Cameron and Eli, even though the book focuses on the pairing and loss.

Another thing I loved about Oberlin was how people emerge from that egg of learning all goopy with desire to make change in the world— to find the work that most honors their powers. We *all* have powers, energies, talents, raw material. What we choose to do with that material is work, and work is not a four-letter word.

No disrespect to Harvard, of course.

What's next for Clementine and Eli? What about Clem and Claudette? Do you think you would ever return to these characters? Where do you think they are now?

I would love to hear what you think, actually. Write and tell me. I often think of my characters' post-book trajectories, and I even write them sometimes, but for this particular moment, I think I'd rather give readers some credit and let them decide for themselves—if the fictional dream (à la John Gardner) was continuous, the best honor of a reader to author would be to dream it on.

What is your current mood, and what would you include in an "Adjective Sandwich" to convey that mood?

This is my favorite question. I was so honored when I wrote to Ma'ayan Plaut and she sent the recipes for the sandwiches in the novel. Today, I'd make Anticipatory: Thinly sliced crusty multigrain bread spread with three-berry jam from the local jam-man, grilled asparagus, smoked turkey, and just a little bit of mini-Winnimere cheese (from Jasper Hill—a Greensboro, Vermont, creamery!). (Sweet, smoky, slightly bitter, tender, tangy . . .) I'd press it in the panini maker and eat it with a mug of Tra Que Chai my sister Claudia sent me from San Diego. Since mini-Winnimere is very rare, you could use goat cheese instead, or even just the thinnest slice of cheddar. I hope Ma'ayan writes a book. I'll get copies for each of my sisters.

Which writers have influenced your work the most, and why? If you could only read one book for the rest of your life, what would it be?
Laurie Colwin, Barbara Kingsolver, Eugene Ionesco, Shakespeare and his leeks, my high school art history class and Janson's *Art Through the Ages*, Tom Lux's poetry, *Ten Ever Lovin' Blue Eyed Years with Pogo*, Alice Monroe, *National Geographic,* Tolkien (my dad read them all aloud to us), Frog and Toad books (those in Mom's voice), Annie Dillard, Elizabeth McCracken's *Here's Your Hat What's Your Hurry*, Robert Frost, the Little House on the Prairie series, *Black Beauty*, Annie Proulx, and the ever-favorite bathroom reading of childhood: the comics, *JAMA,* and *New England Journal of Medicine.*

The one book? Gasp. What a horrible question. I suppose I'd say *Gregory and Lady Turtle in the Valley of the Music Trees* by Laurent de Brunhoff.

But that's today. Ask me again tomorrow.

Are you working on anything new at the moment?
Oh, yes, always. Multiple narrators—multiple secrets, a girl about to leave for college vanishes and each neighbor has seen a different departure through their windows.